CROOKED LETTERS

Diamonds in the Rough • Book 2

LORI COPELAND

CROOKED LETTERS formerly A Case of Crooked Letters, book two of the Morning Shade Series

Copyright © 2003 – 2016 Lori Copeland.
Published by: Sunny Day Publishing.
Springfield, MO

Library of Congress Cataloging-in-Publication Data Copeland, Lori.
Crooked Letters / Lori Copeland / Edition 3.

Cover – Sweet 'N Spicy Designs
Sharon Kizziah-Holmes Publishing Coordinator

ISBN: 0-9854923-5-X
ISBN-13: 978-0-9854923-5-9

CHAPTER 1

Ever notice that everyone is trying to accomplish something big, not realizing that life is made up of little things? Somebody other than me said that, but the older I get, the more I realize it's the truth.

My name is Maude Diamond, and I'm struggling with a lot of little things in my life. I look back on the last eighteen months and thank God for a strong heart, because otherwise I'd have never survived life's upheavals: my husband's unexpected death, my eighty-seven-year-old mother-in-law's moving in with me, my only daughter coming home after her philandering husband's demise. I don't recall who said it—I only know that I agree: Life is a test, and I didn't take very good notes.

Gunshots coming from the living room deafened me. Stella had the TV jacked up to sonic blast. Outside my office window, fall trees put on a splendid display, temperatures in the low seventies—much too nice a day to sit in the house and work. But work I must, because suddenly I hit sixty and I find myself with a full house, a bushel of bills, and a wagonload of responsibility.

It wasn't supposed to be this way.

Looking out my office door I could see that Cee's—that's my thirty-one-year-old, recently widowed daughter—poodles had each other in a canine death lock in the middle of the front-room floor. Captain, our newly acquired cat, sunned himself in the bay window, his tail switching calmly back and forth. But I know the temperamental feline's mood, like those of the three women in this house, can change in a heartbeat.

I've decided that God is still teaching me after all these years. After Herb's death I believe He tried to impress on me the importance of love. Shamefully I admit maybe I didn't give that one commandment a lot of thought. Oh, I loved Herb, and I love our daughter, but I've had to work on loving other people, opening up the doors of my home, my personal domain—and my heart— without resentment.

I'm still working on the lesson.

I tried to focus on the last paragraph I'd written. *Concentrate, Maude.* Monthly bills weighed heavily on my mind. My agent, my publisher, and popular television evangelist Jack Hamel had been so fired up to hire me to ghostwrite Jack's newest book that I thought they would move heaven and earth to hand-deliver the contract and advance royalties check. But twenty years in the writing business had convinced me literary agents and the publishing world worked on their time, not my time.

Hitting Control S, I leaned back in my chair, giving the top of my graying head a good scratch. Why do brainy things make your head itch? Or throb? Or at times feel like it's going to explode—blow up and scatter nasty-looking particles all over the desk? I grinned, proud of the fact that as bad as it was, I could still smile.

"Stella!" I yelled. "Can you turn it down a notch?" Like my mother-in-law could hear anything over the car chase and *rat-a-tat-tat* of machine guns going off in the living room. I often wondered why she didn't like chick flicks—quiet movies with quiet people.

I knew the moment I heard Arnold Schwarzenegger's voice I was in trouble. My mother-in-law hadn't heard a word I said. How many times was she going to watch that old movie?

Sighing, I got up and walked into the living room, tying the sash on my corduroy robe. Why did I even bother to try to concentrate? If I'd ever had flashes of muse, they had flown out the window years ago. Now I wrote out of obedience. Writing is hard, lonely work, and don't let anyone ever tell you different. Baring your heart and soul on paper for others to criticize and pick apart is not easy.

I know I sound harsh and ungrateful; it's a phase I go through periodically. I whine and complain and feel completely out of control when a deadline looms, like now, but writing is what I do. I'll be all right once I get over "deadline fever." Jack Hamel's book had to be on the publisher's desk by February 1. One glance at the calendar and I knew I had a little over three months to complete the project, then get back to my own work.

Often I worry that Maude Diamond's stuff isn't worthy of a single tree that it takes to make paper. But God must have thought I could help or that my work would speak to someone, so when anyone asks if I'm *passionate* about writing, my answer is "I'm passionate to have written."

That's the difference.

"Stella!" The stench of roast boiling dry came to me. "Can you check the roast? I think it needs water!"

"Okay!" My mother-in-law roused herself out of the recliner and shuffled into the kitchen.

The poodles split apart and broke into a lope, chasing each other around the coffee table. A potted philodendron toppled to its side, and the animals tramped dirt into the carpet. And it was only 9 A.M. I turned and went back to my office.

Stella returned from the kitchen and sat down.

When she wasn't involved in amateur town sleuthing— which, at the moment, she wasn't—Stella seemed without purpose. A fish out of water. A squirrel looking for a nut to crack. Reaching for the crocheted afghan on the back of the chair, she swathed herself in the yard of red yarn and lay back, her upper plate resting lopsidedly across her chest.

What a picture that made.

She and Morning Shade's self-appointed law official, Hargus Conley, had cracked the furniture-moving-bandit case three weeks ago. Now Stella was back to waiting for death and gossiping over coffee at the local Citgo every morning.

This small Arkansas town isn't a hotbed of crime, so cases for an elderly woman come few and far between. Actually, there's only been one of any consequence since I've been here—the night Mildred Fasco's grandfather set fire to the gas station to protest inflated pump prices. My. Was that thirty years ago? Herb and I had been newlyweds. How much could regular have been back then? Sixteen—eighteen cents a gallon?

But there was the furniture-moving-bandit case last summer. That turned out to be Simon Bench, who has a case of terminal neatness. He'd gone into neighbors' houses and rearranged furniture, replaced knickknacks, and even hung new drapes at one place.

Tired of trying to write, I reached for the morning paper. I had carried it to my office to keep Stella from making off with it. After she had finished reading the obituary column, she felt she had wrung all the juice out of the news, so to speak. If I wanted to read it I had to grab it before it hit the trash.

The front-page lead article was about a chain letter that apparently everyone in town had received—everyone but me. A chain letter? These days? I wondered how I had missed out on that. Why would anyone mess with a chain letter anyway? They were nothing more than a pyramid scheme, and illegal to boot. I suppose some chain letters are harmless, like the ones that ask for an apron or a handkerchief, although who in this modern age wore an apron or used a handkerchief?

I read the article carefully, learning that it was your typical chain letter. The person who received it was supposed to send five dollars to the top name. Five dollars they might as well burn—and a lot of money, considering how broke I was at the moment.

I took a little time to multiply five dollars by Morning Shade's population—ninety families—and the amount was hefty. I could sure use that much cash, but I quickly scuttled the thought. I didn't think I could come up with an excuse for the windfall that God would find acceptable.

But it was a nice thought while it lasted.

Propping my chin in the palm of my hand, I stared at the blank computer screen, trying to figure out how I was going to write Jack Hamel a best-seller when I couldn't *buy* one for myself.

Whoever said when a person gets older the best years of life are still ahead couldn't have been serious.

Either that—or I'd missed the point completely.

CHAPTER 2

Across town, CeeCee Tamaris stood on tiptoe, straining her five-foot-two frame to slide a flyer into the metal mail case. Morning Shade's daily postal routine was in full swing this morning. She smiled at a whistling Ty Hardin, who pushed a cart across the polished floor. She liked Ty's attitude, the boyish twinkle in his blue green eyes, and the way he stayed out of her way—but always close by if she needed a box or a heavy cart moved.

If anyone rightfully deserved to wear sackcloth and ashes, Ty did. Iva Hinkle said Marlene Walker, Ty's young bride, had died in a school shooting three years back, and Ty couldn't get over it. The couple had been married little more than two months when a young freshman brought a gun into the Little Rock school cafeteria that fateful morning. Three families were forever altered that day: Ty's and those of two other husbands who had kissed their wives good morning and left without knowing their lives were about to change.

CeeCee's thoughts turned to the disappointments life had thrown her—sliding curveballs, actually.

This would be her first Christmas without Jake.

The thought stung and threatened to spoil an otherwise good start to the fall morning. Even if Jake had proved to be a no-good, overinflated-ego, skirt-chasing jock, that hadn't made his death any easier. Cee shoved catalogs into the case and bit back ready tears. She had to admit her mood hadn't been the most charitable lately, but then thinking about the holidays always put her in a funky mood. That and the extra fifteen pounds she'd put on since she came home. You could add the staggering amount of mail increase for the approaching holiday season, and now some nut had started sending out chain letters—least that's what they looked like. She wished she could tell that idiot just how much extra work his or her criminal act had created for hardworking mail personnel.

She stuck the last envelope in the case and tried to make a convincing argument that her Hanes weren't cutting off circulation to her thigh line: they'd simply shrunk in the wash.

Iva Hinkle was giving her the eye this morning. She'd been on the job almost four months now, and the postmistress—and close friend—still kept a sharp lookout for mistakes. Happily CeeCee had made very few. She took to mail delivery like a catfish took to Wheaties balls. She glanced at the clock to see how time was running: 9:15. Perfect. It took her a little over three hours to sort the route by flyers, sizes, box holders. She focused on the canvas laundry cart that contained parcels. For the next thirty minutes she'd red-band the packages by addresses before she pulled down her mail and stacked the rubber-banded bundles into long cardboard trays, packed back to front. On any given day she'd deliver anywhere from fifteen to twenty boxes of mail.

Iva called from behind the cage, "Got anything interesting this morning?"

"Same ol' same ol'," Cee said.

Iva and CeeCee went way back. Even though they were three years apart in age, they'd become friends at Morning Shade High School. CeeCee got married shortly after a brief college effort, but Iva had continued her education, never marrying, and though Cee wasn't in the habit of speculation, she thought Iva was too set in her ways to answer to any man at this stage in her life. At thirty-something, Iva had a good job— ran the town's small brick post office and took care of her invalid mother evenings and weekends. She told Cee that she was happy, but Cee wondered how anybody could be happy working and taking care of an ailing mother.

Sighing, she eyed a letter with illegible writing, thankful that her own mother was healthy—though she couldn't imagine how her dad could have been so irresponsible and not taken out life insurance. Money had always been an issue in the Diamond household, and CeeCee guessed that Dad had thought with Mom's writing income she'd never have a financial worry. But she'd watched new lines form around her mother's eyes—millstone lines, Grandma called them. And CeeCee feared that she'd put a few there herself lately.

"I hope we don't have an early winter," Iva mused, her gaze focused on the fall display outside the front window. "I dread the thought of snow and ice."

CeeCee nodded. "Me too. Especially if I have to drive on the stuff."

"You won't have any trouble. Those postal vehicles are built to go."

CeeCee was glad she didn't walk the route. "I still like summer—heat and all."

"Maybe we'll luck out this year and have a mild winter." Iva glanced up and smiled as a customer entered the building.

CeeCee stacked the last of her route and numbered the trays. A few minutes later she put the trays into the parcel carts and wheeled the day's work out to her Long Life Vehicle.

There wasn't a sign of winter on this late October morning. Overhead an azure sky blanketed the sleepy town of Morning Shade; a warm, acrid-scented breeze carried the smell of drying leaves. Another fifteen minutes and she'd loaded the cardboard trays three to four across the back of her vehicle and as high as needed. By ten o'clock the day's mail was off and rolling.

Pulling out of the parking lot, CeeCee took a deep breath and realized that for the first time since Jake's death, she felt fairly human, and she'd have to say the feeling was welcome. Family and friends said that in time she'd be as good as new. She doubted that inflated optimism the moment she'd heard it. Sure, her marriage had stunk. Jake had stunk, and he hadn't been husband material, but nothing smelled as bad or lasted as long as death.

She leaned over and popped a book on tape into the CD player. By eleven o'clock she was humming along, sipping on a sixty-four-ounce Diet Pepsi in a plastic cup that she'd bought at the Citgo. A sack of salt-and-vinegar potato chips rested on the seat beside her.

She had a good job. In a few months she could get her own place and get out of Mom's hair. Not that her mother ever let on that she was a burden, but Cee knew. She just knew.

Straight ahead she spotted the Barneses' Norwegian elk-hound, and she felt that funny curl in the pit of her stomach. That dog gave her fits. There he was, standing sentinel at the mailbox, waiting to tear into the bumper of her LLV. There were three dogs on her route she'd just as soon were on somebody else's—the Barneses' Norwegian elkhound and the Fergusons' two German shepherds.

Those dogs were rocket fueled. Even if she worked up to a fairly decent speed—enough to slam-dunk mail in the box and floor the truck before the animals noticed—those shepherds nailed her every time. The elkhound's record was nearly as good.

Neither rain nor snow nor ... er ... something, she told herself as she approached the Barneses' mailbox, would impede her from delivering the mail. She felt superior this morning. All Mrs. Barnes had today was a flyer and a Sears sales catalog. She figured she could throw those in the box and be past the twenty-inch-high, fifty-pound pest before he could catch her. Mashing down on the gas pedal, she made a run for it.

The hound's eyes focused on the speeding vehicle. He sat up straighter, jowls dripping with saliva, senses zeroed in on the approaching bumper. CeeCee reached the box doing around thirty—way too fast she knew but figuring that if she wasn't smart enough to outwit a dog she'd best get a different occupation.

The hound sprang at the split second CeeCee's hand snaked out, jerked the box open then shut. Teeth clamped around the hard rubber bumper and the LLV shook.

CeeCee threw her head back and laughed, pressing harder on the gas pedal. No way could he hold on. They had this battle every morning.

The mail truck approached the Millses' mailbox fairly flying, truck shaking like a GE juicer—the pest was really annoying now. The postal truck picked up speed with the hound still hanging on. The race was neck and neck. Man against beast.

CeeCee spotted Hubert Mills coming out of the house and thought, *Okay. Now what?* She shot a quick glance at the mail tray and to her relief saw nothing for the Mills address. She blew by like a sonic blast, leaving Mr. Mills reeling at the edge of the road, scratching his head, staring after the truck like it was an alien spaceship.

Sneaking a peek in the rearview mirror, she decided she should have said something—hollered something. Mail trucks are not supposed to shoot by postal patrons, particularly not with hounds hanging off their front bumpers.

But, hey, it's the hound's fault, she reasoned.

Settling back, she reached for her Diet Pepsi and tore into the bag of chips.

The hound gave up before she reached the crossroad. He let go of the bumper and dropped to his belly in the middle of the road, tongue lagging. CeeCee glanced in her rearview mirror and shouted, "Yes!"

The hound was gathering strength for a new day.

Well, she thought. *I'll be here tomorrow and the next day and the next. CeeCee Tamaris is back in town!*

*   *   *

"'Swing low, sweet chariot, comin' for to carry me home ...'"

"Huh?" Stella Diamond sat straight up, fumbling for her glasses. "Is it time, Lord?"

"'Swing low, sweet chariot...'"

It took a second for her aging eyes to adjust to the blaring television screen. Arnold Schwarzenegger was gone; now some man dressed in a tuxedo stood on a podium singing an old gospel hymn.

Relief flooded Stella. Land sakes. She'd thought for sure it was *time*.

Hitting the remote control's Mute button, she detangled herself from the afghan and closed her eyes, disappointment replacing relief. Maude's office door was closed; she'd have to be quiet and not disturb her daughter-in-law. She sniffed the air, assuring herself the roast was cooking properly.

She sat back in the recliner and put her head in her hands.

If she died right now it would be so peaceful. No pain—just a quick getaway. And that's what she was looking for at her age. Hassle-free death; the only way to go.

Lord, this is Stella. It was always nice to remind Him who needed His time. *I'm eighty-seven and useless as snow tires in the Bahamas. I get under everybody's feet, and it's downright impossible to stay out of the way twenty-four hours a day.*

The phone rang. *Doesn't anyone ever leave a body alone?*

She stuffed her upper plate into her mouth and leaned over and picked up the cordless receiver. After a couple of attempts she found the Talk button and pushed it.

Hilda Throckmorton's grating voice came across the line. "Stella?"

"Yeah?"

"I'm glad I caught you at home."

"Yeah." Like she had anywhere important to go. After morning coffee at Citgo with Pansy, Frances, and Simon she'd pretty well shot her day's agenda. Except for bridge a couple nights a week and Farkle on Friday nights.

"You're aware the church's annual spaghetti supper is coming up?"

"Again?" Hadn't they just been through that brouhaha? The older you got the quicker time passed; for Stella it seemed like she was on a fast freight to Beulah Land.

"Time *does* get away from us, doesn't it? The girls and I have been thinking, Stella. You'd be absolutely *ideal* to chair the committee this year."

Translated to mean: *Congratulations. You're the elected chump.*

When had "the girls," meaning the women of Hilda's Guild committee, come up with this? Seems like she'd already taken her turn chairing the event two years ago—and once was enough. Granted, funds from the spaghetti function played a large part in the church's yearly budget, but the whole pasta-and-garlic-bread thing gave Stella a headache.

How to get out of it?

The old excuse machine was rusty; she hadn't seen the attack coming and she should have. Stella prided herself on details— always alert for the unexpected, the vaguely-implied-but-never-voiced sort of thing.

"What do I have to do?" It didn't really matter; she didn't want to do it. She'd learned a long time ago that women could be vicious. Couldn't make 'em happy if you gave them the moon with their name written in gold on it, and the females of Living Truth Community Church could be downright aggravating when it came to working arrangements.

"Oh, very little," Hilda chirped. "As chair you can *delegate* practically everything."

Right, Stella thought. She was too old to swallow that one. What Hilda was saying was if Stella could hog-tie one more stressed-out soccer, basketball-practice, ballet-practice, aerobic, yoga

overworked mom who still had five minutes left in her day to volunteer for another committee, she had it made. But she was up to the challenge.

The gig would be a piece of cake. She glanced at Maude's closed office door. Plus it would get her out of the house.

Stella felt sorry for her daughter-in-law. Herb had been a negligent numskull. She'd raised him smarter than he'd proved to be. When they'd found him dead in a hotel room last year, who'd have ever thought he'd have been so irresponsible? Hadn't left poor Maude a lick of life insurance or 401(k). Maude got by the best she could, but Stella knew the upcoming holidays and extra expenses were weighing heavily on her mind. Stella sure wasn't in any position to help out financially—had to leave Shady Acres and move in with Maude because her daughter-in-law didn't have the funds to keep her in the residential home, and she sure didn't have the funds to stay there.

You can't stretch a $253-a-month pension the way you used to.

Some folks had the erroneous notion that a writer made a lot of money. Well, maybe some did, but Stella didn't think Maude was one of them.

Stella would give her eyeteeth to be back at the residential care center with Simon, Pansy, and Frances. Not that she minded living with Maude—and now CeeCee, since she'd moved back home—but a body craves privacy. If she wanted to take her teeth out, scratch in unbecoming places, and sit around in her Hanes all day, she ought to be able to do it; she was eighty-seven years old. Stella Diamond had earned the right to be a slob in private. She'd even earned the right to say no to these committee chairs, but seeing how she had nothing better to do with her time she supposed it wouldn't kill her to help out.

"Do I get to pick my own committee?" she asked.

"Well... yes. I have a few who have already volunteered—"

Stella cut Hilda off at the pass. She'd been through that, and no thanks. She'd assemble her own workers and make sure they showed up when they promised. Too often she'd been left holding the bag at the last minute; a whole basement full of hungry people and about as much organization as a dogfight. "I'll choose my own workers, thank you."

"Well... you are the chair," Hilda conceded.

And don't you forget it, Stella thought. But she would. Hilda was as touchy as a new blister, and Stella knew she was taking on a big headache by accepting the chair. She took the job anyway.

"When's the first meeting?"

A hint of coolness crept into Hilda's tone. "Since you're chair I suppose that's up to you."

Well, now—that was okay. Maybe for once Hilda would stand back and let somebody else give the orders.

"Okay," Stella said, feeling a little power happy. "We'll meet next Wednesday morning. I'll have my workers lined up and raring to go."

"Well do you mind if *I'm* on the committee?"

Hilda sounded a *little* on edge now. Stella couldn't remember a year when the busybody wasn't on the committee, and as much as she'd like to remind Hilda that others were capable of cooking spaghetti, Stella wasn't mean-spirited—most days. Besides, if Hilda wasn't on the planning committee she'd take over the decorating committee. *Best give her a job where I can boss her—like beverages. Ice and foam cups. She can't do much harm there.*

Chuckling, Stella wondered why she was feeling so wicked. Guess it didn't matter; as long as she felt anything it meant she was still sucking in air.

She punched the Off button a few minutes later, realizing that she was chairman of the annual church spaghetti supper. What a hoot.

Yawning, she took out her teeth again, picked up a true-crime paperback, and leaned back to pass another hour. Days could get long when you were her age—that's eighty-seven breathing down the neck of eighty-eight. Hard to believe she'd made it this far.

CHAPTER 3

I opened my eyes to see Captain marching back and forth on my bed, rumbling deep in his chest like a runaway freight. Throwing the blanket aside, I reached for my robe. *I might as well get up and feed the cat,* I thought. Either that or be tromped black and blue by the overweight rampaging bully of Morning Shade's back alleys. Captain ruled the feline world, and he did a pretty good job of ruling my household.

The sun was barely up, but Stella had beaten me downstairs. I heard her complaining as she came in the kitchen door from getting the morning paper.

"Dumb dogs. Can't even go outside without falling over one of them. I never kept dogs in the house, Maude. Can't understand why you do."

"You know why. This is Cee's home too, and they're her dogs." My daughter had been through enough when her husband, Jake "Touchdown" Tamaris, had died unexpectedly, leaving her deeply in debt. I couldn't deprive her of her dogs too. "Omelet all right for breakfast?"

"Fine with me. Too late to worry about my diet. At my age it doesn't matter what I eat. I'm living on borrowed time now. Throw some mushrooms and cheese in my omelet. Hang the cholesterol. Tomorrow the doctors will be telling us all that fat's good for the arteries." She spread out the paper on the table, opening it to the obituary column.

I set the table, working around her.

"John Larson's funeral is tomorrow. You know him?"

I stopped chopping mushrooms. "Don't believe I do. Where'd he live?"

"Ash Flat."

I stared at her, exasperated. "Why do you expect me to know anyone in Ash Flat? I just shop over there occasionally. I don't live there."

"It's not on the other side of the world. Thought you might have met John—looks like he's got a pretty good write-up. I wonder how they do that. Some folks get fifteen, sixteen lines, and others only get a mention. Poor John and Velma—it says here that's his wife. She must still be living. I heard once that some women watch the obit columns and when they see that a woman's died—bam! They move in for the kill. Gold diggers. Every last one of them— shameless women looking to take advantage of lonely widowers."

"Velma didn't die. John did." I dumped the mushrooms into the sizzling skillet and wondered why Stella was so fixated on other people's business.

"I know. John was only seventy-eight. Still just a pup. I'm eighty-seven. Should have gone before this man."

CeeCee walked into the kitchen in time to catch the conversational drift, which wasn't all that difficult since we started every morning with the obits, or the "daily deaths," as Cee called them.

I couldn't decide if Stel was sorry the deceased had gone on, or if she was taking a sneaky pleasure in the fact that she was still here.

CeeCee pulled out her chair. "You're young for your age, Grandma."

Stella sniffed. "That's all you know, young lady. I've lived so long all my friends in heaven probably think I didn't make it."

I had to laugh. Stella could be funny sometimes. Frenchie, one of the poodles, yipped for a bite of toast, and Captain, who thought he had a monopoly on table scraps, spat a warning. Frenchie yelped and hunkered under CeeCee's chair. Claire, the smarter of the two dogs, which wasn't saying a whole lot, took refuge behind the waste can.

I sidestepped Captain, who evidently had decided since I was the one preparing the food, it would be good to wrap himself around my ankle, quite a feat for a cat his size. This house got more like a zoo with every passing day. All we needed was a pair of monkeys swinging from the light fixture, and if CeeCee ever ran across some, she'd bring them home with her.

I placed omelets on the table, mushroom and cheese for Stella, cheese for Cee, and started to prepare my own.

"Have you heard? New people moved into the old Harris place." Cee paused to take a drink of milk. "They've got a couple of kids, both girls, and a dog. Just what I need—another dog on my route."

"The old Harris place is haunted," Stella said.

"No it's not," I scolded. "I don't believe in ghosts."

"Neither do I," Stella admitted. "That's just a tale that was going around years ago. I think it turned out to be squirrels in the attic." She cut a bite of her omelet. "Better than bats in your belfry."

I ignored that and sat down at the table, slipping Captain a crust of buttered toast. He crunched it, growling contentedly. Frenchie uttered pitiful yelps, which the cat ignored with all the aplomb of Prince Charles on parade.

"Are either of you planning to be here for lunch?" I asked, mentally running over what I had on hand.

"Not me," CeeCee said. "I'm taking a salad. I need to lose fifteen pounds."

The same fifteen she'd lost three times in as many months, but I didn't say so. I was losing the battle of the bulge myself due to too many hours of sitting in front of a computer instead of exercising. Maybe I'd join the new aerobics class at the senior center, but I wouldn't count on it. I'd bought a new exercise book last week—*Get Your Body in Shape in Three Easy Steps.* I didn't think they meant the steps to the refrigerator, which was where I usually ended up. When it came to exercising, I'd rather read about it than do it. Same with writing; I'd rather read than write.

"I've got a guild meeting this morning," Stella reminded us. "I'm the new chair for the spaghetti dinner."

"So you've said, Grandma." CeeCee winked at me.

Again and again and again, I thought, reminded of the children's song, "the wheels of the bus go round and round ..." I hope I never get to the point I'm relaying the same information day after day.

CeeCee changed the subject. "Have you heard anything about those chain letters everyone is getting?"

I shook my head. "Just that they're getting them. It's the oddest thing." I paused. "I didn't get one—did you?"

Both Cee and Stella shook their heads, but I noticed Stella was a little slower on the uptake this morning.

"No one seems to know who started the letter," I commented. "It was signed *Pigeon,* so you know it's a fake name."

"Well, whoever did it could be in big trouble. A chain letter is just a Ponzi scheme. The ones at the top get money; the ones at the bottom get cheated." CeeCee dipped into her omelet. "Mmm. This smells good, Mom."

Stella peered at Cee over her glasses. "A chain letter isn't crooked. All you have to do is send out the letters and the money comes in. What's wrong with that?"

CeeCee swigged milk. "It's like this, Grandma. A lot of people who start the letters put their name at the top, only sometimes it isn't their real name, and the five names listed under them, well, that's them too, using a fictitious name. It was invented by a guy named Ponzi, and it's called a pyramid scheme. The names at the top get money, and the people at the bottom get zilch, because the chain fizzles out before they get anything."

Stella didn't say anything more, just sat there looking stubborn. I made a mental note to tell her for goodness' sake not to send any money if she got a letter from this Pigeon person. We didn't have any extra cash to throw around on chain letters.

Stella pushed her lips out in a pout. "Pansy wants to stop for lunch at the Citgo after the meeting, so look for me when you see me coming."

Fair enough. Maybe I'd get some work done today if I could have the house to myself for a change. The sort of constant going and coming we had around here hadn't been conducive to the muse.

Stella had finished her breakfast and gone back to reading the obituary page. "Linda Appleby died. She's the same age as me. Do you think I should have agreed to chair that spaghetti dinner? You know, it's three weeks away. I'd hate to think they'd have to get a replacement at the last minute."

"I'm sure you'll still be around when the dinner's over," I said. "You're tougher than you think."

CeeCee carried her dishes to the sink. "I have to run or I'm going to be late. If you go to the store today, Mom, pick up some chips, okay?"

"Sure," I agreed, thinking that eating salad for lunch wouldn't do her much good if she pigged out on salt-and-vinegar chips when she got off work.

CeeCee left, and Stella started on her second mug of coffee. "Tell you what, Maude. That Throckmorton is one bossy broad. I'm surprised the sun can come up in the morning without her permission."

"Now, Stella, I'm sure she means well."

"Oh, her intentions are probably good, but I've heard the road to you-know-where is paved with good intentions."

I had more sense than to touch that. "You're the chair. It's up to you to make the decisions."

"I've got some ideas." She pushed out her lower lip again. For a refreshing change she had both lower and upper plates in today. "This just might be a dinner to remember."

I didn't doubt it a bit. Put Stella and Hilda together, each determined to have her own way, and the resulting fireworks would rival Washington, D.C.'s Fourth of July spectacular.

My mother-in-law stumped into the living room a short while later and picked up her purse. "You'd better come with me, Maude. I might need backup."

"I would, Stella, but I have to work. I have to go through all of Jack's notes and try to decipher his writing. You'll have Frances and Pansy to support you."

Stella riffled through her purse. "Now what did I do with that little notebook I keep my thoughts in? It's got everything I know in it. If I've lost it, I've lost my mind. It's a terrible thing to get old, Maude, but it comes to us all if we live long enough. You'll find that out one day."

Just a big ol' bundle of sunshine.

"*I* think you left your notebook on the coffee table."

She found the spiral and stuck it in her purse, a pensive expression on her face. "Do you think Hilda's really going to let me run the spaghetti dinner?"

"Oh, I'm sure she will. After all, she's the one who appointed you."

"Yeah. She may regret that. Don't forget, I'm scheduled to play bridge with Simon and Pansy and Frances tonight." She let the screen door slam behind her.

I was relieved to see her functioning again. For a while it looked like she'd been entombed in her recliner. After the furniture-arranging, burglar mystery had been solved, she seemed to lose interest in life, but the spaghetti dinner had rejuvenated her. I had a hunch this would be the liveliest dinner in Living Truth's history, but it *was* thoughtful of Hilda to ask Stella to chair the dinner. If I knew Throckmorton—and unfortunately I did—she would still expect to run the whole shebang. I wished her luck; not many could tell Stella what to do and enforce it. My mother-in-law not only marched to her own drummer; she called the tune.

Hilda considered herself the elected leader of the women: actually she didn't have enough leadership skills to pop corn, and she hadn't tangled yet with Stella.

I wiped down the kitchen counters and wandered into my office. The proposal for my next M. K. Diamond mystery should be mailed tomorrow, but I couldn't force myself to get started on it. I really believed God had given me the ability to write, but I was out of fresh ideas. The literary well had run dry. Some days I wanted to quit, but other days I knew I never would. I'm a writer. It's what I do. And for the next three months I was going to be writing Jack Hamel's book.

Instead of sitting down at the computer, I swiped a brush through my hair, shrugged into my coat, and drove to the Cart Mart to order my Thanksgiving turkey, which would be at least three pounds bigger this year because my household had expanded. When I entered the Cart Mart, I was struck by the large display of pumpkins and candy. I always love this time of year; change was coming, but it was welcome change.

I spotted Hargus Conley, Morning Shade's self-appointed lawman, in the snack aisle. If I hadn't promised Cee I'd get chips, I'd have tried to avoid him, but trying to slip past Hargus was like trying to sneak a mackerel past Captain.

Hargus prides himself on being gimlet-eyed. Stella insists on calling it pie-eyed, although I've never seen him drink anything stronger than soda.

He tipped his hat. "Morning, Miz Diamond. How's the world treating you?"

"Fine, Hargus, super. Yourself?"

"Doing good since I cracked that burglary case." He jacked up his pants and shook his head, his expression turning sly. "Never thought a dignified-looking man like Simon Bench would take part in something like that. And my own momma. Gave her a talking-to, I did. Bet she'll think next time before she pulls something like that."

"I'm sure she will." Frankly, I hoped none of them ever got involved in sleuthing again. Trying to catch the burglar had given Stella a boost and had done wonders for my writing, but although I knew it had been a prank, the next time it might have more lasting repercussions. There were days when I wanted to hang Stella, but I didn't want to hurt her.

Hargus peered at me through narrowed eyes. "You sure you're feeling all right, Miz Diamond? You look a mite peaked."

"I'm fine, Hargus." Give me time to concentrate on my work, and I'd be fine, but with Stella and CeeCee popping in at the weirdest times, plus two high-strung poodles and a cantankerous yellow tomcat who could give the Mafia lessons on terrorizing, there was precious little peace at the Diamond household.

"Well, just asking." Hargus took a bag of barbecue chips from the shelf and dumped it in his cart. "Got to get moving. Takes a lot of time to keep an eye on a town this size. You'd be surprised at what all goes on around here."

He wheeled his cart in a figure eight and strode away, pants at half-mast. It wouldn't surprise me a bit if he lost them somewhere between the cookie aisle and the soft-drink center. I don't know why Pansy doesn't tell her son to hitch those things up! As for how busy he is, that must be wishful thinking. Nothing ever happens in Morning Shade.

I got two bags of chips for CeeCee and stopped at the meat counter.

"Morning, Maude," Walt Richards, the meat-department manager, greeted me. "How are things out your way?"

"Just fine, Walt." I thought of how many times I'd used that word today. A nice, generic word that didn't mean much. I could be going through the worse crisis of my life, and I'd probably answer that question the same way. *Fine. Super. Jim-dandy.*

Sometimes, first thing in the morning, I ask, "How are You

today, Lord?" I wonder if anyone ever asks the Father what He's doing and if things are going His way. "I guess I need to order a Thanksgiving turkey."

"We can handle that. What size did you have in mind?"

"I don't know. Big enough for maybe half a dozen people without having enough left over till Christmas." I hadn't made out my guest list yet, but I always had friends and neighbors in for the holiday.

Stella wouldn't eat much, but driving the mail route all day gave CeeCee a rousing good appetite. This would be her first Thanksgiving without Jake, and I wanted the day to be special for her. Jake hadn't been much of a husband, but his death had been hard on Cee. I loved my daughter; I just wished she'd stop turning my home into a shelter for wayward animals.

We finally settled on the size of a turkey, and I drove home to work on Jack's notes. The man could use a cursive lesson— or maybe a half dozen. I put the groceries away and fed the poodles before settling down to work. Captain perched in his favorite spot on top of the file cabinet where he could watch me. As long as my fingers hit the keys, he slept. Let me stop typing and he glared at me out of those malevolent green eyes.

"You're a tyrant, you know that?"

He growled low in his throat and stretched as if I had given him a compliment. Dumb cat. I leaned back in my chair and sighed. Writing was so hard.

It didn't used to be. I could remember when I was eager to start a new book; the ideas came faster than I could type.

I peered at Jack's scratchy notes.

I couldn't get interested in writing, so I spent a few minutes reading and answering e-mail and surfing the best-seller lists, where my books still failed to show up. Finally I switched off the computer. For want of something better to do, I drove to Ash Flat, purchased three books on time management, stress, and burnout, and spent the rest of the day reading.

Time management was a lot like exercising—easier to read about than actually put into practice. I studiously poured over the material, followed the simple little arrows: Stress leads to burnout; burnout leads to depression.

I had them all.

Giving up. Losing perspective. The drive for control.

Been there; done that. I closed the book. No new insights— just guilt that I'd spent thirty dollars and blown the whole afternoon trying to figure out a way to be more productive. At the moment I'd *buy* a mystery just to get Stella involved so I could get motivated.

Something was seriously wrong with my thinking process.

CeeCee and Stella hadn't returned, so I dragged my heels back to the computer to work—or at least present the *appearance* of working. Five minutes later, after ruining my eyes trying to decipher the chicken tracks Jack Hamel called writing, I gave up and called him.

He answered the phone himself, and his deep baritone sounded as dignified and assured as a successful television preacher should sound. "Hamel here."

Jack's last name suddenly reminded me of the popular 1977 Woman's Olympic Championship figure skater, Dorothy Hamill. Remember the Hamill Camel? I always wanted her haircut, but no matter how many times I told the hairdresser "wedge," my cut turned out to look like an ugly, uneven "shelf."

"Jack? This is Maude. Do you have a minute?"

"My time is your time, my good woman. What can I do for you?"

For starters he could come down to earth and develop some penmanship skills. "I'm having trouble reading your notes, Jack."

"Why, whatever could be wrong?" His dignity dropped a few levels. Probably few people criticized Jack Hamel. Well, a new experience was good for everyone.

"It's your handwriting, Jack. I can't read it."

"Why, Maude—"

I interrupted. "Surely I'm not the first person to bring that to your attention."

He was silent for a moment, and then he chuckled. "My wife won't let me write a grocery list. All right, Maude I'll send you new notes, and I'll take care to make them more legible."

"Thanks, Jack, I appreciate it."

I switched off the computer after a good ten minutes of work and went to the kitchen to start dinner, thinking about those time-management books. A total waste of good money. In actual work hours, I'd probably put in fifteen working minutes today.

Shoo-wee. I had to increase my output.

CHAPTER 4

Stella and Pansy walked into the guild meeting, held this morning in the Living Truth fellowship hall because donuts and coffee would be served afterwards. The room was full of the racket associated with women's meetings. Sort of like a gaggle of geese in a windstorm. Above the noise Stella could hear Throckmorton's voice sounding off like an air-raid siren.

Pansy elbowed Stella. "That woman would make a champion hog caller."

Stella stifled a snort. Like she'd told Maude, she had her doubts that Hilda really meant to let her make any decisions about the spaghetti dinner. If she did, it would be a first for Hilda.

Stella twisted her lips in a wry grin. Throckmorton couldn't lead a taffy pull. Not without making a mess.

Frances shifted her purse and a hymnbook, allowing the two women to sit down in the metal chairs she had been saving for them.

"Hilda's in rare form this morning, isn't she? She's going to take over the spaghetti dinner from you, mark my words."

Frances's jet-black dyed hair was coiled on top of her head like a beehive. As usual she wore a print dress with a lace collar, this one in soft shades of blue and lavender that complimented her fair skin. Somehow, no matter what Frances wore, she still looked like what she was: a retired schoolteacher. Confident. Assured. Stella could swear Frances's perfume carried the faint but pleasant hint of paste.

Pansy, seated on Stella's left, looked like her name; she had a soft, cushiony lap and eyes as blue as the flower for which she was named. *And then there's me,* Stella thought. Short, scrawny, nothing like the pretty woman she used to be. And she *had* been pretty... but that was a long time ago. Nothing pretty about eighty-seven.

Stella brought her attention back to Frances's statement. "I've got a few tricks up my sleeve. I may be old, but I'm tough. Living to be eighty-seven isn't for sissies."

"Ladies, ladies," Hilda boomed. "Let's take our places so the meeting can begin. We have a special treat, which I won't go into right now since we have business to take care of first."

Stella shifted in her chair, wondering what the mayor's wife had up her sleeve. You could bet she was up to something. Stella had never met a woman who worked so hard to keep things stirred up. It would be different if the things she stirred amounted to a hill of beans, but most of the time they didn't amount to anything. Just caused a fracas.

Hilda paused dramatically, her florid face stretched in an expansive smile. "I'm sure you know our annual church spaghetti dinner draws the whole town, and the proceeds account for half of the church's yearly income. Therefore, it is very important that everything goes smoothly."

She paused to consult her notes, her voice sliding into a phony, sweet tone, which didn't fool Stella one bit. "This year I've asked Stella Diamond to chair the dinner."

There was a scattering of applause, and Stella gripped her purse, preparing to stand up and approach the podium.

Hilda forged ahead, running a calculating eye over the guild members, sliding right past Stella as if she didn't exist.

"Makes me feel like I actually have died and don't know it,"

Stella muttered. "Like it's my shadow sitting here."

"Hilda is a little short on manners," Frances whispered. "If she'd been in one of my classes when I taught school, I'd have taught her to follow parliamentarian rules."

"Now concerning the spaghetti dinner," Hilda continued.

Stella sat up a little straighter, thinking it was her moment to shine.

But Hilda still had the floor, and it would apparently take a bulldozer to move her. "I think we'll put the drinks over there." Throckmorton pointed to a white linen-cloth-covered table. "And we're serving bread sticks this year instead of garlic bread. Bread sticks are more refined."

Refined? Stella stiffened, her nose twitching. Maybe where *she* came from, but garlic bread was church tradition for the spaghetti dinner. You couldn't just change tradition without so much as a by-your-leave. Someone had to do something, and as the chair, Stella guessed it was up to her. She got to her feet, clutching her purse with nervous fingers. This wasn't her style. She cleared her throat, capturing Hilda's astonished attention.

"We're having garlic bread. I can't eat bread sticks. Hurts my lower gums."

Hilda bristled. "Really, Stella, I believe bread sticks would be in order—"

Stella jutted out her jaw, the way Maude said she did when she was fixing to get stubborn. Well, Hilda hadn't seen stubborn yet. "I'm the chair, and we're having garlic bread, and I'm putting the drinks over there." She pointed to an unadorned, plain brown table on the opposite side of the room. Tablecloths would come later.

Hilda's face turned rose red. "Well, as I was saying—"

Pansy sprang up. "If Stella is the chair, why isn't she up there giving orders?"

"That's right," Frances chimed in. "Let Stella talk!"

Stella sat down in a hurry. It was nice to have friends who would stand up for you, but they were missing a good opportunity to keep quiet. She didn't have anything to say yet. Mostly she was still thinking.

She dug out her little notebook and flipped through the pages, trying to look confident, ready to fake it if necessary. She'd had lots of experience at faking it. Live to be her age and you could bluff your way through anything, but she wasn't what she used to be. Matter of fact, she wasn't sure she ever was what she used to be. Who could remember that far back?

She didn't need to worry. Hilda had no intentions of surrendering the floor. She chugged her way across the room to a group of people sitting on the front row, and her voice climbed a couple of octaves, like she was getting ready to emcee a catfight. "We have some special guests with us this morning: our new pastor, Pat Brookes; and his charming wife, Elly; and their three children." Hilda motioned for the pastor and his family to come forward. "You all just stand up here so everyone can get a good look at you."

Everyone present already knew who the visitors were, considering men and children seldom attended guild meetings. Pastor Healy had recently taken a two-year leave of absence to work in Mexico in the mission field. He claimed the Lord had called him, but Stella figured it was the only way he could get any relief from Hilda telling him what to do.

Hilda shooed Elly Brookes ahead of her, like a tugboat followed by the *Queen Mary*. Stick a pin in her and she'd zap around the room like a runaway balloon. Stella got so tickled thinking about it she almost missed what Pansy whispered.

"Good-looking man. Hope he preaches as good as he looks."

"I like a dark-haired man," Frances said. "Seems like they're more trustworthy."

Stella snickered. You could expect that sort of comment from someone who had never married. Elly Brookes was a slender little thing, one of those quiet-faced women who didn't show much emotion. Reserved. Exact opposite of Hilda.

"She's sort of quiet," Frances said.

"Supposed to be a tireless worker," Pansy mumbled.

"Well, she'd better learn to look out for herself, or Throckmorton will work her to a shadow."

Stella ignored the reprimanding look Hilda sent her way.

The Brookes children seemed well behaved, even shy. Sari, the five-year-old, looked like her father, with dark hair and dancing blue eyes. Might be a handful if you ever got her started. Ten-year-old Jonah was your average boy, brown hair like his mother's, open friendly face. It was Abel, the thirteen-year-old, who caught Stella's attention. Quiet-faced, like Elly. Good-looking boy, but not one to put his thoughts on display. All in all, the new pastor and his family seemed to stack up just fine.

If Hilda didn't scare them off.

When the meeting concluded, Stella walked to the Citgo with her two friends. She only half listened to them talking, her mind on Maude. She hadn't realized the holidays were so close, but all this talk of the spaghetti dinner reminded her the event was held just before Thanksgiving.

Just before Thanksgiving; five weeks before Christmas.

Lately Maude had said just enough for Stella to suspect that her daughter-in-law was worried about Christmas expenses this year. She hadn't revealed much, but Stella was sure Maude was having serious financial woes.

With all this time on her hands, Stella ought to be able to do something to help out. Her pension wouldn't make a dent in a milk bucket, but if she set her head to it, there was surely some way she could contribute to household expenses.

But look what had happened the last time she tried to come up with a way she could help. Got herself into a mess with this bunch of illegal chain letters, that's what. Not exactly helpful, and Maude would land on her like duck on a June bug if she only knew. Stella sighed. And she'd been so careful—so crafty. Hitched a ride to Ash Flat with Hargus Conley, opened a post office box under an assumed name. Brilliance in motion.

She had some thinking to do. She'd thought using a fake name, Pigeon, at the bottom of the list would help, because she didn't want Maude to know what she was doing. She'd been careful to put Pansy's and Frances's names under hers so they'd get in on the good fortune, too. She'd never dreamt she was doing anything wrong! CeeCee's announcement had stunned her—why, she could get in big trouble for writing a chain letter!

Think, old woman! What was she going to do now?

She was too old to go to the Big House. Though she'd be safe there. The young women inmates weren't that hard up for female company.

But what would Hilda say when she found out she'd let a criminal chair the spaghetti supper?

Well, no real harm had been done. Not a soul knew she'd written those letters, so nobody could implicate her. All she'd have to do was let the talk die down. When folks saw they wouldn't be getting a second letter, the crisis would blow over and she'd be in the clear.

Drivel. There must be something to bad luck and chain letters. She'd sure enough been hit with calamity.

*   *   *

CeeCee decided she never wanted an indoor job. The stretch of pretty autumn weather was cool but clear, perfect mail-delivery conditions. After four months, she'd settled into her route and decided there, wasn't any better way to earn a living. People were friendly, and her rural patrons had started to look for her every day. They'd smile or throw a friendly greeting her way. She'd forgotten what small-town rural America was like.

She smiled, turning the corner in her LLV. She'd landed the perfect job—or it would be if it weren't for the dogs.

She'd taken Grandma's advice and invested in a sack of dog biscuits. Where there was a will, there was a way, and all that jazz.

She'd soon have those dogs eating out of her hand—more or less.

She stopped at Victor Johnson's mailbox and honked. After a few moments, he came bustling out, pulling a denim jacket over his faded overalls. Standing about five eight and so scrawny a good puff of wind would blow him into the next county, Victor was one of CeeCee's favorites.

"Howdy, CeeCee. You got me a present?"

"Sure do, Victor." She reached behind her and lifted a cardboard box with air holes. "Looks like a box of bees. I'm going to be glad to get rid of this package. I keep wondering what would happen if they got loose."

"You wouldn't have nothing to fear, CeeCee. Bees are real sociable."

"That's what I'm afraid of. I'd prefer to be sociable with something that doesn't make its point with a stinger. But Mom sure appreciates the fresh honey, Victor."

Victor chuckled and took the box and started back toward the house. "Glad to hear it—got more honey than I know what to do with. But you tell your mom I'm waiting for another invite for fried chicken and hot biscuits."

"I'll tell her!"

The next stop was her own house. She checked to see if her mother had received anything that looked like it might contain an advance check. Mom never complained, but Cee had noticed the worry lines etched in her forehead. Money was tight. Bills had to be paid, and the publishing business was notoriously slow to pay.

CeeCee also knew she was an extra burden and so was Grandma. Mom wouldn't refuse to let them live with her—it wasn't her nature—but you could bet the two of them added to her worries. She put the mail in the box. Nothing resembling a check, worse luck.

A new man had moved into the empty house on the corner of Elm and Spruce. CeeCee riffled through Gary Hendricks's mail, seeing what it might tell her about him. No mention of a Mrs. or a feminine name, so maybe he was single.

And good-looking, she decided, as she spotted him putting up storm windows.

CeeCee slid his mail into the box: a Scout magazine, a seed catalog, a flyer for missionary work in Ethiopia. He turned and waved, flashing a million-dollar grin. CeeCee grinned back and waved. *Hey, not bad.* Medium height, with blow-dried brown hair, and an open friendly manner. Really attractive smile. Nice muscles filling out his sweatshirt. A very good addition to her customer list, and one she was looking forward to getting to know. In a town the size of Morning Shade, where everyone knew everyone else, she was sure to run into him somewhere. She drove away, craning her neck to look back at Gary Hendricks, new man in town, surprised she would even be mildly curious. Since Jake's death she hadn't looked at another man—not with interest.

She spared a second glance at Gary Hendricks in the rear-view mirror.

According to his mail, the man was a God-fearing, patriotic, clean-cut, possibly eligible bachelor who loved to garden.

Hmm.

Leaning back in her seat, CeeCee rammed her hand into the sack of chips. Yep, she had the coolest job in Morning Shade.

CHAPTER 5

CeeCee came in tired and hungry. We sat down to pork chops, mashed potatoes and gravy, and homemade biscuits. I had been in a cooking mood tonight, so there was also a freshly baked cherry pie cooling on the counter.

"Mmm." Cee looked at the table. "That sure looks good. And I'm ready to eat. It's really busy at work, and the holiday season hasn't even started yet."

"Any more chain letters show up?" I quipped.

CeeCee and I both jumped when Stella's fork clattered to the china plate. Frenchie set up a howl, and Captain went nuts, bounding from the armchair to the sofa to the windowsill in the living room. It took a full five minutes to restore house order.

Sitting back down at the table, I stared at my congealing supper. I love pork chops and mashed potatoes; I could eat them stone cold, which I was about to do.

"I haven't noticed any more," CeeCee said. "Asking for money went out years ago—I don't know who came up with the idea to start again."

Stella looked up from her plate. "You're sure chain letters are mail fraud?"

"Positive. Why, it's taking money from unsuspecting

victims—promising to make them rich when there isn't a shot in Little Rock they'll get anything but a few dollars."

"Sounds to me like a body could get rich quick," Stella argued. "And most folk could spare a few dollars."

"Oh, Grandma." CeeCee took a sip of tea. "Those letters are just one more way to bilk an unsuspecting John Doe out of his money. And the sender has the audacity to scare the victim by predicting—" she punctuated the air with quotation marks— "'dire consequences—your hair will drop out, your arches will fall'—if they don't respond."

Stella dropped her gaze back to her plate.

I sighed. "You know better than to take chain letters seriously, Stella. I thought the post office had stamped them out years ago—except for e-mails. I must get fifty 'pass this along if you love Jesus' letters a week. Makes you feel like a heathen if you delete the thing." I picked up what remained of my pork chop and savored the tender meat, my tongue probing the juicy moistness close to the bone. Briefly I eyed the last chop on the plate until my conscience reminded me the scales were up another pound this morning. But I'm fairly certain they aren't accurate—weigh four to five pounds heavy. I reached for the chop.

I hadn't noticed, but Cee had left the table and returned carrying a piece of white, legal-sized paper.

"Ironically, they handed this out at work today. Listen to these odds:

1 person mails 200 pieces.

5% response = 10 people playing.

10 people mail 200 pieces = 2,000 pieces out there.

5% response = 100 people playing.

100 people mail 200 pieces = 20,000 pieces out there.

5% response = 1,000 people playing.

10,000 people mail 200 pieces = 2,000,000 pieces out there.

5% response = 100,000 people playing."

Stella brightened. "Well, there you go. If a hundred thousand people all sent five dollars to the top name, he'd have five hundred thousand dollars!"

CeeCee shook her head. "Grandma, think about it; doesn't a *hundred thousand people* sound a little optimistic?"

Doing a little mental arithmetic, I decided to side with my daughter. "That's the equivalent of Bakersfield, California, responding to one chain letter. Maybe even as many as all those folks who followed Moses to the Promised Land, and that's a bunch."

Both CeeCee and I looked up as Stella's fork clattered to the plate again. We exchanged anxious looks. Twice in one meal Stella had dropped her fork.

"Are you .. . sure you're feeling all right, Stella?" I mentioned this warily because my mother-in-law could freak at the thought of imminent illness. But Stella didn't look so well. Her face had turned as white as the Corning Ware potato bowl.

"A person could get life for sending one of those letters," Stella muttered.

I laughed. "Well, not life, but I sure wouldn't want to be caught mailing one. More peas?"

Stella shook her head and pushed back from the table. "I think I'll rest now."

"Grandma?" Cee frowned. "Are you *sure* you're all right? Do we need to call the doctor?"

Stella feebly waved the idea aside. "I'm fine—think the pork must've upset my stomach."

I frowned. "I cooked it thoroughly." Never would I undercook pork. It could give you worms. I'd grown up with that knowledge. The same held true for milk and fish—never eat the two together. I didn't make the rules, but I sure kept them.

"Life," Stella repeated and shuffled out of the kitchen. "Stupid pigeon!"

I looked at Cee. She looked back. Stella wasn't making a lick of sense. If she kept this up I was going to call the doctor. Lifting my shoulders, I said, "Cherry pie?"

CeeCee nodded. And that was the last said about life and chain letters, but not the last of my worries.

Stella definitely wasn't Stella lately.

CHAPTER 6

Why is it, since I'm basically of sound mind, I pick the cart with a wobbly wheel nine times out of ten?

Thump, thump, thump.

I moved down the canned-goods aisle, my eyes searching for a better brand of green beans. Stella complained that if she wanted to eat sticks she could, and more cheaply than me buying an off-brand that was nothing but stalk.

Like she was a green-bean aficionado. I paused before the waist-high display of vegetables and considered my choices: expensive and more expensive. Grocery prices were going up every day. The Cart Mart had good bargains, but still my grocery bill was getting higher every week and we weren't eating any better. I'd learned one trick though: always look at the bottom shelf. More expensive items were always placed at eye level, cheaper ones farther down.

Before Duella and Luella Denson ever entered Cart Mart I heard the colorful twins coming. They owned and ran an antiques business and were sharp enough to drive a hard bargain when necessary, but they were as honest as the day was long.

Devoted to each other, they were always together, even on a trip to the grocery store.

Duella's Southern-accented tones jumped the fruit aisle, past the peanut-butter-and-jelly section, and shot right through the cereal display.

"Good morning, Milly!" Duella chirped. Milly was Cart Mart's oldest part-time checker.

Hoisting Luella's wheelchair through the mechanized doorway, Duella stopped to help Luella out of her chair and into the motorized shopping cart, before pointing her fraternal twin due north: produce department. Luella drove the cart like she was a contender at the next NASCAR event.

Carl Jenson had managed Cart Mart for well over forty years. Two years ago, he'd invested in a motorized shopping cart for the store, and by that one act Cart Mart was catapulted into the twenty-first century. Carl's innovative, pioneering spirit was the talk of Morning Shade until everybody got downright sick of the subject.

I'm old enough to remember the day Carl moved to Morning Shade. A tall, fresh-faced man with a Texas-friendly grin, he'd sported a crisply starched and ironed white shirt and a blue, yellow, and white-checked tie—Cart Mart's logo colors.

Similar to writing, the grocery business can wear a body to a nub.

Dealing with the public day in and day out falls one notch lower than reaming septic tanks, Carl once told me. Armed with mops and dustpans, the mighty grocery clerk attacks aisle spills, broken glass, split milk, and children's accidents—not of the grocery variety, if you get my drift.

These battle-hardened militia are witness to severe parental abuse inflicted by children snared by the candy display prominently featured in checkout lanes. They might as well put free puppies in a toddler's path. Carl once made the comment that he didn't know a child could twist his body in so many different positions on a hard concrete floor, or a parent's face turn so many varying shades of red in the process of manhandling thirty pounds of kicking deadweight back into a wire cart and strapping him down. And the sound of a toppling three-hundred-can display of V8 juice is plain bloodcurdling.

Over the years I'd began to notice that Carl no longer wore the crisply starched and ironed white shirts, and the feisty blue, yellow, and white-checked ties. These days he wore Dockers wash-and-wear slacks and a pullover. The trendy spit-polished loafers were now no-nonsense shoes with thick rubber soles.

There ought to be a medal for the invisible store clerk, who commandeers the battle to put mashed potatoes and meat on the family dinner table. Something like a Badge of True Grit or Purple Medal of Guts. Something to let the weary aisle warriors know they're appreciated.

By the time Duella and Luella rounded the dairy aisle I'd already dropped two cans of Green Giant green beans, a box of powdered sugar, and two boxes of fruit gelatin into my cart, and I was headed for butter and eggs.

Luella hit the brakes, nearly standing the motorized shopping cart on end, when she spotted me. Duella followed on her sister's heels with her arms chock-full of pickles, a squeeze jar of Hunt's yellow mustard, and a can of black olives. She dumped the items in the cart basket. "Maude!"

I stopped, cart thumps dying away. I knew getting tied up with the two sisters would cost me valuable time, but I couldn't be rude. When I'd been more monetarily flush a few years back Duella had helped me find the early-nineteen-hundred washstand that now sat in my foyer. She had connections through her store, The Antiques Shop, and she found me the washstand with a solid-oak base, a single raised-panel door, and three drawers—prettiest thing you ever laid eyes on. It is probably the most valuable piece of furniture in my house, and I love it.

After dumping the grocery items into her cart, Duella straightened, touching her hand briefly to the scarlet fedora with a black, jewel-encrusted pin decorating the front of her hat. Luella sat stiffly in the cart, dressed in a dark gray outfit with white pearls. Her hair varied from month to month in various shades of plum to oh-my-goodness red, depending on whether Duella got a good do on "Sister's" color. Today it was sort of autumn russet. Duella's snow-white, wiry bob frizzed in an over processed do that more resembled a wad of steel wool than human hair. I wondered if that's why she always wore a hat. Red, usually with feathers and sometimes flowers and, like today, a jeweled pin. Duella was the only person I knew that could pull off heavy Max Factor pancake makeup, bright orange rouge, and lipstick and not stick out like a canary in a flock of blackbirds.

"Haven't seen you in the store recently," Duella chirped. "Still writing?"

"Still writing," I concurred. Why do people always ask if I'm "still writing"? Writing isn't something you move in and out of like a factory job. Do well-meaning friends hope to hear me say, "Nope, can't get a contract to save my life."

There are times I would love nothing *better* than to say that—and mean it. But those are my nonproductive, I-hate-writing days. I don't know what I would do without writing . .. other than restore my sanity.

"Business at The Antiques Shop brisk?" I countered brightly.

Duella's smile gradually turned into a grim line. "Rather slow, dearie." Then she brightened. "But with the upcoming holidays we're certain work will pick up. Can you believe Christmas is a mere six weeks away?"

I couldn't believe that—didn't even want to think about it. Herb and I had always given Stella and Cee a good Christmas. We weren't extravagant—well, yes, we were. We always overspent, caught up in the ringing bells and the gaily lit streets and sidewalks. Morning Shade was small, but during the holidays our town resembled a miniature New York City—nearly, but without the traffic and other hassles. Every shop and eating establishment put up trees and hung greenery.

My thoughts saddened. It was going to be slim pickings around the Diamond household this year. Even with the anticipated relatively large advance check on Hamel's book, I had to pay 15 percent in agent fees, taxes, and office expenses. Deduct 10 percent for the Lord, and the money wouldn't go far. Now that Herb was gone I'd learned a new *word: frugal.*

I didn't like the word.

"Well, ladies, I have to be going." I pushed my cart on down the aisle, trying to look hurried, which wasn't hard. I was always hurried, rushed, behind, and running late.

"Do stop in and see us," Luella trilled. "We have a lovely new four-drawer chest that would look magnificent in your bedroom, Maude."

"Thanks—I'll try to get in one of these days." Briefly I wondered if Duella and Luella were hiring part-time Christmas help. The idea appealed to me since I love both women, and antiques are my passion. I made a mental note to phone Luella soon and inquire about it.

When I got home I put the groceries away, thinking about Stella's strange behavior. Something was bothering her. And if she wasn't sick, then I needed to find out what had put her in this mood.

Ever since that silly chain-letter business had come up, she'd seemed distracted and perturbed. I sucked in my breath as a previously overlooked thought hit me. Great balls of fire! Did *she* send five dollars in answer to the letter? Surely not. Stella didn't throw money away, and she was far too street savvy to fall for a chain-letter scam.

Or was she?

I lifted a lamp and gave the table a hit and a miss with the dusting cloth. I was in a-hit-and-miss mood today. I took a swipe at the top of the television and thought of the old joke: "Hey, Mom, is it true you're dust until you're born and then you return to dust when you die?" "It's true, Jimmy." "Then somebody's either coming or going under my bed."

Odd how little it takes to amuse me. That must be a sign of something, but I'm not sure what. Senility, probably.

If, as I suspected, Stella had fallen for the ruse and sent money, then that would explain her peculiar behavior of late. She'd naturally feel silly for responding to such a hoax, and she'd know that I didn't approve of such nonsense.

A plan started to take shape in my mind. If I answered the chain letter, as much as I hated to, I could make Stella feel better about herself plus pull her out of her bad temper. When I confessed what I'd done, Stella would have a good laugh and confess what she'd done, and the whole incident would be cleared up.

I was so elated with my brainstorm that I hastily discarded the dust cloth and went in search of pen and paper. I found both, crammed in the kitchen catchall drawer along with rubber bands, matches, keys that fit nothing, old candy, and a half-dozen assorted ballpoint pens that wouldn't write. Actually I felt better about the whole conspiracy when I decided I would drive to Ash Flat, open a post office box under a different name, and sign all correspondence with something like ... *Sparrow.* I would be Sparrow. I sent the letter to Pansy, Frances, Simon, Mildred, and Harriet—all good friends who were able to take a joke. It wouldn't hurt any of them to have an extra five dollars in their pockets this time of year.

I rummaged through my purse and came up with a five, which I sent to Simon, the first name on the list, added *Sparrow* at the bottom instead of my name and addressed four new envelopes to Pansy, Frances, Harriet, Mildred, and as a joke, two more—to Hilda and Stella. Stella wouldn't fall for the ruse, but I didn't want her to feel left out.

Changing into my Reeboks, I threw on a sweater and briskly walked to the mailbox at the corner before I could change my mind. The moment I released the lid and heard the letters *plop* to the bottom of the blue-and-white receptacle, I felt like an anchor had been lifted from my chest.

Maybe now Stella would become her old self, and Cee and I could stop second guessing her really bizarre moods.

CHAPTER 7

Stella tucked her purse under her arm and trucked toward the church. Maude had offered to drive her earlier, but she'd refused. Her legs weren't broken; she wasn't feeble, though she might be a sight better off if she were. Seemed to her the good Lord was playing tricks on her, blessing her with a body that deteriorated more every day but with the mind and spirit of a sixty-year-old.

Just wasn't fair.

She climbed the steps of Living Truth and opened the heavy, oak-paneled door. A gusty wind rattled the sparkling aluminum awnings. These awnings had been last year's guild project, and as predicted by Hilda, they made the redbrick church stand out like a cockroach on a wedding cake against the browning lawn. Clumps of yellow and bronze mums ruled the walks, zigzagging into and around the structure. Already Stella could hear high-pitched female voices floating up the basement stairway. Throckmorton's nasal twang soared above the others.

You need to hit me over the head with a two-by-four on this one, Lord. I need a change of heart, but land, that woman gives me the hives. Thurvis Throckmorton must wear earplugs!

Stella entered the basement and saw the small committee already seated.

"Ladies! Ladies!" Hilda clapped her birdlike hands, her majestic blue-shadowed eyes darting about the gathered crowd.

"Excuse me ... excuse me." Stella threaded her way to a seat halfway down the center row. She'd sit next to Harriet Strong today; she wasn't in the mood for Mildred and her war stories of recent gallstones. Sure, gallstones were a blight, but how many times could you tell a story and keep it fresh? Particularly about something like gallstones. Stella sat down, settling her purse on her lap.

Harriet leaned over and whispered. "You're late."

"Had to let CeeCee's dogs out." Stella wiggled her brows. "You know. Morning constitutional."

Harriet nodded sagely.

Once Hilda had quieted the room she jumped right into the meeting. "Ladies, as we all know, the spaghetti dinner is a mere two weeks away. This morning, we'll address the bare bones of the—" Stella cleared her throat.

Hilda didn't seem to notice Stella's mucous reproach. "Er ... this morning's meeting. Now, I have been thinking, and I have come up with a delightful theme for our special evening."

Clearing her throat more conspicuously, Stella pursed her mouth, shifting slightly in the creaky, metal folding chair. Eyes shifted in her direction, then focused back on the speaker.

"A Night under the Stars." Hilda clasped her hands and beamed.

Stella stood up. "I thought I was in charge of this shindig." She ignored the murmurs around her. "How come I'm not heading up this meeting?"

With a flash of petulance, Hilda made a bowing, sweeping gesture toward the podium. "Of course, Stella ... dear. I was merely giving the opening remarks."

"My foot."

The cool thing about being old is that you could skip the niceties and pretty well say what you wanted. Folks didn't like it, but they passed it off as "senile," "cranky," or Stella's personal favorite, "medication is affecting her mind."

Well, *duh.*

She wasn't on much medication—just that blood-pressure pill that was supposed to prevent her from blowing a cork, but she had her doubts about its effectiveness. No. She was just plain ill-tempered when someone butted in, and nothing could rile her quicker than Hilda's butt-in-ski-ness.

Hooking her purse over her arm, Stella threaded back through the line of folding chairs. "Excuse me ... excuse me." Clear of the metal jungle, she marched to the podium. Once there, her eyes scanned the expectant faces peering back at her.

"First of all: A Night under the Stars. Is that hokey or what?"

The women exchanged quizzical glances, some lifting shoulders, others expressing no opinion.

"This supper is two weeks into November," Stella said. "There could be *two feet* of snow on the ground by then." She knew that was stretching it, but Hilda was not going to have the last word on this one. "The weather could turn out to be El Nino's revenge, and wouldn't *we* be the fools. The star thing sounds like a summer picnic."

"It doesn't usually snow that early," Midge Grainer hesitantly offered.

"But it *could.* " Stella shifted the handle of her leather purse to her left arm. "So, what say we just call it Spaghetti Night?"

Hilda's lips formed a perfect pout. "Spaghetti Night? You're *not* serious."

"Serious as taxes."

"Really, Stella," Shirley Shupbach put in, "Spaghetti Night? How festive is that? The dinner is our main yearly fund-raiser."

"How are we supposed to entice a larger crowd with a generic name like Spaghetti Night?" Minnie Draper sniffed and dabbed at her nostrils.

"I say we take a vote." Hilda peered innocently back at Stella.

"Majority rules," she trilled.

Stella stiffened. If she wasn't a lady she'd call Hilda potty names. "If I'm the chairperson, then I should name the event."

Voices of protest drowned in the ensuing ruckus. Finally Stella stiffly threw up her right hand.

"All right!" *Bunch of knuckleheads.* "We'll vote on the name. Anyone else have a suggestion other than—" she glanced at Hilda—"A Night under the Stars, or my suggestion, Spaghetti Night?"

Two ladies on the back row tossed out names far worse than the previous two. Stella halted the suggestions and called for a vote.

"Everyone in favor of A Night under the Stars raise your hand."

Hands shot up.

Squinting, Stella reminded Harriet Strong that she wasn't wearing her glasses and would Harriet count? Harriet reported back momentarily. "Eight votes for A Night under the Stars."

Stella frowned. Harriet was a dingbat; she'd never been able to balance her checkbook, let alone count votes. "How could that be, Harriet? There's only nine of us present."

Hilda Throckmorton beamed. "All who disagree?"

"Aye," Stella snapped.

"Eight against one." Hilda wrote it down in the minutes. "The annual spaghetti dinner is now officially A Night under the Stars. Shall we move on, ladies?"

"Sauce," Stella introduced sourly. She could live with a hokey theme, but she wasn't about to give in on the sauce. "I recommend that oregano be left out this year."

"Left out!" Hilda lifted a hanky and fanned her face. "Why ever for? That sauce is my grandmother Blake's old family recipe—why, for goodness' sake, if we were to leave the oregano out we might as well use a new recipe! The mayor would have a fit!"

"The mayor's your husband. All in favor of using a new recipe?" Stella asked.

When hands shot up, Hilda sprang to her feet. "Now, just a minute!"

"Oh, come on, Hilda," Minnie Draper said. "We've used Grandmother Blake's sauce for the past ten years. Give someone else a chance, will you? My mother makes the best Alfredo sauce this side of the Mississippi River."

"Alfredo?" Hilda looked faint. "Minnie, this is a spaghetti dinner."

"The name suggests barbecue and baked beans," Stella reminded. Now that Hilda had gotten her choice of names for the event, she was going to have to live with it.

"Why don't we have both this year?" Shirley suggested. "Make it a pasta smorgasbord with salad and garlic bread."

"Garlic disagrees with lots of folks," Stella cautioned.

"No garlic bread!" someone shouted.

Stella's hand shot up for order. "I didn't say *no* garlic bread. I'm just suggesting that this year we also have, maybe, hot rolls and butter—" And yes, she knew she had insisted on garlic bread earlier, but the chair had a right to change her mind.

"It wouldn't be the same," Pearl Jenson cried out.

The room broke into animated disagreement, women rising from metal chairs to get in each other's faces. Stella stepped over and pulled a chair closer to the podium and sat down. They hadn't discussed salad dressing yet; there again Hilda's grandmother apparently was the Martha Stewart of the thirties.

By the time the meeting broke up nothing had been settled about the upcoming spaghetti dinner except the name, which Stella didn't like.

Harriet Strong walked out of the church with Stella. "You should have put a stop to Hilda's interference. After all, *you're* the chair."

"I might as well be a brick wall," Stella grumbled. "Hilda hears what she wants to hear."

The two women walked home in bright sunshine, a perfect

Indian summer afternoon. But two weeks from now, the wind could be howling and snow flying. Arkansas weather was fickle. A Night under the Stars could turn into Nightmare on Main Street.

Stella chuckled.

"That Hilda is so bossy," Harriet complained.

"Never met a woman like her," Stella agreed. "If I didn't plan on meeting the Lord any day now, I'd give that woman a piece of my mind."

Harriet nodded. "You're always good to speak your mind."

"Actually I shouldn't be chairing this supper at all." Stella paused, peeling out of her light jacket. "I should be thinking about getting a part-time job."

Harriet turned, jaw agape. "At our age—your age? Why in the world would you want a job?"

Stella wasn't about to tell her friend that Maude was in financial straights—nope, Maude's personal business was as safe with her as a crow in the gutter. Folks thought writers were rich; if you wrote books, that equated in most folks' mind to a bulging bank account. Little did they know that Maude had to watch every cent she spent. Her writing income arrived sporadically. It took months from the time a book was contracted to having an actual check in hand. When Herb was alive it didn't matter so much. His income saw them through the lean months. But now that Herb was gone Maude had a lot of responsibility on her shoulders. She was too proud to complain—Stella knew that—but she'd watched the way Maude pored over the bills that arrived on a daily basis, and she'd watched the way her daughter-in-law would look the other way when she walked past Wal-Mart's cosmetics aisle. When Herb was alive, she'd bought mascara and lipstick like it was going out of style.

Conversation slowed as Stella walked toward the Diamond house sitting on Culver Street. She might be old as dirt, but there must be *something* she could do to generate a little income.

Detecting. That was her one true ability. The job didn't pay beans—actually didn't pay anything—but she loved the work when she could get it. But other than last month's case, whose culprit turned out to be Simon Bench, there wasn't much hope for anything big time happening in Morning Shade. Hargus Conley pretty well hogged any cases remotely curious—which were practically nil anyway. In her opinion the town would be a sight better off if Hargus stuck with his chain-saw art and left the law alone.

She'd thought she had a solution for making money with her idea of chain letters, but now it looked like that bright idea might buy her a one-way ticket to the state pen. If that wasn't just her luck—try to do a good deed and end up in jail.

The way things were going Hargus would be the one to arrest her. Now wouldn't that brighten her day?

Maude glanced up from her computer when Stella let herself into the foyer.

"Hey—you're home early. Thought the meeting would last longer."

"Nope, it's over." Looping her purse on the hall tree, Stella toed off her shoes. "Doesn't take long for Hilda to get her way."

"Oh, dear." Maude sighed. "I hope you ladies didn't argue the whole time."

"Not the whole time." Stella climbed the stairs to her room, her mind still percolating on a job. There must be something she could do other than take up oxygen and argue with Hilda Throckmorton. A person didn't live to her ripe old age without an occasional resourceful idea.

Surely to Moses there was something ...

Stella sat on her bed, holding an envelope in her hand. She'd spotted the letter on the coffee table as soon as she entered the house. A letter for her? She didn't get many letters. Most of the people she knew had gone on to that big homecoming in the sky, where she figured she'd be joining them before long.

She ripped the envelope open and stared in surprise at a

replica of her chain letter.

Someone had sent *her* a chain letter, and it was signed *Sparrow.*

What was going on here? She read the message, hardly believing her eyes. They wanted ten dollars! Double what she had asked for. Words jumped off the page at her: "Woe if you are the unfortunate one to break the chain."

Woe? She'd give them woe! She hadn't written any more letters since she had found out that they were considered mail fraud. Now here was someone trying to cut in on her territory.

She shook her head. What territory? She didn't have a territory. Chain letters were against the law.

Since she had sent the first letter, it might be smart to stay out of this. Let Hargus find this perpetrator.

She almost snorted. Hargus Conley couldn't find his back pocket with both hands. Still, this was serious business. Like it or not, she'd have to confide in Hargus. No penny-ante copycat bandit was going to best her. She'd sent her letter out of concern for Maude; this forgery was plain old highway robbery.

CHAPTER 8

"Stella?"

Ever notice how a person can be underfoot 98 percent of the time, but the 2 percent when they're needed you can't find them with a fine-toothed comb? Besides, I'd called my mother-in-law's name so many times lately that I was starting to feel like Brando in the movie *A Street Car Named Desire*. "Hey, Stellaaaaaa!"

I opened the back door and let Frenchie and Claire out, hen turned my thoughts from Jack Hamel's sermon notes to the evening meal. Jack didn't believe the way I did: I believed that salvation was a gift from God. Undeserved. Yes, but no less a glorious gift. Jack approached evangelism with a baseball-bat mentality—"verbal whippings," Herb used to call them. Scare the devil out them. Not me. I believed that salvation and trust went hand in hand. I thought if emotions propelled a person to acceptance, then maybe that feeling would fade rather quickly. But if the heart accepted—if the heart truly accepted—then the walk might not be perfect but it would be lasting and genuine.

I had put a chicken on to fry when Cee came home a few minutes before four o'clock, all worked up. When I saw the way my daughter's face was flushed and sweat rings stained the back of her postal shirt, I turned down the stove burner and pulled up a chair.

In my considerable life experience, problems take on a new perspective when shared over a glass of iced tea with someone who loves you.

"Bad day, hon?"

"Mom, you wouldn't believe the utter *losers* in this world!"

I realized that I'd forgotten something, so I got up and took two glasses from the cabinet and filled them with ice, then poured clear sweetened tea. Tea's different today; ever notice that? In my youth I'd watch Grandma Parley—Parley's my maiden name—I'd watch Grandma Parley bring Lipton tea leaves to a rolling boil and then turn off the burner. No cold water and tea bags sitting in the sun for Grandma. She'd dump a cup and a half of sugar into the pan, stir it, and then let that jet-black brew sit for most of the afternoon.

I closed my eyes and wondered why the simpler things in life were no more. Nowadays folks drank their tea sugarless or sprinkled a package of aspartame in the glass. No wonder everybody was in a perpetual bad mood. You need sugar to keep your spirits up.

I put Cee's glass in front of her and sat back down. "You met someone today? A man, I presume." I hadn't heard my daughter talk about losers since her brief college stint.

"Listen to this, Mom. I'm driving along on my route, and the day's going pretty well. I'm gaining ground with the dogs, though it's costing me thirty bucks a week in dog biscuits. But the Fergusons' shepherds were actually waiting for me this morning." She leaned over and took a sip of tea. "That's good, Mom. Lots of sugar."

"The only way to make decent tea."

"Well, as I was saying, here I am making good progress. I figure I'll even get off early today. Then I spot the Hendricks box."

"Hendricks—the man who recently moved in on Spruce

Street?"

CeeCee nodded. "I don't know why, but all of a sudden I'm looking for him—you know, like a teenage girl hoping to catch a glimpse of her favorite football player?"

I smiled, inwardly taking a breath of relief. Cee was going to be just fine. For weeks I'd worried that she'd lie down and give up after Jake's death, but the young woman sitting before me with cheeks flushed a rosy red almost resembled my old Cee. I knew if I got a part-time job these moments would be few and far between, and in a way I resented that. I had all I could do to write three thousand publishable words a day; now I was going to add to that stress by taking on a part-time job to help with mounting bills? I knew that these were special moments with my daughter, and they would cease. She'd be coming home from work when I was leaving. And by nine o'clock, we'd all be in bed, dead to the world.

Listen to me go on, Lord. You know I don't resent a thing; I'm glad to serve my family.

I smiled. "Did you see him—what's his first name?"

"Gary. Gary Hendricks, and yes, I saw him. Standing behind his front-door curtain peeking out. Waiting for me."

"Now that's charming," I said. "Rather old-fashioned; I like that in a man—"

CeeCee interrupted my praise. "When I opened the box to put his mail inside, I found a lovely, plump caramel apple wrapped in red Saran Wrap and tied with a red silk bow."

I couldn't help it; I was starting to get excited. Not only was Cee pulling out of her doldrums, but she was actually showing interest in the opposite sex—something I would have bet my last floppy disk wouldn't happen right away. I suddenly felt giddy— the way I did when I got an advance check. Really happy.

Yet my daughter's face was anything but pleased.

"Naturally I was flattered. Here's this hunk giving me a gift— though gifts on my route aren't unusual, I'm finding out. Mrs. Moseley left a plate of freshly baked oatmeal-raisin cookies in the box last week, and the week before Carol Trent gave me one of those bells made out of plastic canvas and yarn she'd made to hang on my car so I wouldn't lose it in parking lots."

"The apple," I pressed. "Do you suppose this Gary is the domestic sort?" Wouldn't that be nice? A man who cooked. Possibly even cleaned. And while I was dreaming I'd just throw in laundry and vacuuming. Why not? Herb would have helped me more, but he was never home that often. I'd heard about men who thrived on domesticity, but I'd never met one in person—

I realized CeeCee was still talking.

"Oh yes," she said, twisting her mouth into a knot. "Gary definitely made this particular gift. I smiled and waved to acknowledge that I'd received it. He smiled and waved back." She picked up her tea and swigged heartily before setting the glass down with a jarring thump. I frowned, discreetly eyeing the glass to see if it had chipped.

The feeling that this "gift" wasn't what it was cracked up to be began to sink in … though how a simple caramel apple could cause the stress now embedding itself in ruts in my daughter's features escaped me.

CeeCee's eyes narrowed and she leaned back in her chair. "I sat that beautifully wrapped caramel apple on the seat beside me and thought of nothing else the remainder of the route. After work, I ran for my car and tore off the Saran Wrap and bit into my gift."

"And?" I smiled, recalling the days of my youth when it was permissible to trick-or-treat, and kind folks handed out homemade caramel apples and popcorn balls. Now if a child dared to go house to house, their goodies were rushed to a local medical clinic and x-rayed before consumption.

My daughter's face sobered, turned as grave as the sight of a mourning hearse.

I leaned forward, concerned. "What? Was the apple rotten?" What *idiot* would caramel a rotten apple? Why, the mere thought made me mad. I'd have to go over there and give Mr. Hendricks a piece of my mind, point out that juvenile pranks were not appreciated here in Morning Shade. Especially pranks that involved my daughter.

"Oh no, the apple wasn't rotten." CeeCee met my expectant gaze. "It wasn't even an apple. It was a big stinking white onion."

I jerked back like I'd been shot. *Onion?* Gary Hendricks had carameled an *onion,* wrapped it in red Saran Wrap, stuck on a pretty ribbon, and made a fool of Cee?

My blood bubbled.

"Why that's ... awful," I said lamely. "What sort of man would resort to such childish tricks?"

Stella shuffled through the doorway just then, carrying a sizable bundle of cards. I turned and looked at her, realizing she'd been hiding all afternoon in her room. Now I knew what she'd been up too.

"Chicken's burning, Maude."

"Oh!" I jumped up and grabbed a long-handled fork and jerked the lid off the popping skillet. Standing back, I turned the pieces of meat, frowning when I saw the blackened undersides.

"Did I hear somebody talking about onions?" Stella asked.

CeeCee glanced at the bundle and said, "What you got there, Grandma? Early Christmas cards?"

"No, ma'am," Stella said. "Just a few notes I've written to dear friends."

I mentally groaned. Stella's friends would not want to hear Stella's final words of wisdom; they heard them every year around the holidays.

"What about the onions?" Stella set the cards beside her purse and then moseyed back to the table.

Between me and CeeCee we told her about Gary Hendricks's not-so-funny prank.

Stella shrugged. "Sounds to me like he's trying to get your attention. I had a boy put a snake in my school desk one time, trying to get my attention."

I turned the last chicken thigh, and then lowered the flame under the skillet. "And did he?"

"I think I got his more. I picked up that garter snake and wrapped it around his neck." Stella snorted. "Don't know if they ever saw that boy again. Last I heard he was streaking out of town still trying to uncoil that snake from around his neck."

Well, the older generation had odd ways of courting.

Stella pulled out a chair. "I had an aunt once who used to peel whole onions and eat them."

CeeCee shuddered. "That's nauseating, Grandma."

"Yep. Salted that onion down and ate it like an apple." Stella grinned. "Maybe your fella has a hankering for onions instead of apples."

"Grandma, Gary Hendricks is not my fella. Please don't insult me."

"Stella," I rebuked, "don't antagonize her. She's upset about this. That man ought to be ashamed of himself. Anticipating a Red Delicious and biting into an onion couldn't be pleasant."

"My aunt liked it," Stella contended.

CeeCee shuddered again. "Gary Hendricks is a loser. And to think I found him mildly attractive."

"I understand he's been asked to be the new Scout leader." I shook my head, wondering if the committee had made a mistake. Ever since Harold Logan's triple bypass the young men in Morning Shade had been leaderless, but far better to be leaderless than be led by a moron.

"That's the thing about men," I said, lifting the skillet lid to turn the meat again. While I was at it, I tested the boiling potatoes, satisfied they were nearly done.

"What's that, Mom?" Cee asked glumly.

"When it comes to men, you never know if you're going to get a Red Delicious or an Egyptian onion."

"Amen," Stella said. "But my aunt liked onions. Preferred them over apples. Folks are strange."

Amen, I silently added.

Not that anyone in particular came to mind.

*   *   *

November began to slip away, and I still hadn't made out my Christmas card list. I was still getting rid of Halloween candy. If I put it off much longer I could send the cards for April Fool's Day. Predictions of a winter storm by late afternoon caught my ear, and I shoved the breakfast dishes out of the way and spread out the morning paper, using my napkin to wipe away a smear of blackberry jelly dotting the obituary page.

Stella had already checked the column to see if she was still breathing. She had left the pages out of line as usual, a pet peeve of mine. It would be nice to read a morning paper someone else hadn't already thumbed through.

A handful of sleet splattered the windowpane. I got up to look out at the rapidly worsening weather. Cee was out there driving in this. The roads were already buried under a thin coating of ice. *Dear Lord, keep her safe.* I didn't want her driving her mail route in this weather, but no one had asked for my opinion. My daughter was a grown woman and becoming more independent every day. I dumped feed into a bowl for Captain and set it on the floor, knowing full well I had to feed him first or fight him away from the poodles' dishes.

Captain crouched over his chow, defending it from all comers, head lowered and rumbling deep in his throat. The lion walked again. The poodles gulped their feed, knowing from experience that if the cat finished first, he would come after theirs. A dog's life wasn't all it was cracked up to be in the Diamond household.

Stella appeared in the doorway looking plaintive. "Maude?"

"Yes, Stella?"

"Have you seen my lower plate?"

"Not lately." If she'd keep her teeth in her mouth where they belonged, she'd know where they were.

She pushed her lips in and out. "I have to find them. Tonight's the spaghetti dinner."

So help me, I had forgotten. In this weather, too, and Stella was in charge. I'd have to take her.

She pulled out a chair and sat down. "Do you think anyone will come tonight?"

"Oh, I'm sure they will. You know the whole town looks forward to the spaghetti dinner. It's the number one social event."

"An old woman like me shouldn't be out in this weather. What if I fall and break a hip?"

"Don't be morbid, Stella. Cee and I won't let you fall. And maybe the weather will ease up before evening." I didn't mention the possibility of a winter storm watch. Why worry her more?

"Probably get worse."

She was in one of her gloomy moods, sure she had one foot in the grave and the other on an ice cube. It had been wonderful for her to have the spaghetti dinner to keep her occupied, but after tonight she would be underfoot again. I had an idea for a solution, but I wasn't sure how she would feel about it. Might as well drop a hint and see how it flew.

"I hear there's a new senior day-care center in Ash Flat."

"Humph." Stella took out her upper plate, turned.it over, looked at it, and put it back in her mouth. "That poodle made a mess on the floor."

Frenchie looked guilty, and I grabbed a handful of paper towels. The dogs were housebroken, but the stress of living with Captain had left Frenchie with a weak bladder. That, plus the sleet peppering the windows, and I could sympathize with the pup. I didn't want to go outside today either.

"Never thought I'd have to live with a poodle that messes on the floor," Stella complained.

"Would you give it a rest?" If I had to choose which one was the more irritating to live with—my mother-in-law or a poodle with an incontinence problem—Stella would win in a walk.

She had ignored my mention of the day-care center, and maybe it wasn't such a good idea. With winter coming on, I wasn't prepared to lock myself into driving to Ash Flat every day. Stella would miss more days than she'd attend, plus the senior day-care center was too close to Wal-Mart. When I'm worried, I go shopping. And right now, with Christmas around the corner and no advance in hand, money was too tight to indulge in my favorite stress-busting therapy: impulsive spending. Once I thought I just had to have a fifteen-inch stir-fry skillet—lands, it was only $9.88, marked down from $12.95. When I got it home it occurred to me the skillet would serve a small battalion. I stored it in the attic. But it was only $9.88.

"You get any writing done today, Maude?"

"Not yet, Stella."

How could anyone expect me to get anything done with the television blaring at the decibel level of a 747 at takeoff? An ivory tower this wasn't.

Stella leaned back in her chair. "I guess I'd better rest so I'll be ready to work this afternoon."

"Probably so." I should be so lucky.

She picked up the discarded newspaper and leafed through it, hunting for the obituary pages. "Did you read the paper this morning?"

"Not that part of it." Why read it when I knew she would give me a line-by-line account?

"Mabel Armstrong died. Didn't say why. Probably old age."

"How old was she?"

"Seventy-six. Younger than me." She peered over her glasses, like a ruffled owl. "The Grim Reaper's breathing down my neck, Maude. I can feel him coming closer."

"That's the draft from the ceiling fan." I had turned it on hoping it would circulate the air, but I didn't think it was working.

"You just don't know," she mourned. "When I open my eyes in

the morning, I pinch myself and see if it hurts. If it does, I know I'm still alive."

"Well, I guess that's one way of finding out." Probably worked just as well as a cat doing a tango across my stomach, which was the way I woke up most mornings. Captain had an internal clock that never missed a feeding time.

I picked up the dishes and carried them to the sink. "What do you want for lunch?"

Stella perked up at the mention of food. "Something light. I don't want to ruin my appetite for the dinner tonight. We're having garlic bread."

"That's good. I like garlic bread."

"Hilda thought bread sticks would be more refined."

"There's nothing refined about bread sticks. Garlic bread goes better with spaghetti, although it does tend to repeat on a body, wouldn't you say?"

"I've never had that problem." She shook her head. "Well, I don't have anything serious against bread sticks—just wanted to ruffle Hilda's feathers. Garlic bread is traditional though. Sticks to the ribs and stinks up the breath."

I laughed. "It does that, all right. It's going to be right fragrant in the church fellowship hall tonight."

Stella grinned. "Too bad we can't bottle the air and sell it. We'd make a fortune."

"It would never replace Chanel No. 5."

Stella chortled. "Well, it would be an improvement over that Essence of Violets Hilda drenches herself with. It's enough to give violets a bad name." She got up to leave the kitchen, but paused in the doorway. "Maude, when I die I want you to have my rosebud tea set."

I stared at her, overcome. "Why, Stella ..."

She nodded. "I mean it. I don't know what would have happened to me if you hadn't let me live here. Likely I'd have wound up in one of those nursing homes over in Ash Flat. I may be old, but I'm not ready for that."

"I've never regretted inviting you to move in here." Which I
hadn't. I might get irritated at her, and sometimes I wanted to swat
her, but I couldn't imagine life without her. Funny, how our
greatest blessings come in the most unlikely wrappings.

"I know I'm a bother sometimes, and I'm a financial burden
too, but you've always made me feel welcome. That's why I want
you to have the tea set after I'm gone."

"I'd be honored to have it, Stella, but I hope you enjoy it for
many years to come."

The set was made of fine Bavarian china. Its fluted cups with
dainty pink rosebuds on a cream-colored background were rimmed
with what Stella called "fourteen caret pure-dee gold," and it was
her prized possession. That she wanted me to have it brought me
close to tears.

"Well," she said, "I just thought I'd let you know. I'm going to
look for my teeth."

I sat at the table for a while, listening to the sleet hissing at the
windows and watching the poodles try to look invisible while
Captain surveyed his kitchen kingdom, crouched low, belly almost
to the ground, green eyes slanted with malice. The king of the beasts
was on the prowl.

I nudged him with my toe. "Behave yourself."

He jumped and then tried to look as if nothing had happened.
All innocence—and a complete fraud. If I didn't intervene from time
to time, he would make the poodles even more miserable than they
were now.

I thought about Stella and CeeCee and how their coming here
had changed me from a fretful widow worrying about living alone
to a woman with people to share my life. I thought about how
blessed I was and how good God had been to me, and I apologized
to Him for all the times I had whined when things were going
wrong. I needed to remember I lived under the shadow of His
wings.

I got up and checked the pantry. Canned chicken-noodle soup and tuna sandwiches for lunch, and tonight we'd make up for it at the guild's annual spaghetti and garlic bread dinner. Now if Cee would just get home safely, my cup of blessings would overflow.

After lunch I drove Stella to the church, where the ladies were to meet at one to prepare for the evening festivities. Back home I sat down at my computer with Captain perched on top of the file cabinet in his role of self-appointed straw boss. He stared at me with those green, unblinking eyes, until I stuck my tongue out at him.

"Go to sleep. I'm working. Believe it or not, thinking is work."

He shifted his attention to the window, watching a bedraggled sparrow scratching through a half inch of sleet to find the bird seed. I pulled out my notes for Jack's book and tried to concentrate. If I was to get this book done by February first, I was going to have to come up with a better working plan.

Someone rang the front doorbell, and the poodles erupted in a yipping frenzy. I waded through dogs and opened the door to find Maury Peacock, my neighbor on the left, shivering in the foul weather. He wore sock suspenders and Bermuda shorts. His scrawny legs resembled those of an anorexic chicken. I knew this was his usual garb, but I'd have thought twenty-nine degrees and sleet and snow might suggest long pants were in order.

"Howdy, Miz Diamond," he greeted me. "You doing all right?"

"Doing fine, Maury. Yourself?"

"Fine, fine, just fine."

I eyed him uncertainly. He might be fine, but I had my doubts. He'd been acting strange lately. Two weeks ago he'd had surgery on an ingrown toenail, and I knew he was taking Valium and Vicodin. I suspected that might have something to do with his behavior.

Now he held out a measuring cup. "Could I borrow a cup of salt? I'm making corn bread."

A cup? Must be a big batch of bread. "Does the recipe call for a cup of salt?"

"Don't use a recipe. I've been making corn bread most of my life. Just make it from scratch, and it turns out good most times. I'm making this batch to feed to the birds. They like my corn bread."

He was going to have a bunch of thirsty birds on his hands if he put that much salt in the bread. I took the cup and invited him in. He trailed me back to the kitchen, eyeing the blue-and-white curtains and the red geraniums on the windowsill. "I always like your kitchen. It looks so homey and nice."

I took a quick appraisal of the kitchen, surprised. It did look good. CeeCee had lined up Stella's copper molds around the top of the cabinets, and a white ironstone bowl of fresh fruit sat in the middle of the table. Captain added a nice touch, sitting in front of the poodles' food dishes, looking so sweet and innocent it was almost disgusting. Surely the poodles thought so.

I put two teaspoons of salt into the cup. "Here you go, Maury. This is enough for one batch of corn bread. If you need more later, come on back."

He took the cup, not seeming to mind it was short of the amount he had requested. *"I* sure thank you, Miz Diamond. You going to the spaghetti dinner tonight?"

"We'll be there. Stella is the chair."

"She'll do a fine job too. Well, I'll see you tonight then."

He left and I sat down in front of the computer, my concentration totally shot. I'd be lucky to get this book done by the Fourth of July.

CHAPTER 9

Women's laughter filled the Living Truth Community fellowship hall. Ladies bustled about their self-appointed tasks. Actually most of them had helped with so many church dinners they didn't need anyone to tell them what to do, but that didn't stop Hilda from barking out orders like a drill sergeant. Mayor Throckmorton had even rolled up his shirtsleeves to help.

Large pots of spaghetti were ready to be served. Sauce bubbled, distributing tantalizing odors of tomato and basil. Frances and Pansy were in charge of salad, and the oven was full of the last batch of chocolate-mayonnaise cake. Previously baked cakes were cooling, ready for the fudge icing to be applied. Thick wedges of garlic bread were ready to pop into the oven when the cakes came out.

Hilda had sniffed when she saw the garlic bread, her lips screwed up in a frustrated knot, but she hadn't said anything. Stella grinned, knowing Hilda had a reason to be ticked. That bread wasn't her only downfall. The drinks were where Stella had wanted them too.

It felt good to win one.

Now Hilda bustled off to oversee the seating arrangements. "Don't place the chairs too far apart. Remember we're expecting around one hundred and eighty-five hungry people, if everyone shows up."

Harriet Strong cast a worried eye at the window. "Weather's real bad and going to get worse if the weatherman's right."

"Might keep people away," Stella said. She wouldn't be here herself if Maude hadn't brought her. Truth be told, it wasn't a fit night for man nor beast. Why would anyone risk an accident or broken bone to eat spaghetti, even if it was good spaghetti?

Hilda rounded on Stella. "Don't even think such a thing! Where's your faith?"

Stella bristled. "I've got faith, but the weather is bad—didn't I tell you the weather would be bad? Didn't I say we should call it Spaghetti Night, then there'd be no—"

"All right! Enough already about the weather!" Hilda sniffed. "So it's spitting snow. Big deal."

She'd think *big deal* when nobody showed up. And Stella would be blamed because she was the chair. How did she let herself get talked into something like this? Should have known it would be a disaster.

Hilda charged across the room muttering something about ice, and Stella clamped her mouth shut. She had expected the woman to revert to form, so this bossy, rule-the-roost-and-flog-anyone-who-got-in-her-way attitude wasn't surprising. Stella knew Pansy and Frances were disappointed that she wasn't saying anything to straighten Hilda out and let her know who was in charge, but Stella had made a pact with the Lord. No matter how badly Hilda acted, she was going to show Him she could control her tongue. With His help, of course.

Probably be a surprise to Him too. She wasn't known for tact or patience. Always start out the way you intended to keep on— that was her motto. Saved a lot of time in the long run.

Harriet and Pansy were talking about the chain letters. Stella listened, pretending to arrange silverware. Turned out mailing those letters was anything but clever. But she'd say one thing for them—they were bringing in money. She had already received ten dollars, which she'd put in an envelope marked "Christmas Expenses and Various Other Things."

Of course she couldn't tell anyone about the money and where she got it. That would just be buying a one-way ticket to the county hoosegow. She'd heard all Hargus ever served his prisoners was hot baloney and store-bought bread. Not that there had ever been more than one prisoner and that was just Al Barnetto, who had made Hargus mad by cutting in front of him at the stock-car races. Barnetto didn't stay in jail much longer than a couple of hours, but Hargus had to feed him. Al swore it was the sorriest grub he'd ever had.

"I threw my letter in the trash," Pansy said. "I'm not giving any money to someone who calls himself Sparrow."

Stella frowned. Didn't Pansy understand she could make a small fortune just by writing a few letters herself and mailing them out? Of course, she couldn't mail them in Morning Shade. Stella had already covered this area. She might be old, , but you could say one thing for her: she didn't do things by half measures. If they ever caught her, the entire town could give witness against her. Well, she wouldn't go quietly.

"I don't know," Harriet said. "I've heard there's bad luck attached to breaking a chain letter. I'd be afraid to risk it."

Stella perked up. That was more like it. Not that she believed in bad luck. She'd just tacked that on because it was sort of tradition for a chain letter.

Frances joined them. *"I* haven't decided what I'll do about mine. It's a lot of money. My social security check and pension don't stretch all that far. If I thought I'd get anything back it would be different, but I can't afford to throw money away."

Stella paused in slicing chocolate cake. She hadn't thought of that. Maybe some of the folks she'd sent letters to couldn't afford to give money. Well, they didn't have to send anything, but some of her earlier excitement faded a little. Was she taking advantage of other people in order to help Maude? And what about the copycat letter writer? Doubled the amount. Made her mad just to think about it.

Mildred Fasco brought more dessert plates and started moving the filled ones to the front of the table. "I hope this weather doesn't get any worse. I have to drive to Little Rock in the morning."

Stella deftly lifted a slice of chocolate cake with fudge icing and slid it on a plate. "Whatever for?"

Mildred filched a bite of cake that had fallen away from the piece Stella cut. "Rebecca, my granddaughter, is coming to spend the holidays with me."

"The one from San Francisco? That's nice. She'll be a lot of company for you."

A lot of trouble more likely. Stella remembered Becky. Pretty, feisty, and could stir up more friction than Hilda Throckmorton could ever dream of. When it came to riling the waters, Hilda was a pure amateur compared to fourteen-year-old Becky.

Mildred was still talking. "My daughter's been seeing an insurance broker, and they unexpectedly decided to get married. He has a lot of money, and they're off for a six-week Mediterranean cruise. Naturally they wouldn't want Becky tagging along on a honeymoon."

Couldn't fault them for that, Stella silently agreed. Becky could be a pain anytime. She'd wreck a honeymoon. Take her along and it could be the shortest marriage on record.

Stella cut the last piece of her cake and Mildred took the empty pan and handed her a full one. "I'll enjoy having Becky. I hope staying with me won't be boring for her."

"I'm sure you'll make Becky's holiday a happy one," Stella soothed. "The good Lord has a way of working things out."

The good Lord was going to have His hands full. Poor old Mildred. That ungrateful daughter of hers had pawned her juvenile delinquent off on Grandma Fasco and hightailed to a foreign country.

Pretty crafty.

CeeCee threaded her way through the overheated room, carrying her plate to a center table. A quick look around revealed Gary Hendricks headed in her direction. She mentally groaned.

Grabbing her plate and glass of tea, she hurriedly scooted to the far end of the table, where she hunched over her food, trying to look inconspicuous.

Too late. The Scout leader squeezed into the seat next to her, flashing that smile she had first thought attractive, but which she now found obnoxious. It was surprising how your perception of a person could change once you got to know them. Gary didn't wear well.

He twirled spaghetti around his fork, sliding her a sly look. "Did you enjoy your apple?"

She stared at him in amazement. How *could* the man be such an insensitive clod? Why bother to answer? He wouldn't recognize an insult if he fell over it.

Gary turned to the man next to him and boasted about the prank. CeeCee burned as he explained in detail how he had dipped the onion in caramel until it looked tantalizing, then carefully wrapped it in Saran Wrap and tied a pretty red ribbon around it. The other man grinned and glanced at CeeCee as if he wondered how she was taking it.

She would like to show both of them how *well* she was taking it.

Too bad this was a church function, or Mr. Smart Mouth Hendricks would be wearing a spaghetti hairpiece. She'd dump a plateful over his head and walk out. But since Grandma was the chair, she'd try to control her natural inclination. She bit into a piece of garlic bread so savagely her teeth snapped together.

Gary finished his tale, throwing back his head and giving his braying laugh, slapping his knee as the hilarity of the practical joke overcame him. CeeCee picked up her plate and glass and stalked off. Let him have his fun. She didn't have to put up with him, which turned out to be all she knew about it, because every way she turned he was there, sticking closer than a license plate. He trailed her around the hall, getting in her way and making a pest of himself.

"Hey, CeeCee? What would you get if you crossed a gorilla with an alligator?"

She sighed impatiently. "I have no idea." *And I care even less.*

"I don't know either, but you'd better not cross him." He brayed.

She stared at him in exasperation. "That doesn't make sense."

His elbow jabbed her in the ribs. "But it's funny, no?"

"No. Look, Gary, go play in the street. I'm not interested, okay?"

"You don't mean that." Cocking his head slyly, he grinned at her. "Playing hard to get, huh, babe?" He pretended to magically draw a long string of spaghetti out of her right ear. *How romantic.*

"Make that impossible."

She turned away to speak to Iva and Ty. A wet ice chip hit her cheek. She turned and glared at Gary. "Will you stop that?"

He laughed. "Chill out. It's just a *joke.* "

" *I* don't like your jokes." She saw her mother helping Stella put on her coat and hurried to join them. "Let's get out of here. I've had all the fun I can stand."

Mom raised an inquiring eyebrow, but CeeCee ignored her. She slipped her arm through Stella's. "Come on, Grandma. I'll walk you to the car. The spaghetti dinner was a success. You did a great job."

Stella smirked. "Well, I had a lot of help, some of which I could have done without."

When they reached the doorway, CeeCee glanced back. Gary crossed his eyes, flashed her a goofy grin, and stuck his thumbs in his ears, wiggling his fingers. She turned and walked off, but she could still hear him yelling.

"See you later, CeeCee!"

Stella paused and CeeCee urged her forward. "Keep moving, and don't look back. You never know what might be gaining on you."

Peering over her shoulder, Stella walked faster. "That fellow isn't hitting on all four cylinders, is he?"

"Not even close, Grandma." CeeCee shot Gary one last leave-me-alone look. "Not even close."

CHAPTER 10

I opened my eyes to soft gray dawn filtering through the blinds. My hand automatically reached out to touch Herb, and then I remembered.

Captain licked my face, and I figured I might as well get up and fix breakfast. There'd be no more sleep for me until I fed the cat. I'd never admit it, but I had become fond of the disreputable old monster—and his morning affection was really more than Herb had ever given me. Somehow the cat and I seemed to have a lot in common, although I'd like to think I was better behaved.

I brought in the paper because I didn't want Stella out on the ice. I knew it would take more than a winter storm to keep her from reading the obituary pages. She'd get the newspaper if she had to crawl out to the curb where our paperboy usually tossed it.

To my surprise, Cee came down early too and sat at the table watching as I fixed breakfast. I'd made refrigerator bread dough yesterday and now had cinnamon rolls rising ready to be baked. On a cold November morning the scent of fresh-baked yeast bread would revive anyone's spirits.

CeeCee pushed back her hair and yawned. "Did you see Gary Hendricks last night? I can't believe the way he behaves."

Stella looked up from the paper. "What'd he do this time? Put hot sauce on your spaghetti?"

CeeCee sounded bitter. "What *didn't* he do would be more like it. The nerd had the nerve to ask how I liked my 'apple.'"

"I'll bet you told him," Stella commented absently, one eye on the obit page.

"No, because he didn't give me a chance to answer. He started telling the guy next to him all about it, like it was something to be proud of."

I slid the pan of rolls into the oven and mixed icing to drizzle over them after they baked. "Is that all he did?"

"No. He followed me all around the room, telling me stupid jokes and acting like he thought he was the hottest thing since chili peppers. And ice chips. He actually flipped ice chips at me! Can you imagine anything more juvenile?"

I laughed, and she looked offended, but her sense of humor got the best of her. "And did you hear him yelling that he'd see me later? Not if I see him first. Half the town probably thinks I'm going out with him."

"And the other half thinks you're crazy," Stella said.

I took the rolls out of the oven and set the breakfast casserole I had made earlier on the table. "Well, a good man is hard to find."

"Purt near impossible," Stella agreed.

CeeCee dipped into the casserole. "Mmm. This smells good, Mom."

"New recipe. Eggs, sausage, cheese, mushroom soup, and corn tortillas. I thought it would be a nice change."

"Very nice."

Captain paced back and forth, yowling for a sample. Stella seemed preoccupied this morning. Well, that would change when she found out what I had done. Somehow since I'd had a couple weeks to think about my impulsive decision, I had been a bit preoccupied myself. *Lord, don't ever let Cee learn what I've done.* She would clean my kettle but good. Probably repeat every thing I've ever taught her about obeying the law. That's the problem. Your children never forget a thing you said to them. They just repeat it back to you, word for word, when they grow up.

CeeCee wrapped a couple of cinnamon rolls in a napkin. "Uh-oh, look at the time—I've got to run. Luckily the highway crew worked all night, so the roads are clear. You stay inside, Grandma. It's slick out there."

CHAPTER 11

"**B**e back at 1:00."

Stella stared at the sign hanging lopsided on Hargus's door, then checked her watch. One-thirty. She'd have Hargus's hide nailed on a fence if she were running things. She had important matters to discuss, and the town law enforcement was nowhere in sight.

Well, she'd wait. Didn't have another thing to do. She sat' down on the front porch of City Hall and prepared to do battle. Hargus had moved into a cubicle there last week so he could be closer to the action.

Half an hour later she checked the time again. Two o'clock. Fine "law official" they had. What would happen if there was a real emergency?

At three-thirty, Hargus's pickup rounded the corner and sped up the street, skidding in the icy slush.

Dozing, Stella suddenly snapped to attention when the old truck wheeled into a parking space and refused to die. Hargus doubled his fist, thumped the dashboard soundly, and the engine finally knocked and sputtered to silence. He calmly climbed out of the cab, slammed the door, took a hitch in his trousers, and strode toward Stella.

"It's about time you showed up."

Ruddiness tinged Hargus's round baby cheeks. He shot her a hard look. "Had an emergency—couldn't get back on time."

Stella consulted her watch. *Emergency, my foot.* He reeked of Pennzoil, which meant he'd been wasting time down at Luther Peacock's garage, messing around with that piece of junk they raced every night starting in late April and running until late fall. But she wasn't going to rile him. Right now, as bad as she hated to admit it, she needed the goofus on her side.

Hargus stepped around her and opened the door to City Hall. She didn't know why; it was time to go home for most working folks. She trailed him inside and shut the door behind herself.

He turned, acting half surprised to see her. "You need something?"

"No, I'm an aggravating cosmetics saleswoman wanting to sell you some lip gloss."

He shrugged. "You ought to get a life, Stella Diamond."

She let that pass. Pulling up a chair, she planted herself in front of his desk. "We need to talk."

Stepping to the small refrigerator, he pulled out a soda. "What kind of business do we have? Ain't had any business with you since I solved the furniture-moving mystery."

"We," she corrected tersely. *"We* solved the mystery."

"Whatever." He sat down and propped his size-seven shoes on top of the desk. Taking a swig of his drink, he eyed her. "What d' you want?"

Now this was the hard part. How was she going to tell Hargus that she'd sent the first chain letter? He'd laugh himself stupid— no, couldn't do that, he was already there. Clearing her throat, she decided to meet this bull head-on.

"Okay, there's no easy way to tell you so I'm not going to sugarcoat my words. You listen, and you listen good because I'm not going to repeat it a second time."

At this, he removed his feet from the desktop, sat up straight, and slid to the edge of his seat, curiosity reflected in his eyes.

"Are you listening?"

"Don't I look like I'm listening?"

It was a wonder to her all that sugary soda hadn't plugged up his ear canals.

"Okay." She took a deep breath. "I sent the first chain letter because I thought I'd be helping Maude out. If I'd given the idea more thought, I'd have known it was stupid, but nobody ever accused me of being overly bright." She looked up. "If you know what I mean."

He nodded, absently taking a gulp out of the bottle and looking as intelligent as he could look, which wasn't saying much for Hargus.

Now that she had his ear, Stella plunged headfirst into the purpose of her visit. "I need help, Hargus. Somebody is sending chain letters, asking for ten dollars a person."

"So?" The news didn't seem to faze him. "Nobody has to send money if they don't want to."

"No, but it's not fair. I sent the first letter because I thought I would be helping Maude—she's been in a bit of a financial quagmire since Herb died—but the moment I found out that chain letters are mail fraud I didn't write another one." She whipped her hand across her throat in a cutting manner. "Cut it off—just like that. Now there's a copycat bandit trying to infringe on my territory."

"So what?" Hargus took another swig, clearly enjoying her discomfiture, but little did he know that didn't surprise her. She'd expected his reaction. That's why she had been so reluctant to tell him about the letters. It really burnt her that she needed his help. She took a deep breath and struggled on.

"So I want you to find out who's sending the letters and put a stop to it. Chain letters are serious business, mister, or didn't you know that?"

"I knew that," he contended.

She bet not, but like she said, she needed his help. "So?" she prompted.

He cocked his head. "Will I find the copycat bandit?"

"That's what I'm asking."

He threw his head back and brayed like the donkey she knew him to be.

Her lip curled with contempt. "I don't see a thing funny about this, Hargus."

He momentarily sobered, then broke down, laying his head on the desk, pounding the scarred oak with his fists, his shoulders heaving with mirth.

She didn't think it was that funny. In fact she didn't think it was funny at all. "Okay, okay, you've had your fun. Now answer me—will you help me or not? I'd work on the case, but if Maude was ever to find out I sent that first letter she'd be embarrassed arid mad as a hornet—at me." Stella didn't even want to think about that. Maude didn't lose her temper very often, but when she did, look out, sister.

Lifting his head, Hargus stared at her, then rolled his eyes and brayed again, his big old teeth flashing in the late-afternoon sunlight. Reminded her of Joe Taylor's prize mule, except the mule had the edge on brainpower.

Stella sat through the humiliation, letting him have his fun. When she'd had enough, she said calmly. "You remember the time you told Pansy you were going to Little Rock for a law convention, but actually you and Luther spent the entire weekend on the gambling boats?"

Braying ceased. Hargus fixed his eyes on her. "No."

"Do too."

"Do not."

"Do too."

Springing to his feet, he smacked the desk, his face as red as a sun-ripened tomato. "How come you can't stay out of my business?"

Stella primly straightened the hem of her dress. "I never told your mother. Not yet, anyway." It'd been on the tip of her tongue many a time, but she'd saved the information for a rainy day. Today it was raining cats and dogs.

Hargus wasn't laughing now. Good. Maybe they could get down to business.

He sat down, pushing the half-empty bottle to the back of his desk. "What do you expect me to do? Nobody knows who sends those stupid chain letters."

"Nobody's ever tried to find out, have they?"

His shoulders rose halfheartedly.

"Well, you're going to be the first. Ask around. Do a little snooping—you're the law, aren't you?"

Again his shoulders lifted without enthusiasm.

Stella stood up, hooking her purse over her arm. "This is important, Hargus. Whoever is sending the letters is taking advantage of my mistake. Folks in Morning Shade don't need to be fleeced. You've got to put a stop to this before it goes any further."

"You should have thought about that before you sent the first one."

She reached out and whacked him across the shoulders with her purse. Stunned, he fell back into his chair. "You're going to get me out of this—and if you ever tell a soul what I've done, I'll come after you, Hargus. I'll hunt you down like an animal."

"Ohhhhh." He pretended to cower with fear. "Blackmail, Stella?"

She bent closer to the desk, smiling. "I'm your worst nightmare, Hargus. Remember the church picnic when you were sixteen? Old man Hawkins lay down on a park bench and dozed off. Some wiseacre called the coroners office and told them they had a pickup at City Park?"

He scowled, his heavy jowls drooping. "That's wasn't me."

Her smile widened. "Was too—I heard you make the call on the pavilion pay phone."

"Oh, all right! I'll *help* you. Satisfied?"

She nodded. "Now I am."

Throwing her a surly nod, he got up and stalked out of the office, leaving her to lock up. Didn't even finish his drink.

Well, she didn't mind. She secured her purse more evenly on her arm. If it wasn't for Stella Diamond, Morning Shade would be a hotbed of crime. At least she had Hargus on the case. If her luck held, he'd track down the copycat bandit and put a stop to the letters.

Then she'd sleep better.

CHAPTER 12

Sometimes I think Stella is one fry short of a Happy Meal. Her peculiar preoccupation of late wasn't like her; she was always looking for a new case. And come to think of it, I could use a little motivation—aka inspiration—that wonderful, magically illusive term writers feed on. Like hungry sharks on a piece of chum.

But far from inspiring, Stella crept around the house, shoulders hunched, looking downright guilty about something. Had she spilled sugar in the flour canister again? Left eggshells in the carton? Drunk out of the milk carton? What? Had I made her life miserable by demanding perfect quiet during my work hours? I hoped not. I'm not an ogre—not on a regular basis.

I hated the notion that my muse was never more evident than when Stella was involved in a case, but face the truth I must. My creativeness and Stella's sleuthing went hand in hand. Still, I didn't honestly want her involved in risky business, if there was such a term in Morning Shade. Just hanging around with Hargus Conley was risky enough; if he didn't pull those pants up, catastrophe was waiting to happen.

What I hated most was Stella's blank stares of late, the kind where she faded into la-la land when she was talking. She'd always been clear in her thoughts—too clear at times. But lately you have to ask her things twice—sometimes three times—— before the question penetrates.

Even Cee mentioned it. "What's up with Sam Spade?"

I hit Control *S* and leaned back in my office chair, thinking I hadn't heard that name in years. Cee'd come in from work and now stood in the doorway eating a handful of Oreos.

"You'd noticed too?"

"Who could miss it?" She shook her head as she broke a cookie apart and licked the creamy middle. The familiar gesture brought back of rush of memories: the way my four-year-old begged for "Rolos." I swallowed a sentimental lump in my throat.

"Grandma's looney as a bat in a henhouse, and that's not like her. Is something bothering her?"

"If there is, she hasn't mentioned it."

Nonetheless, I decided to investigate her distracted state over dinner that night, which turned out to be as useless as a button on a hat.

"Peas, Stella?"

Stella stared at her plate. "If I wanted to eat sticks—"

"I said *peas.* Not green beans."

She glanced up. "Oh. Green beans. Yeah, I'll have a spoonful." I ladled the vegetable onto her plate, studying her from beneath lowered lids. She definitely had something on her mind tonight.

"You feeling well?"

Stella shrugged. "Did the doctor call?"

I stared back at her, pursing my lips. "Should he? Have you been in to see him this week?"

"No, course not. I'm healthy as an eighty-seven-year-old horse."

"Then why would the doctor call, Grandma?" CeeCee passed a plate of steaming pork chops.

"He did?"

"No, I said ..." CeeCee paused and gave me a distressed you-take-it-from-here look. "What did you want to say, Mom?"

By now Stella had me so confused I was trying to remember whether the doctor had called. I was fairly certain he hadn't.

"I asked if you were feeling well," I said, trying to get back on the subject. "You seem distracted these days."

"Me?" Stella picked up the shaker and salted her tea. I leaned over and took the shaker out of her hand and replaced it with the sugar bowl.

"Nothing's bothering you?"

"Nope."

"Anything going on with Simon, Pansy, or Frances?"

"Nothing unusual."

CeeCee ladled cream gravy over mashed potatoes. "Well, the oddest thing happened to me today. I was delivering mail on Spruce, and I heard this ... noise ... like people squabbling in loud, angry voices, coming from 3662."

"Did you investigate?" I asked. Seemed Cee had a new adventure to share every evening, and I never had anything worthwhile to offer. Writing and deletions were not exactly hot topics. Maybe I ought to give up writing and look for a postal job. The pay would be more regular—if I could find a postal service crazy enough to hire a sixty-year-old woman. Most folks were on their way out at sixty, not filling out employment applications. Nope. Even dear, sweet Iva Hinkle couldn't pull enough strings with the higher-ups to help me.

CeeCee shook her head. "I didn't get out of the truck. The people who live there are sorta strange. Two weird-looking men and an older woman moved in a few weeks ago. Newspapers are always lying around the yard. Last week they parked this junky old pickup in the side yard, jacked up the frame, and took off all four tires. It's a real neighborhood eyesore. Until then I rarely saw signs of life around the house, except one time the woman put a letter in the box and money for a stamp. Only I don't know where she's been living the last ten years. She gave me a quarter for postage and wanted it to go airmail."

I took a bite of peas. "Think that's who you heard arguing?"

CeeCee's hand paused with her fork in midair. "I'm. not sure. It was just loud noise—I couldn't make out anything they were saying. They had the front-room window open, because the weather was so nice today." She smiled and changed the subject. "Come on, Grandma. I always share my day. You share yours. What have you been up to lately?"

Stella sat up straighter, prickly now. "Nothing. Who told you I was up to anything? I haven't got a new case—whoever told you I did was dead wrong. Was it Hargus? Is he blabbing my business—"

"Hey!" CeeCee threw up the white flag. "Easy, Grandma. Nobody's said anything. Mom and I were just wondering what you've been doing lately to occupy your time."

Relief flooded Stella's features. She reached for a piece of bread. "You know—planning that silly Night under a Snowbank."

"Well," I said, glad to know that Hilda Throckmorton was the cause of Stella's diversion, "the dinner went off well, and I'm glad to hear you ladies are getting along."

"I didn't say we were getting along," Stella reminded. "But as a matter-of-fact, we do get along fine as long as we do what Hilda says."

I smothered a grin. Stella hated it when I laughed at her problems, but hey, hers were the only problems I *could* laugh at and not end up crying; mine and CeeCee's had deeper roots.

*   *   *

Saturday morning, I dragged myself out of bed earlier than usual. Always one to shoot off my mouth before I thought. I'd volunteered to take the church teens on their annual visit to City Hall, which included a visit to Hargus's eight-by-eight cubicle and to Morning Shade's fire department (one old truck that was on its last legs).

Still, it would be nice to free my brain for one blissful

morning—no consideration of word count, plot, or deadline. Best of all, no worrying about things I had little control over. Like money. I knew full well that though the Lord was seldom early, He was always on time, and that would be the case this holiday. Some didn't believe in a God who loved them personally. The Father was slowly reinforcing my belief: He loves me personally. And when I concentrated on today and not on tomorrow, I was a happier person.

I stood for a long time under the showerhead, letting the steamy water clear my mind. Thanksgiving was next week. I mentally went over my guest list: I'd invite Maury Peacock and Victor Johnson, dear souls. Both men were lost without their spouses. Funny how I'd invited both men every year and baked their favorite pies and put chestnuts in the dressing the way Victor's wife, Susie, used to, but now, for the second year, I would share the emptiness in their hearts. Chestnuts only served to remind us of happier days. But mercy, if Ellie Peacock could see Maury in those black suspenders and Bermuda shorts, she'd sit up in her grave. And all that medicine the poor man took—why, he didn't know where he was half the time.

Stella would want to invite Simon, Patsy, and Frances to share the day. Of course if Pansy came, then Hargus would follow. My eighty-four-inch round oak table that had once belonged to Herb's grandmother would be filled to overflowing. But wasn't that what the holidays were about? Family, good friends, love, and the warmth of the season.

Shortly before nine as I was backing the Buick out of the drive, Stella was coming down the walk from her morning Citgo coffee klatch, purse dangling from her arm. I rolled down my window. "I'm on my way to take the teens to City Hall this morning!"

Stella stopped where she was and just stood there.

Letting the car engine idle, I realized that she was still in her strange mood. She'd gone off on tangents occasionally, but she usually came back to earth in a few days.

She was knee-deep in true-crime novels lately, and I suppose murder and chaos wouldn't automatically include chain letters, but my mother-in-law had lived long enough to know the absurdity of such a scheme. Why, I bet she'd gotten a hundred chain letters in her lifetime. Should I confront her about her blowing five dollars and try to ease her guilt, or should I keep silent and let her distracted state blow over? One glance at the dashboard clock made up my mind. I pulled the transmission into reverse, waved, and backed onto the street.

"Be back shortly after lunch," I called. Cranking up the window, I shifted into Drive and took off.

It was five minutes after nine when I parked in front of the church. Teens milled about, hair spiked with heavy gel, boys wearing shirts and pants three sizes too big, hems dragging the heels of untied sneakers. If there was a Prince Charming in the bunch he'd be hard to spot. One lone boy was wearing a Scout uniform.

The church had a nine-passenger van. When I saw Gary Hendricks's blue Cavalier wheel into the parking lot I mentally groaned. I'd forgotten that he was the new Scout leader. I watched the good-looking young man turn off the engine then slap a club like security device over his steering wheel. Obviously this man was new to Morning Shade.

The teens crowded into the church van—five girls and two boys. I sat up front with the youth leader and driver, Ralph Moss, picking cat hair off my tweed jacket. I wasn't accustomed to wearing fur, and the practice annoyed me. I like Captain, but two dogs and a cat was a bit much for someone who'd never owned a pet, much less lived with three.

Hendricks, apparently satisfied that his Cavalier would be waiting when he got back, sprinted toward the idling van and crawled in.

"Morning, Ms. Diamond!"

"Good morning, Gary." I still burned when I thought about that prank he'd played on Cee. When I was younger I would have said something like, "Been caramelizing any onions lately?" But sixty was way too old to be catty—though I slipped once in a while and got in a good one. Gary snapped the back of my seat belt as he scrambled into the backseat. I suppose he thought he was being funny. I didn't.

"Everyone belted up tight?" Ralph asked. He adjusted the rearview mirror.

Groans and the distinct snap of metal inserted into metal followed the youth leader's remark.

Ralph had always reminded me of Ralph the Mouth on TV's *Happy Days*. The retired mechanic had the same build, same sandy-colored hair, and talked a mile a minute. This morning was no different as we made the five-minute trip to the small cinder-block building known as Morning Shade's City Hall.

As I got out of the van, I remembered why I'd decided I'd never remarry.

Ralph the Mouth.

Though I missed Herb desperately, I didn't miss smiling pleasantly, nodding, and agreeing with statements I didn't agree with in the least. Ralph told the kids he liked their "look"—that he would have dressed that way himself in his youth, but his parents would have grounded him for weeks.

I thought the remark was rather a backhanded insult, but the kids thought Ralph was cool. Ralph had given me a conspiratorial wink, like he thought he was cool too, and I was privy to the information.

When he was letting the kids out of the back, I heard Ralph say, "You're going to trip over those shoestrings and break your neck." Then he grinned. "Reeboks, aren't they? Awesome."

Mildred Fasco's granddaughter, Becky, was along today. She and Sunday school classmate Kendra Larkin kept to themselves. I had a feeling Kendra was on her best behavior, awed by the young sophisticated San Fransican. Kendra's dad owned the local hardware story, and he ran a pretty tight ship at home. Kendra wouldn't be hanging around Becky much, if I knew Pete Larkin.

I felt sorry for Becky and the tumultuous life she'd lived. Folks divorced, mother remarried and off on a holiday cruise with her new fifteen-years-younger-than-her husband. Without Becky. I knew the brittle facade the young girl presented was a Band-Aid—a very big Band-Aid to cover her hurt. After all, wasn't this the beginning of a new family? Surely Becky had reasons to wonder.

City Hall's visit passed without incident. I watched Gary Hendricks make paper airplanes out of local-interest flyers and sail them around the room. Mayor Throckmorton didn't laugh—but he did remind Gary that printing costs were sky-high these days.

Hargus took us on a tour of the police department. I couldn't imagine why law enforcement fascinated Stella. I'd go nuts in this small confinement, but she thrived on the Mayberry-like atmosphere. Pictures of America's most wanted plastered the wall. I studied the silent fax machine and telephone and wondered if they ever rang. Poor Hargus. I decided I'd call every week using the pretense of a research question. It was the least I could do for Pansy.

Hendricks shot off a few rounds of rubber bands at Becky and Kendra; if looks could kill, the Scout leader would be pushing up dirt right about then.

The grand tour ended at the fire department. Eighty-five-year-old Herbert Owsley showed us around the truck. I'd seen the vehicle so many times I knew the dents by heart, so I wandered off to the pop machine, intending to buy a Dr Pepper, except I didn't have the correct change. While I was rummaging in the bottom of my purse for coins, Gary walked up, recognized my problem, and promptly kicked the stuffing out of the dispenser.

I thought Herbert was going to throw up.

He immediately aborted the tour and strode over to unlock the machine, amid a loud jangle of keys from the fifty or so dangling off the dog-leash-snap apparatus he had hooked to his belt. The heavy leather weight sagged on his skeletal frame. He gave Gary a look that would fry meat. I was just plain embarrassed by the whole episode. Cee's instincts had been right on about this guy. I had never been more convinced of her good judgment.

Instead of apologizing for his inappropriate behavior, Gary took the can of Dr Pepper, shook it violently, and we all fell back several paces when he jerked the top off and soda spewed liked a fountain.

The Scout leader brayed.

Grabbing a tissue from my purse, I calmly wiped Dr Pepper off my coat and wondered if, when they'd handed out brains, Gary mistook them to say *trains* and it left the station without him.

*   *   *

I stopped off at the Cart Mart for groceries before going home. Seems like I spend half of my life in a grocery store. I read somewhere that an army travels on its stomach, and I'm here to tell you the Diamond women are good little soldiers. A slinky female on *Oprah* the other day claimed she was good to her body because she exercised. I'm good to my body too. I give it everything it wants to eat.

I was pushing my cart down the cookie-and-snack-cracker aisle, trying to decide between Oreos and Wheat Thins with the Wheat Thins losing the battle when I ran into Hargus.

Literally.

I was sauntering along, pushing my cart and reading the brand names on cookie boxes, and he was bending over picking up a box of Little Debbies. The point of impact and a startled grunt from the law officer brought me up short in a hurry.

"Oh, Hargus. I'm so sorry."

He hitched up his pants, and I could see he was fairly biting his tongue. "That's all right, Miz Diamond."

He said it, but one look at his face and I knew he didn't mean it.

"I should have been watching where I was going. I really am

sorry."

"Uh-huh."

I never knew one word could sound so sarcastic.

"Where's Stella?" he asked.

Where indeed? I hadn't seen her since I left home this morning and even then, while you could definitely say the body was present, the mind seemed to have taken a hike.

"I haven't a clue."

"Clue?" He narrowed those squinty eyes at me. "What do you mean, clue?"

I blinked. "Well... *clue,*" I stammered, feeling guilty, although I couldn't exactly say why. "Meaning I don't know."

"Oh." He looked like he was thinking, although with Hargus it's hard to tell. "Well, it's like this. You know them chain letters?"

I swallowed. Oh, well, yes indeed I knew them chain letters, but I certainly wasn't going to discuss what I knew with him.

He reached for his hip pocket and I froze. Was he going to whip out a pair of handcuffs right here in the cookie-and-cracker aisle of Cart Mart? Just because I had rear-ended him with a grocery cart? I bristled, ready to do battle.

He brought out a grimy letter and handed it to me.

"Oh." My anger subsided in a hurry. "You got a chain letter."

"That's right, and me an officer of the law. It's like they're just daring me to catch them. Well, I say, bring 'em on. I'm up to anything they throw at me. Birds don't intimidate me in the least."

"I don't think that's the reason behind the letter," I said, trying to soothe his ruffled feathers. "They probably just needed another name to send one to."

"And that's another thing." When he shoved his face toward me, I backed up a step. "Hummingbird wants *fifteen* dollars. Do you know how much money that is?"

Well, yes, considering how much I spend for groceries, I had a pretty fair idea. Probably enough to keep him in soda for a couple of weeks. Before I could say anything though, he snapped the letter out of my hand and shoved it back in his hip pocket, almost causing a sartorial disaster. He grabbed his pants just in time to avoid total exposure.

"You tell Stella this is the last straw. She don't need to worry no more. I'm going to catch this sneaky, conniving crook before he can lick another postage stamp."

Another hitch to his pants and he whirled, quickstepping out of sight. I stared after him, openmouthed as he rode into the sunset, or in this case, pranced out the front door of the Cart Mart.

That boy was definitely a couple of bricks short of a wall.

*   *   *

Around four o'clock on Monday, I pulled a meat loaf out of the oven, trying to balance the phone receiver between my ear and shoulder. On the other end of the line, my agent, Jean Sterling was trying to explain why the contract would be delayed again.

I sat the baking dish on a trivet, listening but feeling very little sympathy for the reason. It didn't matter *why* it wouldn't be in my mailbox this week, only *when* it would be there. I thought of the thick manila envelope lying on my desk crammed with Jack Hamel's illegible notes. I was expected to take those notes and erratic ramblings and make them into a best-seller. I'd verbally agreed to do so, and my word is my honor, but it seemed to me that an author should be allowed a *but* without seeming to be a diva.

Jean's soothing tones, with a hint of finality, came over the wire. "I'm going to ask that your check be sent with the contract. That will at least save time."

It would, I had to agree. Sometimes the length of time between signing the contract and receiving the first half of an advance could take months. Sometimes when I lie in bed at night and wonder how ends will meet, I think about the folks who have the security of a weekly or monthly income. The average author can seldom live on his or her writing income; but for those who do, they live in the dark on when money will arrive.

Once a manuscript is written, it begins a lengthy and often frustrating process. Sometimes it feels like the book is being read by a committee, and I'm expected to satisfy six or seven different reviewers who each has suggestions for revisions. Then when I do get feedback on the manuscript, I often have to write the book a second time—time that isn't factored into my monetary or physical writing schedule.

After this work is completed, the book goes back to the publishing house, where it will be reread. Usually this is a speedier but still time-consuming process. There may be more suggestions, more rewrites, but eventually, if the manuscript is accepted, the magic call comes: We accept the book, and we will release the second half of the advance. That's when I do my happy dance. For the next few weeks I'll not be worrying over bills.

But by then I'm behind in my schedule: I have to do an outline of the next book, send it to the publisher, have it read, get suggested changes, make revisions.

My contracted deadline for Jack's book is fast approaching, but at this point I haven't gotten the official signal to proceed—or the first half of the advance so that I can pay my bills until the book is written. I don't want to obsess over a check, but my creditors do.

I assured Jean that I would be deeply grateful if she could pull off the contract-and-check-at-the-same-time feat, but I had my doubts. I hung up, giving the prospect about a one in two hundred chance.

While my mind was on Jack Hamel, I opened the drawer and took out a slip of paper with his personal phone number on it, then punched in the numbers on the keypad.

The housekeeper answered. "Hamel residence."

"This is Maude Diamond. Is Jack in?"

"Mr. Hamel is working and can't be disturbed."

Well, wouldn't that be nice—a guard dog. *That's what you need, Maude, a great big, old, mean, junkyard dog to keep people at bay when you write.* I grinned, imagining the luxury.

"Can you give Mr. Hamel a message?"

"I can."

"Tell him I—Maude—still can't read his notes. Can he have them typed and faxed to me?"

"Oh, Mr. Hamel's secretary is gone for the day."

"Okay, tomorrow is soon enough."

"I'll give Mr. Hamel the message."

As I hung up, the back door opened and CeeCee tramped in, followed by Frenchie and Claire. I frowned when I saw muddy paw prints on the linoleum. "Honey, the dogs have been in their water pan again."

"Sorry, Mom." Grabbing a clean dish towel, Cee doubled over and waddled around the kitchen, wiping up muddy paw prints. "Boy, what a day I've had! Just look at the scratch on my leg!"

I peered over the tabletop, staring at the angry laceration. "What happened?"

"I fell off a porch!"

"You what!"

"Fell off a porch." She pulled out a chair and sat down.

I stopped what I was doing and got the medical kit and cleaned the wound.

After I washed my hands and put the kit away, knowing CeeCee would explain the accident, I reached into the oven and took out foil-wrapped baked potatoes. Personally, I like a potato baked without foil—they're moister—but CeeCee and Stella like the foil.

"Mom?"

I straightened, pushing a lock of hair out of my face with my arm. "Yes, dear?"

"Don't you want to hear about my day?"

"Sure." I set the potatoes down and took off my insulated oven mitt. "What happened? Gary Hendricks again?"

"Mom, you can't believe this guy."

"Yes, I can," I assured her, thinking about the kicked pop

machine and poor Herbert Owsley's face on Saturday.

"I'd decided I was going to do one of my 'drive-bys'—drop
the mail in his box and gun it—but wouldn't you know Mrs.
Fielder caught me just before I approached the Hendricks box. I saw
her standing on her porch, waving at me, so I stopped to see what
she wanted. She came down the walk carrying a plate of something.
You know how good people are to mail carriers; they bake cookies
and make homemade things for them. So that's what I thought was
happening—Mrs. Fielder had baked me cookies."

"Well, wasn't that sweet of Ilda."

"Not so sweet, Mom. The cookies were for *Gary.* Mrs. Fielder asked
if I could deliver them for her since her ankle's been bothering her
lately. It's all swollen and she's wearing this ugly-looking brown
bandage."

I shook my head. Ilda had her nerve. If she was going to bake
cookies, she should have baked enough for Cee *and* Gary. "Why
would Ilda bake Gary cookies?"

"She said something about how he'd gotten her 'sweetie
pie' out of the tree for her yesterday. Said that cat would climb the
Empire State Building if somebody didn't stop her—doesn't have a
fearful bone in her body.

"Anyway, I didn't have the heart to refuse her, so I took the
plate of cookies and drove to the next box, which was Gary's. I was
thinking about leaving the cookies in the box along with his mail,
but then I didn't know how long it would be until he found them, so
I sat there and honked for five minutes. He never came to the door so
I thought, *Great, I don't have to deal with the jokester.*

"I hopped out of the truck and hiked up the walk, balancing the
plate of cookies and his mail. When I got to the door I decided I'd
better ring the doorbell—for courtesy's sake, plus the fact I could see
Mrs. Fielder watching me from her front porch.

"After a third try to rouse the lunkhead, I was about to set the
plate of cookies on the porch, but guess what happened?"

I sighed. "He answered the door."

CeeCee leveled a finger at me. "Bingo. Swathed in this heavy, ugly-looking, massive, furry housecoat with a towel wrapped around his head. I was thinking I'd either disturbed a séance or he'd just gotten out of the shower. Anyway, I handed him the plate of cookies and turned around to leave, but he thought Mrs. Fielder's gift was something *I'd* given him, and the man went bananas! He got this predator look in his eyes and this stultified grin on his face. I started backing up, my eyes scanning the plate of cookies for a signature card, which wasn't there. I turned toward Mrs. Fielder to see if she was still on the porch, but she'd gone inside and shut the door.

"Gary was advancing—looking like a deranged bear in that fur robe—and I was still backing up. All of a sudden I ran out of space and *boom!* I tumbled head over heels down the row of concrete steps."

"It's a wonder you didn't break something! He must have been beside himself."

"Laughing," CeeCee said. "Practically rolling on the porch floor, holding his sides."

"Why, that's awful! He didn't try to help?"

"He might have—I didn't give him the opportunity. I got up and hightailed it back to the truck. He was standing on the porch, his face twisted with confusion. He was yelling, 'Hey! I don't get it! First you play hard to get; then you bring me cookies—what's the deal here?'

"I could have died, Mom. He was yelling at the top of his lungs—everyone for a mile around could hear him. What did he do? I jumped in the truck, rolled up my window, and drove off."

"He proceeded out to the curb in his robe and slippers, cupped his hand to his mouth and shouted, 'What's the deal—are you the kind to lead a man on? I don't care! How's Wednesday look? You free then? You like Italian—I make a mean lasagna!'"

I sank down in the chair opposite CeeCee. I knew my mouth was hanging open. "I've never heard of such a thing."

"Well, you have now," CeeCee said. She stood up, trying to bend her leg under the confining liquid bandage I had applied earlier. "You ever read the book *Men Are from Mars, Women Are from Venus?*"

I had not, but I'd heard enough about the subject that I felt I had read the book—even saw the author on the *Today* show once.

"Well—" CeeCee straightened—"Gary is from Pluto."

I didn't want to make her problem worse, but I had to laugh. Pluto sounded about right for the odd man.

"And you're from ... ?" I teased.

"Morning Shade, Arkansas. Good ole Arkansan. We don't dress in massive furry housecoats and yell at people from the curb."

Well, no, we didn't, but I'd been tempted a few times....

I leaned over and hugged her. It was a real shame that a worthy suitor wasn't spending as much time vying for her attention. Cee needed a man in her life, one who would treat her right. For the longest of times she had insisted that she was from California—the land of fruits and nuts. Jake Tamaris had certainly been a nut, but it was good to have Cee's heart back home and acknowledging her roots.

Morning Shade *was* her home, and nothing would ever change that.

And on the eve of Thanksgiving, that was truly one of my greatest blessings.

CHAPTER 13

On Thanksgiving Day the roads were passable, which was a good thing because I'd invited Maury Peacock and Victor Johnson, as well as Stella's bridge group—Simon, Pansy, and Frances—none of whom would ever see seventy again. Cee was planning to drive around and pick them up. Cee's coworker Ty offered to do it. I'd invited him, too—at Cee's request—and Iva Hinkle and her mother. Iva declined, but said they hoped to spend Christmas with us. With Stella's continuing strange mood I thought the more I could invite the merrier.

I got up early and put the turkey in the oven. CeeCee had made the cranberry salad last night, and Stella had mixed the bread cubes—corn bread, biscuits, and white bread for the stuffing. We were using Stella's recipe seasoned with onions, celery, and freshly ground sage picked and dried from the sage plant at the back of the house. Herb had planted that sage because he claimed the homegrown variety was better than store-bought. He was right.

Emptiness washed over me—so strong that for a moment I had to grip the side of the kitchen counter for support. Herb. This was only the second year he wouldn't be carving the turkey, sitting proudly at the head of the table. I thought of the pistachio salad in the refrigerator—his favorite—and I knew it would be as tasteless as dust in my mouth.

Stella wandered into the kitchen, lost without the morning paper. "Can I do anything to help?"

"Not at the moment, unless you want to set the table for breakfast. It's going to be simple this morning. Just cereal. I don't have time to get fancy."

Stella sniffed. "Anything will do for me. Doesn't matter what I eat now. Should have started to take care of myself years ago. That's the secret of living to a ripe old age."

She's eighty-seven, for pity's sake. What more does she want? CeeCee wandered in, wearing faded jeans and a sweatshirt that said "You have to kiss a lot of frogs before you find a prince."

Bless her sweet heart; she should know.

Stella laughed. "Reminds me of a cup I used to have. One side said 'Love is blind.' The other side said 'Marriage is the eye-opener'."

"Ain't it the truth?" I murmured. Oh, I'd had a good life with Herb, and I missed him, but I was still bitter about his dying without leaving a life insurance policy. Had he not given my future any thought? Why, I wouldn't have to be worrying about making ends meet—I wouldn't even have to write any more if I didn't want to.

I recalled Stephen King's words concerning writing. He said if a writer doesn't find ways of keeping stories fresh and interesting, writing will get old and tired in a hurry. That's what happened to me: I got old and tired in a hurry. Maybe if I'd ever made the best-seller lists—ever did anything that made all the toil and worry worthwhile.... But I knew that kind of thinking was just self-indulgence. Writing had given me more than it had cost me in the long run. God gives gifts, and this was mine. He knew what was best for this child.

CeeCee poured herself a glass of orange juice. "That about covers it, Grandma."

I picked up a pan of potatoes to peel, turned to carry them to the sink, and stumbled over Claire. Potatoes rolled across the floor and I only saved myself from falling by grabbing the table. "Cee!"

"Right. I'll put them in my room." She left with the poodles, and Captain crouched under the table, refusing to leave the kitchen and the enticing food smells. I couldn't blame him, but I couldn't risk breaking a leg. I held out a piece of bacon, luring him to my office. He followed, tail twitching, but when I closed the door, leaving him there, he cut loose with what I took to be a string of cat cursing that fairly curled my hair.

Stella, grinned. "A cat ought not to talk like that."

"I'm certainly glad I can't understand what he's saying," I agreed.

"Seems sometimes like he's almost human, and then other times, he just seems like a cat."

Stella sat at the table rubbing the sage to a fine powder. The sharp pungent odor filled the kitchen, blending with the fragrance of roasting turkey, and onions and celery simmering in butter on the stove.

"Every notice how good Thanksgiving smells?" Stella asked. "It's the best-smelling holiday I know."

"Oh, I don't know. Christmas smells pretty good too, if you add in the scent of greenery and all of the other cooking smells."

"Your kitchen usually smells good," she agreed in one of her rare complimentary comments. "You're a good cook, Maude."

"Well, I had two good teachers—you and my mother." Both good cooks and never too busy to share a recipe or a tip. I hoped I had passed on good culinary memories to my daughter.

CeeCee reentered the kitchen. "Need some help?"

"How about putting the extra leaf in the dining-room table, and then you can get out the plates and silverware." I dumped the onions and celery into the cubed bread and added the sage and enough broth to moisten it.

Cee set out my company plates and arranged the good silverware, carefully polished for the occasion. We used the best for our friends. Stella scooted back out of the way as I removed the turkey from the oven.

"Would you look at that," CeeCee admired. "Martha Stewart couldn't have done it better."

"Probably couldn't have done it as well," I bragged.

I transferred the golden brown bird to my grandmother's platter with the forget-me-not pattern I had used for Thanksgiving for as long as I had been married. This Thanksgiving would be as good as I could make it. Three widows and their friends. Sharing the good times and the bad, but God had blessed us with health, love, and friends. What more could we want?

The guests began arriving. Victor came with a jar of honey from his own bees. Pansy brought a broccoli salad, Frances carried in her famous three-layer coconut cake, and Simon had concocted a fruit and relish tray that was a sight to behold. Ty showed up with boxes of chocolates for everyone, and Maury Peacock walked in carrying a head of cabbage. I took the cabbage and shot Stella a look that threatened her with bodily harm if she said anything. She sniffed but let it go.

Pansy also brought Hargus, his pants at half-mast as usual. His contribution was a six-pack of his favorite soda, which he proceeded to drink. That worked out fine, since no one else seemed to care for it.

After Simon asked the blessing, everyone dug into the feast. I doled out white meat and dark meat as if I had been carving turkeys all my life. I must have absorbed the basics from watching Herb all those years. I still felt weepy when I pictured him standing where I stood now. He had enjoyed the holidays, and they didn't seem the same without him.

We finished the meal with pistachio salad and large wedges of Frances's cake. Hargus ate until I wouldn't have been surprised if he'd popped like a balloon blown up past air capacity, although I should be the last to talk. If I hadn't worn my black slacks with elastic in the waist, I would have been very uncomfortable. As it was, I wasn't sure I could get out of my chair without help.

A disagreement among the men broke out over whether to watch football or car races, with Simon, Victor, and Ty voting for football and Hargus wanting the races. Football won, but from what I could see, the debaters were mostly dozing in front of the TV screen. Maury wandered into the kitchen to watch me clean up.

He sat down in Stella's favorite chair, looking more alert than usual. Not enough so you could say he was back to normal, but the mental fog didn't seem quite so thick.

"Sure was a good meal, Miz Diamond. I appreciate you inviting me."

"I'm glad you could come."

"Sure beats that TV dinner I had planned. I can have it tomorrow."

A TV dinner. What if I hadn't invited him? The poor man would have been sitting at home alone, eating a packaged dinner instead of the feast he'd enjoyed here. I wasn't even sure he'd have the sense to heat it first. He had to get off that medicine before it addled him permanently.

"Would you like a plate of leftovers to take home with you, Maury?"

"I sure would, Miz Diamond. Maybe a little piece of that coconut cake—if you can spare it."

I filled a plate with turkey and stuffing and salads and a second plate with a large slice of cake, one that would serve Maury twice.

Pansy and Frances trotted out to the kitchen, followed by Stella.

Frances pulled a grape from the centerpiece and examined it critically before eating it. "Has anyone received any more chain letters?"

"Not that I know of." Pansy dabbed a spoonful of cranberry salad on a paper plate and added a morsel of turkey. "Good thing, too. Hargus says it's mail fraud."

Stella pulled out a chair and sat down. "I see the Citgo is having a sale on ballpoint pens."

I stared at her. Now that was an important piece of

information.

Maury Peacock nibbled on a holiday cookie. "You need lots of pens to write chain letters. I know. I bought a whole package the other day because I'd used up all the ones I had."

I turned to stare at him about the same time Stella did. We both exchanged a curious look—Stella's more puzzled than mine.

Pansy snorted. "You used every ballpoint pen in your house? Maury, you'd better stop taking all that medicine. It's making you downright squirrelly."

"Probably so," Maury agreed. "Always liked squirrels. Friendly little fellows."

I bit back a chuckle. This group was better than a circus any day. I couldn't figure Stella out, though. Usually she was right on top of any mystery, but she seemed totally unconcerned about the chain letters. I wondered again if she had gotten one and hadn't mentioned it. Surely she wouldn't be foolish enough to send money, but she probably wouldn't tell me if she had.

"Well, back to the chain letters," Frances said. "It's hard to imagine what kind of person would write a letter trying to scare people into giving them money."

"I write letters—every day." Maury reached for another cookie.

"To whom?" I asked. .

"To anyone who wants to get one—"

Stella interrupted. "*I* don't think the person who sent that letter meant any harm. Since there haven't been any more incidents, I'd say it's a onetime thing. Best everyone just forgot about it." She yawned, jotting something down in her notebook. From where I stood it looked like she'd written Maury's name and underlined it.

I eyed her suspiciously. That was a fake yawn if I ever saw one. I'd bet she was up to something, but I knew better than to try to push her. She could be downright closemouthed when she wanted to be.

CeeCee stuck her head in the doorway. "The football game's over and Simon wants to go home. Ty says he'll take him if you ladies are ready to go."

A bustle of leave-taking followed, with everyone carrying away more food than they had brought. Frances offered to leave some of her wonderful cake, and I didn't protest too hard. She cut three slabs, each big enough to cover a saucer, taking turkey and stuffing in return. I figured it was a fair trade. I'd ask her for the cake recipe, but I knew it was a treasured secret she planned on taking to her grave. A shame. Some things were meant to be shared.

After they were gone, CeeCee let the dogs out of her room. I opened the door to my office and Captain stalked out, the picture of offended dignity. Cee filled the animals' bowls and came back to collapse in front of the television. Stella was snoring in her recliner, and I kicked off my shoes and stretched out on the couch with a book, fully intending to doze.

The doorbell rang, and I padded over to answer it.

Gary Hendricks stood there with a basket of fresh fruit. "Afternoon. CeeCee in?"

"Ah... yes, Gary. Come in." Well, what else could I do, although I knew Cee would be furious with me.,

He set the basket on the coffee table. "Thought you might like some fruit. It's better for you than all those fattening desserts."

CeeCee glared at him. "Meaning I'm fat?"

He wiggled his eyebrows. "I like my women pleasingly plump."

CeeCee pressed her lips together, refusing to answer, and Gary edged toward the door. "Well, I'll not bother you. You enjoy the fruit."

He left and Cee indicated the basket. "Probably booby-trapped. I wouldn't touch it unless you like surprises."

Stella eyed the fruit from the safety of her recliner. "Looks edible to me."

"Well, that caramel onion looked good too until I bit into it. I'm telling you, if you're smart you won't touch it."

I left them arguing and went back to the kitchen. At least

Captain and the poodles were quietly eating their special dinner. The day had gone well, and everyone seemed to have a good time. I smiled contentedly. All in all, considering the circumstances and Herb's absence, I'd made it through the holiday with only a few privately shed tears.

And experienced an awful lot of meaningful friendship.

*   *   *

The morning after Thanksgiving I put in a call to Jean, my agent.

"Oh, hello, Maude. Did you have a good holiday?"

"Very good. You?"

"Excellent. I guess you're calling about the new contract."

"Right. Is it any closer to being completed?"

"Well, closer of course, but we're not there yet."

I sighed. The writing business was slower than a centipede on crutches. "Well, if it's ever signed, overnight the check, please."

"Will do, Maude. Sorry I can't be of more help."

"That's all right." I hung up the phone before I said what I really thought. "Sure, I had money coming; sure, I would get it eventually."

Try spending that at the bank.

The doorbell rang and I went to answer, trying to avoid tripping over Captain, who thought he had a duty to inspect all visitors, which wouldn't have been so bad if he had looked presentable. But it put people off to be greeted by an oversized, green-eyed tomcat exhibiting all the affability of a cattle rancher at a convention of People for the Ethical Treatment of Animals.

I opened the door to find a half-drowned Mildred Fasco.

"Morning, Maude. Hope you got a cup of hot coffee."

A handful of icy rain splattered against the window. I watched Mildred shed her muddy boots in the foyer, trying not to resent the intrusion on my writing time. Yes, I was home all day, but that didn't mean my time was free. I *worked* at home. Why couldn't people understand that?

I tried to keep resentment out of my voice. "Of course, Mildred. Come on back to the kitchen."

I rinsed the pot and started fresh coffee brewing, wishing Stella would come home from the Citgo so she could keep Mildred entertained, but Simon wasn't supposed to bring her back for at least thirty minutes. In the meantime, another morning when I should be working was headed down the drain. I had set a goal of two chapters a week. So far I was two months behind.

Mildred twitched her sweater into place and planted herself in one of the kitchen chairs as if she were settling in for the day. Captain watched her every move, eyes slitted as if trying to decide whether to ignore the intruder or attack. Frenchie and Claire sniffed her ankles. I sighed, remembering a time when my household hadn't been run by a bunch of animals.

Mildred wrapped her hands around her coffee cup, looking down at the table. I watched her for a moment, wondering if I should say anything or wait until she was ready to talk. When she didn't make a move I decided the ball was in my court.

"Is anything wrong?"

It was as if I had opened a floodgate. "It's Becky. Hargus caught her and Abel Brookes papering Farley Birks's house last night."

Farley Birks was the high school principal, and I could see that Abel might think it was a good idea, since he, at least, went to school in Morning Shade. But Becky was just here for the holidays, so how did she get involved? Sheer juvenile cussedness, I suspected.

"I guess Hargus was upset."

"Not nearly as upset as Farley was. The rain last night turned all that paper into white mush."

I pictured Farley—thin, precise, toothbrush mustache, and receding hairline—gathering soggy toilet paper off his shrubs and snickered. I couldn't help it.

Mildred managed a grin. "He had this big old bucket, and every time he picked up a handful he'd say something like 'My goodness gracious,' or 'My, oh my.' It *was* sort of funny. Or it would have been if my granddaughter hadn't been involved." She took a drink of coffee and set her mug down on the table. "I had just bought a twenty-roll economy pack, and they used it all."

"They shouldn't have done it, Mildred, but it's not all that big a deal. Farley might be upset, but it doesn't take much to throw him into a tizzy, and he'll get over it. Kids have been toilet-papering houses for years. It's nothing new."

"I know, but Becky's a handful. Seems like she's been bent on causing trouble since her parents divorced three years ago. Sometimes breaking up a family is tougher on the kids than it is on the adults."

"You're probably right. The adults are ready to call it quits; the kids usually aren't. But Becky is a good girl. She'll work it out in time."

Mildred nodded, but her eyes were troubled. "What if she doesn't?"

I stared at her, thinking of all the things I could say but probably wouldn't. It's easy to talk, but it's hard to back up good intentions, and the only person who really likes advice is the one handing it out.

"Teenage rebellion is always a problem, Mildred. And what works for one won't work for another. There is no one clear list of rules that are effective every time."

I should know. Though Cee had no longer been a teenager, no one could talk her out of marrying Jake Tamaris. It hadn't been easy smiling and performing as the mother of the bride when I knew my daughter was making a mistake.

Mildred looked out the window at the pelting rain. "I suppose this latest outburst is because she's upset over her mother's marriage. I think she always hoped her parents would get back together. Now that prospect is gone."

"It's tough, Mildred, but God knows what Becky's going through. He's going through it with her. It may take a while, but He'll help her work it out."

"I know. But it's hard to see her hurting and know there's nothing I can do."

"You can pray."

"Yes, I can do that."

We sat in silence drinking our coffee. When Mildred finally left, it was nearly eleven and time for Stella to come home. No writing done yet. No lunch fixed either. As far as work was concerned, the morning had been wasted, but Mildred needed someone to talk to. We all need someone to listen once in a while. I wandered into the office and looked at the blank monitor screen. How could I finish Jack's book with all these interruptions? *Lord, I know You gave me a talent for writing, and I want to use it for You, but I have a life separate from my writing, and it keeps getting in my way.*

I thought about this. There wasn't any part of my life I wanted to give up. I'd miss Cee and Stella if they weren't here. I'd even miss the poodles and Captain—as long as we don't add to the menagerie.

Of course there were times when I yearned for peace and quiet, but only on a temporary basis. I'd never want to go back to living alone again. Well, not full-time, anyway.

I heard CeeCee's truck and stepped out on the porch to wave. Not much in the mail this morning: a couple of circulars, a letter for Stella, the telephone bill, and an envelope from Peace River Insurance Company. My medical insurance. I ripped it open, fingers stiff with apprehension. Just what I didn't need right now, another bill. The figures swam before my eyes. The premium had nearly doubled from last year. How on earth would I be able to pay for it? But I was afraid not to. What if I got sick? I'd never be able to afford time in the hospital. Not at today's prices, and not to mention the government has made it illegal not to carry health insurance.

What with unexpected bills and sky-high insurance premiums,

my savings account was dwindling faster than a drop of water on a hot sidewalk. Talk about being between a rock and a hard place. This was it.

I wandered back inside and put the insurance statement in my desk drawer so CeeCee or Stella couldn't find it. I was getting a nice little collection of unpaid bills. Maybe I could frame them. What really ticked me off was the fact that the new contract was still sitting on someone's desk. Once it made it through the chain, then there'd be another week before the advance check arrived, even if Jean put a rush on it.

I stared out the window, thinking that the only way I could see to pay that medical premium and meet holiday expenses was to get a part-time job. Christmas was coming and businesses would be hiring extra help. I dreaded the thought of working and then coming home to write, but I could do anything short term. Somehow the thought didn't make me feel any better, but I decided I'd make that call to Luella Denson and ask if they needed help at The Antiques Shop.

I didn't hold out much hope. After all, Luella had told me that, like every other Morning Shade business, their sales were down. But a phone call couldn't hurt.

CHAPTER 14

Across town, CeeCee automatically dropped mail into boxes and wished the day were over. Her throat felt sorer with every passing hour. She stopped at Minnie Draper's to deliver a package and stared at it in dismay. How had she missed the label on this one? *FRAGILE.*

She had what was left of something in her truck. A gray, powdery dust drifted over her hand. The box had a small tear that someone had tried to tape over.

There was, a hole in the box, and the contents were leaking out. She knew Minnie's grandmother in Arizona had died last month. Could this be her ashes? *Urkk!* What was left of her ashes, she amended, watching a haze of fine dust settle over the vehicle seat.

No—the box would be marked "Human Remains." *Whew.*

From the weight of the box, there probably wasn't enough left of whatever it was to fill a toothpick holder, let alone an urn.

She wiped her hand on a tissue. Better deliver this one in person. Apologies were in order. She climbed the steps to Minnie's front porch and rang the doorbell.

Minnie answered on the first summons. "CeeCee, what a surprise. Come on in, honey."

CeeCee held out the box, hole up. "Hi, Minnie. I'm sorry but there's a hole in this box, and I've lost part of your package."

Minnie blinked with surprise. "Say what?"

CeeCee indicated the label. "It says Fragile."

"Oh." Minnie's face cleared. "That's cookies. Christmas cookies. My uncle sends them every year."

"There's a hole in the box. Right there." CeeCee pointed to it. "Some of the crumbs dribbled out. Sorry."

"Land sakes. So they did." Minnie took the box and inspected it critically. "Wonder what happened?"

"I don't know. Minnie, I'm so sorry."

"Now don't you be a bit upset about it, CeeCee." Minnie reached out and patted her arm. "Uncle Harold's cookies are a crime. Seems fitting they would be scattered from here to Arizona. Sort of like my dreams finally came true."

"Well, I suppose that's one way of looking at it," Cee said.

"It's the only way to look at it," Minnie said. "I'll have enough of Uncle Harold's cookies to send a thank-you card, but I won't have to suffer through eating any of them. You're the best postal carrier I've ever had."

Cee drove away, relieved Minnie had taken the damaged box so well. Someone like Hilda Throckmorton would probably have thrown a fit that would have made World War II look like a Sunday school picnic. She left a couple of Christmas cards at the next box. They were still eating Thanksgiving turkey, and someone already had their cards in the mail.

Her head was starting to throb, and her throat was getting scratchier and sorer by the minute. The day couldn't get any worse.

She pulled up at the corner and got out, shouldering her bag. Six houses here and easier to walk the block than stop every few feet. She left mail at each box, skipping Leroy and Genevieve Prescott's house. Their mail was on hold until March when they would get back from Texas.

She walked past the vacant house, aware of loud voices again. Why would there be voices in a house that was obviously empty?

Reluctantly she climbed the steps and tried the front door. It swung open easily, and she hesitantly stepped inside. The stench of bird droppings clogged her nose. She stared in dismay at a cage holding two unkempt, hungry, extremely vocal and agitated macaws. "For goodness' sake."

Squawk. "GOT A CRACKER, SIS?" The red one cocked his head, staring at her.

The green one stuck his beak through the wires and made a nibbling motion. "WHAT TOOK YOU SO LONG, TOOTS?"

CeeCee approached the cage, not sure what to do. She couldn't leave them here, cold and with no food. Apparently the former occupants had abandoned these poor birds. She'd have to deliver them to the pet shelter in Ash Flat when the roads cleared, but for now she'd have to take them home with her. Oh, yeah, this was going to go over real well, on top of Frenchie and Claire and Captain. She didn't want to think of her mother's face when she saw two more mouths to feed.

It took some finagling to get the cage containing the noisy birds into the mail truck. By the time she finished she'd felt like she'd wrestled a three-hundred-pound gator.

She drove straight home—which was against the rules, but she couldn't deliver mail with all that squawking going on in the back of the vehicle—and sat there for a moment, gathering her courage. Finally, she got out and carried the cage into the house.

Mom met her in the front room. *"What* is that?"

The red macaw spotted Captain. *Squawk.* "AHOY MATE! WAR PARTY! WAR PARTY!"

The green one cocked an eye at Maude. "HELLO, TOOTS. HUBBA, HUBBA." Followed by a piercing wolf whistle.

"Catch the cat!" CeeCee yelled.

Captain crouched, ready to leap. The macaws fluttered frantically, apparently sensing danger. Stella shot out a slippered foot, hitting Captain in the rump. Startled, he sprang onto the coffee table. Claire went into a yapping fit, and Frenchie made a mess on the floor.

Maude stared at CeeCee, momentarily speechless ... which wasn't a good sign. Mom was never without words.

"Mom—I can explain—you remember those loud voices I was talking about the other day?"

CeeCee went on to explain her plight even though Maude's face had turned gray. She ended by solemnly promising, "The moment the weather lets up I'll drive both birds to the shelter in Ash Flat."

Maude had only one thing to say. "You'd better." Then she wheeled and left the room with as much composure as two yipping poodles, a hissing cat, and two screeching macaws allowed her.

Stella spared a glance in CeeCee's direction. "You're getting on her last nerve, sissy."

"I know, Grandma. I promise. The birds will be out of here in twenty-four hours, max."

*   *   *

CeeCee opened her eyes the next morning, listening to the brittle snap of tree limbs breaking under their heavy coating of ice. Her throat felt like it had been sandpapered, and her forehead was hot to the touch. Her brain hurt, and she had no medical insurance. Whatever was wrong with her, Mom would have to pay for the doctor and antibiotics. At least until the end of the month when she got her paycheck. She knew her mother had been worried lately. That advance check was late and there'd been a lot of unexpected expenses.

She could hear the macaws screeching and Frenchie and Clarie yapping. No doubt Captain was doing all he could to agitate the situation.

She closed her eyes, remembering the expression on her mother's face when she saw the birds. If it hadn't been so awful, it would have been funny.

And the green bird had whistled at her.

CeeCee stifled a snort of laughter that hurt the back of her throat. Yanking the covers over her head, she grimaced. She couldn't drive to Ash Flat today on these icy roads. She felt rotten. Didn't have the strength to fight her way out of a wet paper sack.

This was one time it would be safer to stay in bed.

CHAPTER 15

Balancing a hot Cup of coffee, holding the screen door open with one foot, and reaching down into a metal box wasn't easy, but my fingers snagged the mail, and I pulled the banded bundle free as the wind caught the screen door and propelled me back into the foyer. Shivering, I walked toward my office, listening to the *gentle flap flap* of my slippers against oak flooring.

"Utilities, phone, cable bill ... "My eye focused on the upper left-hand corner of a white envelope, and I silently groaned—or it could have been audible, I'm not sure. Whatever, I knew without opening the envelope that I had another chain letter. Bless my soul—when was this going to stop? When I was about to drop the letter into the trash I noticed two more envelopes, one addressed to Stella, the other to Cee, all without return addresses. We'd all three been hit with the scurrilous scam.

"Anything for me?"

I glanced up when Stella shuffled into the foyer, a little surprised to see her. I hadn't realized she was still home. Consulting my watch, I saw that it was after eleven. Where had the morning gone? I'd worked on Jack's notes—still no legible faxed information had come through—until I'd taken a coffee break, but I had no idea the morning was practically gone.

I handed Stella her envelope. "Another chain letter."

Stella's jaw dropped. Color drained from her face.

Alarmed, I reached out to steady her slight frame. "Do you need to sit down?" That did it; I was calling the doctor immediately.

Stella pushed my hand away and slit open the envelope with her index nail. Color fused her pale features. "I'm fine—must be my blood pressure acting up."

"I'm calling the doctor—you haven't been yourself in weeks."

"I don't need a doctor. When you're my age nothing on you works right." She pulled the letter out of the envelope and read it. "Fifteen dollars! They've upped their price!"

"What?"

She waved the sheet of paper in front of my nose. "The crooks! They're asking fifteen dollars now. Signed their name *Hummingbird.* That's a lot of moolah for such a tiny bird."

Shaking my head, I dropped my envelope in the waste-basket, surprised when I heard Stella's quick intake of air. "What's wrong?"

"You shouldn't throw that away."

I laughed. "Why not? It's junk mail."

Stella's eyes dropped to the letter she was still holding in her hand. I noticed the paper shook. "It says one man broke the chain, and he lost his entire family to the plague—plus his dog and car a week later."

"Oh, be serious, Stella. You can't believe that."

Stella carefully refolded the letter and slid it back into the envelope. "Poor man. And the real culprit—the sender—got away scot-free. He's probably living on one of those tropical islands right now, leaving the sun and surf just long enough to go to the post office box and pick up his cash every day."

"Oh, for heaven's sake."

Her eyes narrowed. "But when he's caught it means hard time—life on the rock."

"You watch too much television." I picked up my coffee cup and continued into my office. Stella misunderstood this whole chain-letter thing, but I didn't have the patience to go through it with her again.

My eyes caught the stack of unanswered mail on my desk: fan mail, invitations to book signings, requests for updated lists of my books. Every day the pile mounted, but I never seemed to find time to take care of it. It was all I could do to keep up with my fan e-mail, and I felt bad. I considered the bulk of my ministry wasn't writing but ministering to the readers who took the time to write me. Many were lonely and wrote pages upon pages telling me about their life, their marriages and family. If I could, I'd pick up the phone and call each one of them—talk for a while, let them know that somebody cared that they were suffering from cancer, or lost a child, or were in the midst of a painful divorce. But I couldn't. My time was so stretched now I could barely breathe, and it was all I could do to meet deadlines. I wonder if that's what God wanted of me, or if He expected more. More compassion and less busyness.

I knew the answer. God wanted me to love my neighbor as I loved myself. I knew the command. If I could only find a way to pay bills *and* love my neighbor at the same time.

"You know what you need?"

I turned, unaware that Stella had followed me into the room. What's the chance? "What do I need?"

"You need a secretary—someone to help you answer all that mail and the requests for autographed books for libraries and school carnivals. Someone who could help you assemble discussion questions for readers groups and do monthly postcard mailings for your newest book."

Bingo, I thought. That would be nice, but if I didn't have the money to pay my utility bill, how was I going to pay this superwoman office whiz? Maybe an angel would help—I believe in angels. I would like nothing better than to look up from my computer and see an angel bearing a strong resemblance to Denzel Washington licking stamps and feeding faxes into my office machine. But this wasn't the movie *The Preacher's Wife,* and I was, in reality, a struggling published writer who was just lucky enough to get work on a steady basis with no added frills.

"That would be grand," I told my mother-in-law. "I've heard of writers who can afford assistants and publicists."

"Well, you should get someone like that, Maude. You're like a cat chasing his tail—running in circles and getting nowhere."

I'm so glad she noticed, though the comparison wasn't the most flattering. I tried. Believe me, I tried to manage my time better. Look at all the books I'd bought and read. On paper, the books' theories looked great, but in my world they didn't hold water.

"You're lucky, though. You can sit home and do your work— no stress. When I worked I had to be up before dawn, punch a time clock, and work whether I felt like it or not. A writer can work when she wants to."

Okay. Ignorance is bliss. I thought of the ad a publisher might run, and it would read something like this:

Wanted: Best-selling authors. No medical insurance or 401(k) plan, no vacations or holidays, irregular income, 24/7 shift. Royalty statements mailed twice a year—as is. Submit 5-page resume outlining everything you've ever done all your life and how you intend to apply it toward the story you're writing. Due to heavy submissions, allow 4-6 months for reply. No double submissions, please.

I grinned at the idea. Maybe I was in the wrong business. I should be writing classified ads.

"Tell you what I'm gonna do." When Stella pulled up a chair, I could see I was in trouble. "I'm going to help. Don't know why I didn't think of it sooner, but I can write letters. My hand's a little shaky—maybe you can teach me how to use the computer and I'll type the replies. You can tell me what to say, I'll type it, and then you can sign them." She beamed. "How's that for a deal?" `

I couldn't get my mouth to work. Teach her how to use the computer? Tell her what to say? The thought was staggering. I could answer the letters and write a couple of chapters in the time it would take to train somebody—especially Stella.

"That's so sweet of you, Stella, but it isn't necessary. I plan to catch up on my mail one night this week."

Stella's face crumbled. "But I want to help, Maude."

I could see that she did, bless her soul, but how could I make her understand that unqualified help was more of a burden than a help? Lately Stella seemed bent on contributing to the household, and I didn't want her to worry. Since I am the head of this house, worrying is my job, and that is one task where I'm always working ahead of the game.

"Couldn't I handwrite some of the replies?" Stella peered back at me expectantly. "I'd do a good job."

"Don't you and Hargus have anything to work on?"

Stella shook her head. "We're not working on anything." She looked away, and I noticed she seemed unusually preoccupied with a glass paperweight Cee had given me last Christmas. For the life of me I couldn't shake the feeling that she wasn't herself lately—that she still had something bothersome weighing on her mind.

"Well, if you want to answer three or four, that's fine." I felt obligated to give her something to fill her time. "Thank the readers for writing, tell them about my newest release, include a bookmark, and if they ask, send an updated list of all my titles. Put your initials below the signature line and I will sign the letter."

"Okay. Anything else?"

"I always try to answer in a tone like I'm talking to an old friend."

"Okay, I can do that."

Oh, that it would only be that easy, I thought, knowing this was too good to be true.

*   *   *

Stella worked steadily throughout the early afternoon. She sat in her recliner, pad and pencil in hand, glasses perched professionally on the end of her nose, wearing teeth, letters stacked neatly on the end table. Occasionally I got a "Hey, Maude! What do I say to this one?" but in general my afternoon was turning out to be productive.

After a third call to Hamel's secretary I even got a faxed, readable version of the evangelist's notes. I went back through the morning's work and replaced words *like feelings* with *faith.*

Little things a theologian might catch.

Around three o'clock, Stella closed her "office." She shuffled into mine and handed me three handwritten letters, a proud smile on her face.

"Three!" I praised, eyeing the stack of fifty or more still on the end table. "That's wonderful, Stella."

"Read them, sign them, and I'll get them in today's mail."

"Now?" I was looking forward to starting dinner and a brain drain for the next couple of hours.

"Now—I'll have to walk to the mailbox; they pick up at three-thirty."

I figured the letters would all say about the same thing so I read one. Color drained from my face and dripped off the end of my nose.

"Stella ... did you answer all three letters as ... candidly?"

"I did exactly what you told me," she said.

I reread the first letter:

Dear Elizabeth,

Thank you for writing. I am very busy, and I have to have my secretary answer your letter, but nevertheless I like hearing from my readers. You said you get my books at the library— that is nice, but I do not get paid for any books checked out at the library. So if you like my books and want to see me continue to write, you will have to buy them. There are many bookstores around; just open your eyes and look. .

I am sending a bookmark of my newest release. I know everybody can use bookmarks, and use mine freely since the publisher gave them to me and I'm not out any money—which is very tight for me right now.

You asked if I knew where you could get backlist copies of my books. I don't have time to worry about such things, but if you have time to read you have time to research this question yourself. Enclosed is an updated list of my work to assist you in your search. In the future you should be more vigilant. My books come out twice a year, regular as clockwork. They're in bookstores—you have to get down on your hands and knees and look on the bottom shelf in Christian Fiction, but there are usually one or even two copies there, so I don't understand why you say you can't find them. Have you really looked? Just a suggestion for future titles, friend. Yours truly,

Sad

Sad?

Oh. Stella Amelia Diamond: my secretary's initials.

Folding the letter, I mustered a lame smile, wondering if I could get my hands on a brown paper bag. I was hyperventilating now. "Well... thank you, Stella. You were certainly candid with the reader." Make that my ex-reader, if she ever received this letter.

"You know me—I never shy around the subject." She yawned, stretched. "Boy, that about wore me out. Think I'll stretch out on the sofa for a few minutes. Let me know when you've signed the letters. I'll go mail them. Need any help with supper?"

Oh no, I thought. She'd been about all the help I could handle in one day.

When she left the room, I folded the answered letters and shoved them to the back of my files. Sometime this week I'd answer the letters myself. Meanwhile I'd have to think of a reason why Stella couldn't mail them before supper.

Captain stalked through the kitchen, where I was heating water in the microwave for my late-afternoon tea. The green macaw shifted nervously on his perch. *"AWK,* RUN FOR COVER, MATE."

I eyed him sourly. "Yeah. Good advice." His days were numbered. Soon the birds would be at the Ash Flat shelter.

The front doorbell rang, and I left the kitchen and my freshly brewed tea to answer.

My neighbor Maury Peacock shivered on the doorstep. "Howdy, Miz Diamond. Can I come in?"

"Why, of course, Maury. What are you doing out in weather like this?" No hat, no coat. He'd given up the Bermuda shorts, thank goodness, but with his faded jeans he wore a Hawaiian print shirt complete with hula girls and bongo drums in all the tints and hues known to mankind. Probably the closest thing to Joseph's coat of many colors you'll find on this earth.

Maury followed me to the fireplace, where I drew up a chair for him to get warm. He rubbed his hands together, shivering slightly. I waited while he stared into space as if he saw something I didn't. Before I could help myself, I sent a hurried glance over my shoulder, but all I could see was Captain stalking the poodles.

"You stop that right now," I yelled.

Maury looked startled. "Yes, ma'am, Miz Diamond. I sure will. What was I doing?"

"Not you, Maury. I was talking to the cat."

He looked relieved and took a deep breath. "I've got troubles, Miz Diamond."

Troubles? What now? Had he locked himself out? Or worse yet, set fire to his kitchen? I glanced out the window, but everything looked calm.

"What kind of trouble?" It must be something bad to make him look so shaken.

He held out an envelope, and I took it with a sinking heart.

A chain letter. "It's a bill, Miz Diamond. I don't know what it's for, but if I don't pay it, something bad will happen. Somebody that calls himself *Hummingbird.*"

"Oh, no, Maury. Nothing will happen. It's just a chain letter. Ignore it."

"Says so right there." He pointed a stubby finger at the letter. "Bad luck will happen if I don't pay it in ten days, and I don't get my check in time for that. Why, no telling what will happen. I'm worried something terrible."

Oh, great. What do I do now? Think, Maude. Use your head. There must be some way I can get through to him. "Are you still taking your medicine?"

"Yes, ma'am," he said proudly. "Take it three or four times a day."

I stared at him in consternation. Well, my stars. No wonder he was three peas short of a pod most of the time. "Listen, Maury. This is not a bill."

"Oh, yes it is. Says so right there." He nodded like one of those bobble-headed dolls. "Send fifteen dollars to each of those people." He blinked up at me. "I don't even know those people. Don't see how I could owe them money, but I guess I do. Must be some new government program."

I read the letter more thoroughly. Not one of mine gone astray, thank goodness, but I still felt lower than dirt. And the person had upped the ante. Fifteen dollars to five names on the list. Never had I ever suspected anyone would mistake a chain letter for a bill. Had I caused anyone to worry like this? *Oh, dear God, forgive me. I didn't realize what I was doing.*

"I'll tell you what, Maury. I think I can straighten this out for you. Why don't you leave the letter with me?"

"You think that would be all right?"

"I'm sure it will. If you get any more of these letters, you bring them to me and I'll take care of it."

He smiled. "Now that's right neighborly of you, Miz Diamond. I appreciate it; I surely do."

"Think nothing of it, Maury. Glad I could help."

"You'll take care of it before those ten days are up, won't you?" The worried look was back on his face. "I wouldn't want to bring bad luck down on you."

I closed my eyes. *That's right; make me feel even worse than J do now.* "I'll take care of it. I promise."

I walked him to the door and watched until he was safely outside before going back to the kitchen and my cold cup of tea. *Lord, this isn't funny. I tried to help Stella, but what if I've ended up hurting others? I knew it was wrong to send those letters. I just didn't think. Old leap-before-she-looks, that's me.*

The red macaw winked at me. "BUMMER, BABE."

I lifted my cup and took a drink of cold tea. "You got that right, mate."

*   *   *

Sunday morning dawned bright and clear. The sanctuary at Living Truth was filled. Pansy and Frances sat two rows in front of us, and Simon was a couple of rows over. Even Hargus was here today. Hilda Throckmorton cruised in under full sail, looking like the *Queen Mary* in search of a berth. She chugged into a vacant seat near the front and proceeded to put her purse next to her, Bible on the other side, and squirmed around a few times getting comfortable before settling down, head up, shoulders back, patronizing smile plastered in place.

Stella nudged me. "Takes her a while to build her nest, doesn't it?"

I grinned but didn't answer, not wanting to encourage her. She can be outrageous enough without any help from me. She unwrapped a peppermint drop and popped it in her mouth. Peppermint is not one of my favorite scents.

I raised my eyebrows. "Why are you eating candy in church?"

"Keeps me awake."

Oh, well. Given the choice of listening to her crunch hard

candy or have her sleeping on my shoulder, I chose the lesser of the two evils. Stella in full snore could rival the steam whistle on a homebound freight.

The choir marched down to take their seats with the congregation, and Pastor Pat Brookes approached the pulpit, looking solemn and saintly, as was appropriate for Sunday morning worship service. Looks can be deceiving, though. Pat Brookes could laugh and tell a joke with the best of them. Always in good taste, of course.

He held up a sheet of paper, which, by now, had become distressingly familiar. A chain letter. Surely no one would have been dim enough to send a chain letter to the *preacher*. But evidently someone had.

"Before I read my text, I want to say a few words about chain letters." He waved that sheet of paper around like a red flag. *"I understand people in this community have been subjected to a veritable flood of these letters."*

I sighed and tried to sink lower, making a mighty effort to hide behind Frances, which of course was similar to hiding a mountain behind a pine tree. Not that I'm as big as a mountain, but I'm working on it. As if I hadn't been feeling bad enough about sending those letters, particularly after the way poor Maury Peacock had been confused, now I had to be preached at as well. I guess I had it coming.

Pastor Brookes leaned on the pulpit, looking me in the eye. Or at least, that's the way it seemed. Probably just my guilty conscience, but I flushed and slid lower in my seat.

"I suppose you all know this is a form of gambling."

Well... no. I hadn't thought of it that way. Trying to get something for nothing, I supposed, although you did have to buy paper supplies and postage, so you had a little investment involved. But I could see his point.

"People who can't afford to pay out the money will do so, hoping to get rich. It's a fool's game. It's also illegal, and we

Christians are supposed to obey the law."

Talk about hitting a woman when she's down. I was ready to leap to my feet and confess my sin when I noticed Stella making gagging noises and turning a peculiar shade of blue. I whacked her across the shoulder blades and the peppermint drop shot from her mouth, ricocheted off the back of the pew in front of her, and went spinning through the air with the speed of a stray bullet. I watched in horror as it clipped Hilda in passing.

Stella took a deep breath; her eyes bugged out at me. "Thought I was dying right here in front of God and everyone."

I shushed her and turned my attention back to the pastor. If we hadn't known his views about chain letters before, we sure did now. The man was hot.

Later, Stella was unusually quiet as we drove home from church. I didn't have much to say myself. Brother Pat's sermon had left me feeling lower than ditch water. *Oh, Lord, what have I done?* I hadn't realized that a guilty conscience could be such a heavy load to carry.

CHAPTER 16

Late Monday afternoon, Stella hiked in the direction of Hargus's office, purse dangling from her right arm, working up a hefty head of steam. She'd seen nary a thing to indicate that he had taken her seriously. If he had any information about the chain letters, she wanted it, and he was going to give it to her or she would know the reason why. She had a right to the information, since she was the one who had started the ball rolling, so to speak.

CeeCee worked for the post office, and seeing as how chain letters were considered mail fraud, she wondered how her granddaughter would feel if Hargus had to arrest her own grandmother? Bet that would stamp her envelope.

Evidently some conniving mind had seen the potential to make a profit and swiped Stella's idea. Which really ticked her off—or it would if she was still in the chain-letter business, which she wasn't.

She pushed open the door to City Hall and walked in. She found Hargus in his cubicle, leaning back in his chair with his feet on the desk. He had a cola in his hand.

"So this is what you do all day." Stella scooted a chair around and sat down, staring accusingly at him. "Is this any way to control crime in this town?"

He swigged cola, the muscle in his throat working like a

primed pump. "I'm thinking. That's an important part of solving crimes—sorting clues and thinking."

"Thinking about what?"

He smirked. "I ain't telling you anything. This is one case where I don't need any help. I've got my eye on a likely suspect, and it's just a matter of time until this case is signed, sealed, and delivered."

Stella perked up. "You have a suspect? Who?"

Hargus gulped soda and then burped. "That's for me to know and you to find out."

"You're not talking?"

Hargus shook his head. "Not on your life. You ain't poking your nose in where it don't belong and hogging the credit this tune."

Stella bristled. "If that isn't just like you, Hargus Conley— too muley to ask for help whether you need it or not. I'm betting you don't even have a suspect."

"Do too." Hargus jerked his feet off the desk and stood up. "I got a red-hot suspect, and I don't need any help closing this case. So there."

Stella shoved her chair back and stood up to confront him. "All right, be that way, but I've got a few leads of my own, and *I'm* not sharing them with *you*. " She whirled and started toward the door.

"Hey!" Hargus yelled. "I thought you didn't want in on this— thought you didn't want Maude to know what you'd done."

Stella stopped and turned slowly back to face him. "You haven't said anything, have you?"

His grin was pure-dee wicked. "I'm your worst nightmare, Stella. Remember when you were in here a few days ago, throwing your weight around, *blackmailing* me?"

She shook her head. "That wasn't me."

"Was too."

"Okay, so we both got the drop on each other. Looks like we're in this together whether we like it or not."

"What leads you got? I'll charge you with obstructing an

investigation if you don't tell me," he threatened.

"What *investigation?*" Stella jeered. "You don't need my help. You just said so." She would make him eat those words if it was the last thing she did on this earth, and considering her age, it might very well be. Go out in a blaze of glory.

She stormed out the cubicle door and City Hall, and strode up the street, so angry she almost ran over Maury Peacock.

"Hey—whoa." Maury reached out to steady her. "Where are you going in such an all-fired hurry?"

"Sorry, Maury." Stella clutched her purse and sidestepped a patch of ice. *"I* wasn't watching where I was going. What are you up to?"

Maury's features turned serious. "About five-foot-eight. Seems like I used to be taller, but I think I've shrunk."

Stella peered at him over her glasses. "You still take that medicine?"

"Yep." Maury nodded. "Don't bother me none though. Used to make me sort of thickheaded, but my thinking has cleared up real well."

Stella shook her head. *Crazy as a bedbug.* She'd never thought Maury was the brightest bulb in the package, but he had dimmed even more. That's what doctors and their pills did for you. She took medicine herself. Half a blood-pressure pill every morning. Shame to have to live on pills. One more side effect of getting old.

She fell into step with Maury, and together they walked toward Citgo, Maury tipping his hat to everyone they met. She thought about telling him to keep it on—bound to catch cold creating a draft like that. Maury needed a good woman to look after him, but she wasn't in the market for the job. Had all she could do to take care of herself.

"You ever get any of those chain letters, Maury?"

Maury nodded. "I reckon. Got something I thought was a bill. Maude said it was a chain letter and took care of it for me, but I figured out a way to handle it myself. I just send them back marked 'return to sender'."

Stella stopped and looked at him. "What good would that do? There wasn't a return address on it."

"That's the post office's problem," Maury said. "They get paid to make high-level decisions like that."

Stella couldn't wait to pass the information on to CeeCee. She was complaining just the other day about people who made her job harder. She'd be happy to know Maury was one of them. When they reached the Citgo, she invited him to come in and have a latte. Maybe a little caffeine would water down the effect of his medication.

"Don't believe I will. Got to go home and check my mail. Might have got another one of those letters."

Stella sighed. "Well, you might as well open it and see how much the crook wants this time."

Maury took a step backward, his hand covering his heart. "You can't send them back if you open them. That wouldn't be right."

"Whatever." *Nuttier than a jar of chunky peanut butter.*

Maury veered off, heading in the opposite direction. "See you around, Stella. Watch out for slick spots walking home. Can't have you falling and breaking something important."

"Everything I've got is important."

Stella watched him walk away, figuring she could scratch his name off the suspect list. That medicine had him so confused he'd be lucky if he could write out a grocery list, let alone a chain letter.

Looked like she had to work harder if she aimed to solve this case ahead of Hargus.

CHAPTER 17

Late-afternoon sun filtered through the window as I laid comic strips in the birds' cage. If Cee didn't recover soon I was going to *walk* to Ash Flat carrying the cage in my arms.

Squawk. "YOU'RE A BABE, TOOTS!"

The really pitiful thing was that the bird was my only source of male compliments these days.

Beady eyes viewed me quizzically. "BAD NEWS. HUH?"

"The worst, bird. The very worst. Try cleaning *my* cage and see how you like it."

I glanced up as Stella came in from the Citgo. Of course, she'd caught me away from the computer again, but somehow bird cawcaw appealed to me more than writing.

Stella entered the living room minus her upper plate.

I stared at her, aghast. Who would leave the house without all her teeth? "Where're your teeth?"

"On the hall table. I didn't leave without them, Maude; they hurt so I took them out as soon as I came in. Help me remember where I left them."

One of these days Frenchie or Claire was apt to carry them off, and then we'd be in a fix. Teeth cost money. Too much to just leave them lying around anywhere you choose.

"How were things at the Citgo?"

"Fine. Pansy's got the lumbago. Can't hardly get around, poor thing. It's terrible to get old, Maude."

"But the alternative isn't all that swift either."

Stella sniffed. "If that's supposed to make me feel better it doesn't. Wait until you get to be my age. What works hurts, and what don't work can't be fixed. Old age isn't for sissies; I'll tell you that. This younger generation won't have what it takes to make it this far. You'll never believe what I saw down at the Citgo. One of the new girls has dyed her hair *pink*. Bright pink and she has a ring in her *eyebrow*. What do you think of that?"

"It's a fad, Stella. She'll outgrow that sort of thing soon enough. Kids in every generation try to shock their parents."

"You'd think it would scare her witless every time she passed a mirror. Did I tell you that I bumped into Maury Peacock? He's as goofy as they get."

"I do wish he'd stop taking that medicine. I wonder if he's been back to see Sherman?" Sherman Winters had doctored Morning Shade residents for over thirty years..

Stella shrugged. "I thought he might be the one writing those chain letters, but I've changed my mind. He can't think that straight."

I wadded up the soiled cage papers, threw them in the trash, and tried to look stern. "I don't want you getting mixed up with those chain letters. That case of the furniture-arranging burglar was bad enough. I realize it was all a prank, but it could have been serious. Whoever is writing those letters doesn't want to be caught, and besides, basically the petitions are harmless. Nobody's got a gun to anyone's head. They can either send the money or throw the letter in the trash. I wish you wouldn't feel so bad about sending money—"

I caught myself, immediately aware of the slip.

Peering back at me, Stella frowned. *"I* didn't send money."

"Oh—okay. I thought maybe you did and felt guilty about it."

I pretended interest in the local newspaper section. "There's no need to feel guilty—everyone's fallen prey to the scheme once."

"I didn't send money," Stella contended.

"Okay."

"Not much chance of me getting involved in finding out who did," Stella groused. "Hargus won't tell me anything. Says he doesn't want me messing up his case."

"Hargus working on the case, is he?" Maybe this wasn't the best time to tell her about my part in the crime. I put the admission off for another day.

"Sort of." Stella sat down in the recliner, resting her chin in her hands. "I'm just in the way. Too old to be any good to anyone."

Here we go again. "That isn't true, Stella. You still have a lot to give."

Stella sniffed. "I don't know what. Seems like I've outlived my usefulness."

Captain got up and walked over to butt his head gently against her leg. The green macaw whistled. "GIVE US A KISS, TOOTS."

Stella stared at the bird. "Can't even throw a decent pity party around here."

I laughed. Say what you want, but Stel has a good sense of humor. "That's what happens when you live in a zoo. I keep wondering what CeeCee will bring home next."

Stella turned to face the window. Snow had started to fall. "Just got the sidewalks cleared and here it comes again."

I didn't mind shoveling snow; it's being knee-deep in bird cawcaw that I minded. Sighing, I folded the newspaper. "Guess we're going to have a white Christmas, and it's coming way too fast for me."

"Done your shopping yet?"

"Not yet, but when I start my part-time job—" I caught myself at the stunned look on my mother-in-law's face. Oops. I *never* intended to let it slip that I was going to work.

Stella appeared stricken. "You're going to *what?*"

"Oh—it's just an idea," I hastened to explain. "I haven't actually looked for work yet."

"But that's what you meant, wasn't it? I wish I had the money to help out. I know having me here is added expense."

"There's nothing you can do to help, and it doesn't cost any more to feed you than it does CeeCee's animals. This is your home, Stella. I wouldn't have it any other way. Anyway, I'm just thinking about a job. Part-time, just twenty or so hours a week. Maybe I won't have to resort to that if my advance gets here in time. We'll be fine as soon as I get that money."

If only I could believe those brave words. Sure, the advance would come sometime, but not before Christmas. In time for the IRS, but not in time to help me. This was Cee's first Christmas without Jake, and Stella's first Christmas here. I had wanted the day to be extra special, but now it looked like I'd be lucky to buy groceries. Not exactly what I had planned.

Stella's tongue worried her lower lip. "You know, Maude, maybe you shouldn't be throwing your chain letters away. I know they're frowned on by the postal authorities, but truth be told, your luck seems to be getting worse since they started arriving."

I slipped Captain a crust of bread before straightening up and shaking my head in disbelief. "You can't really think a letter can cause bad luck. That's just a silly superstition."

I thought about the money I'd recently sent and mentally berated myself. *Sparrow. How could I engage in such foolishness?* But supposedly, by answering, I'd warded off more bad luck. Ha. Now I needed to find the opportune moment to tell Stella what I'd done.

Stella's eyes turned flinty. "I'm not saying I'm superstitious, but why tempt fate? Maybe you'd better answer the next one. It wouldn't hurt—might even help."

I pressed my lips together, exasperated, but trying to hold back what I really thought. How did she come up with these lame ideas?

"Let me assure you that my present run of bad luck is because I haven't received that advance. It has nothing to do with a chain letter. If I had an extra ten dollars to blow, I wouldn't spend it on anything that silly. So forget it. End of subject."

I mentally crossed my fingers. If Stella was telling the truth and she hadn't sent money—if her recent preoccupation and melancholy were caused by something other than guilt—I'd slit my throat. I was not in the position to throw money around even to cheer Stella up. "Remember what Pastor Brookes said," I reminded her. "Chain letters are illegal, and Christians should obey the law."

Stella made a disagreeable sound, flipping the television to blast-off volume.

The red macaw squawked, *"AWK, WATCH THE CAT!"*

Captain paced the floor beneath the cage, eyes slitted in concentration.

I sighed, remembering how quiet my home used to be before it was invaded by a daughter, a mother-in-law, and a flock of animals. Frenchie skidded into the kitchen, followed by Claire. They scooted around me, overturned Captain's food dish, and galloped back into the living room.

Feeling like the pivot pole in a dog race, I swept up the spilled food and dumped it back in the cat dish. Captain seemed insulted.

"It's clean. The floor's clean. Don't you give me any grief." I emptied the trash and put a stray glass in the dishwasher before going to my office. Captain followed, perching on top of the file cabinet. I turned on the computer and sat staring at the monitor instead of working. The words simply weren't there. How could I write with all these bills hanging over me? But still I could kick myself for my Freudian slip about getting a part-time job. I was really counting on additional income, but knowing Stella, she would worry herself into a snit fit trying to think of a way to help. So maybe I should discard the idea completely. In some ways a job would make my life easier; in others I'd only be adding to my worries.

Lord, I know I'm letting my lack of money drag me

down. You'll take care of me. You always have. It's just that I had such big plans for this Christmas, and now I'll be doing good to make a token effort. But Lord, I really do appreciate Your blessings, more of them than I can count. I have a feeling that even Stella's and Cee's moving in with me was Your doing, and I know I've benefited from it. Be patient with me, Lord. I realize I should be more mature than this, but remember, I'm a work in progress.

I'd have to downplay my reasons for taking a part-time job or CeeCee would be upset too. She was working, but most of her check from the post office went toward the debts Jake had left behind. Jake had made good money, but self-restraint hadn't been one of his outstanding traits. He had spent all he had and borrowed to the hilt on everything he owned. At least Herb hadn't left me in debt, even if he had been so reckless he hadn't bothered with life insurance. Apparently he had expected to live forever.

I clicked on the chapter I had written yesterday. Captain dozed. Outside the window, snowflakes, light as goose down, whirled in the winter wind. I tried not to think of the looming gas bill, not to mention the insurance premium.

God would provide. He always had. He always would. Still, it was hard not to worry. All very well to talk about the lilies of the field and how He clothed them. Those lilies didn't have a Christmas holiday hanging over their heads.

Wednesday night I'd approach Duella Denson after services and ask her again if she had part-time work. Surely business would be picking up and they could use an extra hand now that Christmas was fast approaching. With that cheery thought, I managed to write a couple of paragraphs before supper. At this stage, I'm grateful for anything.

CHAPTER 18

Wednesday evening, CeeCee decided she felt well enough to attend church with me. It would be the first time she'd left the house since she'd come down with strep throat, and she welcomed the outing. Common sense said she was rushing things, but cabin fever said *Go!*

Besides, with both Mom and Grandma insisting she should stay in where it was warm, she was almost duty-bound to go. It …was hard to assert your independence when you lived under your mother's roof. Not that Mom meant to be bossy—most of the time she wasn't, but sickness seemed to bring out a terminal streak of motherhood in her.

Maude came downstairs carrying CeeCee's heaviest winter coat. "I think you should wear this instead of that jacket you have on. It's warmer."

"I'm hot enough to roast already," CeeCee said. "Have a heart, Mom. This coat is warm enough." It was a 100-percent wool.

"No. Now, Cee, you don't want to get chilled and have a setback. I think it would be best if you wore the heavier coat." Maude approached, holding out the gray-and-black tweed coat with black knitted cuffs and collar attached inside.

CeeCee sighed. Might as well give in and wear the coat, even though she hated the thing. She liked layering, lighter coats over a sweater. Now she would swelter and probably take cold, but Mom was in her motherly mode. She knew from experience it would be easier to give in than to argue.

Maude helped her change coats and tied a woolen scarf around her throat. CeeCee felt the sweat trickling down her spine. Stella descended the stairs, holding a brown bottle. CeeCee clamped her eyes shut. Oh, no. Not Mercurochrome, Grandma's wonder drug. According to Stella, it would cure all ills. Real or imagined ones.

Now Stella approached, taking the lid off the bottle. "Sit down over here, sweetie. I want to swab your throat out with Mercurochrome before we leave. Kill those germs."

"No, Grandma. That won't be necessary."

Stella seemed not to have heard her. "I always swabbed Herb's throat with Mercurochrome. Kept him healthy. Open wide and say *ahhhhhhhh.*"

Mentally rebelling, CeeCee sat down on the arm of the couch. If it wouldn't look childish on her part, she would storm upstairs and take off this coat and rinse out her throat with a liter of Pepsi, and go to bed. She sat obediently, trying not to gag, while Stella swabbed her throat.

"See—now, isn't this better?"

"Arrrrgggggrrrrggr."

Maude shut the poodles in the kitchen with the macaws, leaving Captain in the living room. The cat growled deep in his throat, pacing back and forth in front of the kitchen door. CeeCee glanced out the window at the falling snow. As soon as she felt strong enough to make the drive, she was taking those birds to the animal shelter. And if that cat didn't straighten up and fly right, she would haul him off too.

She knew she wouldn't though. Captain had made a place for himself here. Besides, she had tried to ditch him once only to find him sitting on the front steps waiting for her when she got home.

She had a hunch he'd be a hard cat to lose. And she suspected that Mom was starting to enjoy the cat—and the birds—or she'd have taken them to Ash Flat herself.

At the church, they settled into their pews, waiting for the service to start. CeeCee amused herself by watching the people file in. There was Mildred Fasco. Probably she had left her rambunctious granddaughter downstairs with the youth group. Put Becky in the same class with Abel Brookes, the preacher's son, and no telling what would happen.

CeeCee grinned. Last week they'd filled the fishbowl in the nursery classroom with cherry Jell-O. They'd been studying about the plagues in Egypt and tried their hand at turning water into blood. Lona Bridges, nursery teacher, hadn't fully recovered from the experience. Claimed it gave her such a start, like having the Bible come to life right before your eyes.

Gary Hendricks entered the sanctuary. CeeCee spotted him before he saw her and slunk lower in the pew. *Please, Lord, no. Don't let him see me.*

She should have stayed home. Look what it would have saved her. This coat, the nasty taste of Mercurochrome in her throat, and now an encounter with Gary Hendricks.

He turned in her direction, and she immediately shifted her attention away from him. He headed toward her, and she prayed he'd pass on by, but no such luck.

Gary edged his way past the five people between CeeCee and the end of the pew to sit beside her. "Evening, CeeCee. You're looking well tonight."

She grunted a reply, careful not to glance at him. The man didn't need encouragement. Not that he would recognize discouragement either. She'd never met anyone so totally immune to a snub.

She watched in disbelief as he tore a strip of paper off last week's church bulletin and put it in his mouth. A few seconds later he removed the wad of well-moistened paper and hurled it at the back of Frances's head, two rows down. The spit wad bounced off her hat and grazed Pansy's cheek. Her hand flew up to brush away the sudden annoyance.

CeeCee slid lower in the seat. Spitballs! He was throwing *spitballs* in church. And he was sitting next to her. People would think she was with him. Why, oh why, hadn't she stayed home tonight?

Gary flipped another spitball at Maury Peacock, catching him on the back of the left ear. Maury looked bewildered—nothing new for Maury—glancing up at the ceiling as if thinking he had been beaned with a heavenly message.

CeeCee considered kicking Gary. Hard.

He winked at her. "Think I can hit the preacher?"

CeeCee stared in horror at Pastor Brookes, looking so dignified in a blue shirt and tie and imagined him being slammed with a spitball. "Stop it right now!" she hissed.

Stella leaned forward to stare at him, her eyes nailing him to the pew. Gary casually leaned back, trying to hide behind CeeCee. Stella continued to eye him, as if scrutinizing a particularly strange species of insect life.

CeeCee grinned. Trust Grandma. She'd seen that look a few times herself, and it never failed to cow her. At least it had put an end to Gary's infantile behavior. He still hadn't recovered his usual goofy attitude by the end of the service.

After the final prayer the congregation trooped to the base merit for cookies and punch. As usual Hilda was hustling around, overseeing the women doing the actual work. CeeCee had noticed before that the only thing Hilda Throckmorton worked was her mouth. Now she instructed Midge and Harriet on the proper way to serve, limiting the youth and children to two cookies each, although CeeCee noticed Abel Brookes managed to get a double helping.

Becky, pretty and vivacious, egged him on. Stella shook her head. "Mildred is going to have trouble with that girl yet. She's a corker."

CeeCee had to agree, but she had a hunch Becky was venting her frustration at the recent changes in her life. CeeCee accepted the cookies and punch Harriet Strong handed her and followed Stella over to where Pansy and Frances were sitting. Gary started to join the women, took one look at Stella and apparently changed his mind. CeeCee grinned. Maybe she had solved tonight's problem— or Stella had. Too bad she couldn't take Grandma on the route with her.

As usual, Pansy turned the conversation to the chain letters. For once, Grandma didn't try to change the subject. She leaned forward, almost eager to talk about it. CeeCee found the subject boring, so she only half listened.

"Hargus says he has a lead," Stella said. "Any idea who?"

Pansy shook her head. "He won't tell me anything. Said if I knew it I'd tell, and he didn't want anyone helping him solve this case."

"He told me the same thing," Stella said glumly. "I'd think he'd be glad of a little help."

Frances drank her punch, little finger crooked daintily. "This last letter wanted more money. Seems like the price gets higher every time."

"Did you answer it?" CeeCee asked, butting in on the conversation. "You shouldn't, you know."

"Of course I didn't," Frances replied. "I'm not a fool. I worked too hard for my money to spend it on a chain letter signed *Blackbird.*"

"But you stand to get a lot more money back," Stella said.

"I wouldn't hold my breath waiting for that." Frances nibbled on a lemon bar. "Besides, we all know chain letters are mail fraud. I wouldn't take part in anything like that."

CeeCee thought Stella looked guilty. She'd have to talk to Grandma later and see if she had sent any money. She didn't see how. Living on a social security check didn't leave much for frivolous spending. Unless she actually believed she'd make a big profit by investing in the pyramid scheme.

Pansy stood up, gathering her empty plate and punch cup. "Well, it's time to be going. I enjoyed the service tonight, but someone hit me with a spitball. I'd blame Abel Brookes, except the children were all downstairs."

Frances touched her mouth with a napkin. "It ricocheted off me and hit Pansy. Seemed to come from someone behind us."

CeeCee debated telling them what had happened but decided against it. Nothing they could do about Gary Hendricks's behavior. He was a case of arrested development. Stuck in a fourteen-year-old time warp.

After Frances and Pansy left, CeeCee picked up Stella's plate and added it to her own. "I'll get rid of these. Mom's probably ready to go."

Stella nodded. "I'll be glad to get home myself. Get to be my age, you don't need all of this nightlife."

CeeCee carried the dirty paper plates to the trash can, reflecting that if her grandmother considered punch and cookies in the church fellowship hall an exciting nightlife, she led a very sheltered existence. Exciting it wasn't.

Unless you happened to be sitting by Gary Hendricks.

She almost made it back to Stella when Becky dashed past her, chased by a laughing Abel Brookes. CeeCee steadied herself against a chair. The room was too crowded for running, and they were both old enough to know better. She watched in horror as Abel ran into Stella, nearly knocking her off her feet.

He caught her before she fell, and she clutched the back of her chair, eyes flashing. "And what do you think you're doing running in here, young man?"

Abel wilted, apparently realizing he had just run into something he shouldn't have. "Sorry. I didn't mean to hit you."

"Sorry? Well, how sorry would you be if I had fallen and broken a hip? You think about that, sonny." She had a firm grip on his collar, preventing him from making an escape.

Abel looked rebellious. "I said I was *sorry*. I didn't run into you on purpose."

CeeCee noticed Becky hanging around, waiting for Abel but careful not to wander into Stella's territory. She couldn't say she blamed her.

Stella's eyes pinpointed the preacher's boy. "What's your face so red about? Looks flushed to me. You feel all right?"

"I'm fine."

"I don't know. You look puny to me."

CeeCee joined them. "If you're not hurt, Grandma, let it go. We need to get home."

Stella's stubborn streak flashed. "This boy is sick. Feel his forehead."

"I don't want to feel his forehead. Drop it, okay." CeeCee shot a desperate glance around the room, hoping Gary Hendricks wasn't watching. She didn't need him to get involved.

"Go on," Stella urged. "Feel his forehead. It's hot as a smoking pistol."

CeeCee reluctantly placed her hand on Abel's forehead and was amazed at how warm it felt. Grandma could be right. He was flushed too. Why would he be out tonight if he wasn't well?

Elly Brookes approached, evidently aware her son was the center of some controversy. "Is everything all right?"

Stella turned to face her. "Your boy is sick. He's running a fever."

Elly brushed Abel's hair back from his cherubic face. "Yes. He has been all day. But I figured he wouldn't feel any worse at church than he would at home, and he's been looking forward to tonight's activities. I didn't have the heart to make him miss them."

Abel, released from Stella's grip, faded toward Becky. The two pulled a fast disappearing act. CeeCee watched from the corner of her eye and spotted Gary Hendricks walking in her direction, but Maury Peacock inadvertently blocked the path. By the time the two men got untangled, Gary must have changed his mind. At any rate he left the hall, and CeeCee sighed in relief.

Elly smiled. "If there isn't anything else, I must see if Hilda needs me."

She walked away, leaving CeeCee and Stella standing alone. Stella pushed out her lower lip. "Did you hear what she said? That boy has been running a fever all day and she let him come tonight anyway."

"I heard, Grandma. She said he wouldn't feel any worse here than he would at home." CeeCee shook her head. And Elly Brookes seemed like such a sensible woman.

Stella allowed CeeCee to take her elbow and steer her toward the door. "He might not feel worse, but everyone he's exposed to whatever he's got will soon be feeling worse, and you can count on that."

Maude joined them. "Ready to go?"

Stella told her about her run-in with Abel. "That boy is sick as a pup. His mother should have kept him at home."

"Don't fuss," CeeCee warned. She wasn't feeling top of the morning herself, plus she'd belched Mercurochrome for the last hour. She really should have stayed home herself. "We weren't around him long enough to catch anything. If anyone gets sick it will probably be Becky."

"Humph. That's all you know. People my age are vulnerable. Probably spread germs all over me—he almost flattened me, you know. Just might be the death of me. I'm hanging by a thread anyway."

Stella marched down the walk and CeeCee followed behind, keeping a sharp eye out for Hendricks. She wouldn't feel free of that moron until she actually got in the car.

The man was more of a menace than Abel Brookes could ever be.

CHAPTER 19

I must be getting Old. Used to be I could stay up half the night and feel like a prom queen the next day. These days I go to bed at nine on the vague pretext of research reading, but after I've checked the Lifetime movie channel to see what's on, I nod with no hope of making the ten-o'clock news.

Where have the years gone?

What happened to my eternal youth?

I took off my glasses and laid them on the bedside table, then massaged udder cream into my dry hands. Winter winds had them chapped beet red. That and the age spots made me want to cry. And smearing something on my hands out of a bottle with a cow on the label did nothing to boost my morale. Yawning, I scratched my head and sat down on the side of the bed, eventually gaining enough strength to roll into the warmth of my sheets, artificially heated by an electric mattress pad.

Sleeping conditions were important to me—room temperature, bed warmth, the right pillow, and usually I either ran a small fan or my sound machine to block the house sounds: Stella padding to the kitchen in the middle of the night, dogs' nails clicking on linoleum, cars going up and down the street. And since menopause I've always had a window cracked open for ventilation. The mattress pad, fan, and open window fought like Kilkenny cats, but I didn't mind. I was comfortable even if the control light on the pad clicked on and off, on and off.

I lay for a moment soaking up the warmth, thinking about how sickly Abel had looked tonight. You'd think mothers would keep their wee ones home when they were under the weather, but it was a different world than when I raised Cee. In my day if a child was sick he stayed home in bed.

A soft tap sounded at my door, and I opened my eyes. "Yes?" I wished Cee and Stella would leave me alone when my bedroom door was closed. Whatever was wrong could surely wait until morning.

"Hey, Maude?"

Especially Stella.

"Yes?"

"My bed's wet; I had a little accident. Can I sleep with you?"

My heart sank. Accident. Wet bed. Oh my, had we descended to that? How would I cope with Depends along with everything else in my life? Rolling out of bed, I wedged my feet into my slippers, thinking how close I'd come to eight hours of uninterrupted solitude.

When I opened the door, Stella was standing there holding a leaking bottle of drinking water. My eyes followed the drip to the wet puddle forming at her feet.

"My water bottle sprang a leak," she explained. "Now my mattress is wet."

I was filled with instantaneous relief. She'd spilled water— not released it involuntarily—but I also felt annoyed. I'd told my mother-in-law a hundred times to check the water bottle before she drank it. How hard is that?

The puddle at Stella's feet spread onto my carpet. "How did the bottle get a hole in it?"

She shrugged.

Taking the plastic container out of her hand, I plugged the hole with my index finger (how hard was that?) and took the bottle to the kitchen and pitched it. When I returned, Stella was settled in nicely on Herb's side of the bed, her glasses folded neatly next to mine on the bed stand. I just stood there and gawked, every mean thought I could manage kicking around in my head.

Suddenly my sanctuary—my *bed*—was a Holiday Inn? Yanking the lamp chain, I turned out the light and crawled between the sheets.

"I snore," Stella warned.

Like this was a news flash? I plumped my pillow and tried to calm down. Tomorrow was a new day. Sighing, I realized even optimistic thinking failed me right now.

The house settled down to nightly whispers. I lay in the darkness too tired to turn on my fan for background noise. I wouldn't have any trouble sleeping tonight.

I'd been asleep over three hours when suddenly I felt a sharp jab to the left side of my rib cage. In that drifting sphere between half awareness and deep sleep, I winced, thinking somewhere in the dark recesses of my mind that I was dreaming.

I felt the pain a second time—sharp, insistent—and I rolled to my back and lay for a moment, wondering if I was having some sort of attack. Gallbladder? What side was the appendix on ... middle left... right? My hand searched the aforementioned areas.

An elbow caught me again hard, and my eyes flew open. "What ...?"

"Hey, Maude. "

I rolled to my side and came eyeball-to-eyeball with Stella. For a moment I simply stared owlishly at the warm body next to me. Then I asked in a tone as calm as I could muster after being jarred from a sound sleep, "Why are you jabbing me in the ribs?"

"There's somebody walking around outside our window."

My blood froze. Had she actually heard someone or was she, like me, in a semiconscious state? "Are you sure?"

"I'm sure, Maude." Her voice was barely a whisper. "I've

heard it twice. Footsteps—on gravel, around the shrubs."

My heart caught, and I realized that I was the one who had to investigate; Herb wasn't here anymore. "Maybe it's a dog—or a raccoon." The pesky little critters often came around at night scavenging for food. Herb had scared off more than one over the years.

"It was footsteps," Stella emphasized. "Someone's trying to get into the house."

"Okay," I said. We both lay for a moment while I tried to garner up enough courage to investigate. Should I call Hargus? It would take time for him to get dressed and drive over here. By then whoever it was would be gone.

Stella whispered. "Are you going to check it out?"

"Yes."

We lay for another moment, my ears straining to hear the noise. All I could hear was the rhythmic sound of the old furnace clicking on and off. And then there it was—a soft rustle near the windowsill—a fumbling, searching noise on decorative rock.

I don't remembered who threw the blanket back first or highest. In retrospect I believe Stella was out of bed before my feet hit the floor, but regardless we both dove for our glasses on the bedside table.

I fumbled, then slipped the frames on my face and screamed. I was *blind.* I couldn't see my hand in front of my face! Dear Lord— how long had it been since I'd seen the optometrist? Not that long!

Stella had her glasses on, fumbling her way around the bed. "Losing what's left of my eyesight. Can't see a blamed thing!" she complained in a hoarse whisper.

I felt my way around the edge of the mattress, stumping my big toe on the footboard. Biting back a yowl, I grabbed my toe, certain it was a bloody stump. By now Stella had made it to the window—at least that was the direction her voice was coming from. I couldn't see zip. I inched my way over by feel, still freaked by my sudden unexplainable loss of vision. Too many long hours spent in front of a computer screen. I'd known the occupational hazards, but I never dreamt the change would happen so swiftly and be so debilitating.

Between the two of us, we'd made so much noise bumping and groaning that if there was a burglar, he'd be half a block away by now. I bumped into Stella and latched on to the collar of her gown for support. "Can you see anyone?"

"I can't see the windowsill," she groused. She turned and reached out and snatched the glasses off my face. I reacted, clawing for the frames and bending them nearly double in the process.

"Hold on!" Stella bellowed.

"Look what you've done to my glasses!" I yelled. "Bent the frames double!" I couldn't see that—I could only make the damage assessment by touch—but I felt the thin wire bent in half.

"Those are *my* glasses," Stella said shortly. "Here." She whisked off the pair she was wearing and thrust them toward me. When I slipped the frames on my nose, I nearly fainted with relief. My vision was as clear as a bell.

"Oh," I said and wondered why I hadn't thought about a possible optical switch. I guess in all the confusion I hadn't stopped to remember that both pairs of glasses were on the bedside table. Score one for the mother-in-law.

Vision restored, Stella lifted the blinds and peered out the window. The corner streetlight illuminated the ground and made it light as day.

"Do you see anything?" I peered over her shoulder.

"Nothing. Whoever it was is gone."

Duh, I thought. We'd made enough racket to scare Lucifer himself.

Removing her specs, Stella tucked them under her pillow and then climbed back under the covers. She was asleep before her head hit the bed.

I switched on the fan, determined to override any further disturbance with white noise. Stella wasn't kidding. She snored like a lumberjack.

After several minutes I rolled back out of bed, went into my bathroom, and took two Excedrin PM That was before I glanced at the clock and saw that it was ten minutes to four. Great. Two Excedrin PMs and I was due to get up in three hours.

Life can be pretty unfair.

CHAPTER 20

Living Truth Community Hall was full by 9 A.M. Thursday morning. Stella shuffled into the room and took a chair next to Duella and Luella Denson. The long work-tables were piled high with floral wire, ribbons, glue, and red velvet bows. The smell of evergreen scented the room.

"Good morning," Luella chirped. She rolled her wheelchair closer to Duella to make more room.

"Morning," Stella greeted. She picked up a piece of wire and greenery and started to assemble a pinecone wreath.

"I thought Maude might be with you this morning." This came from Luella who was stringing cranberries and popcorn together in a long garland.

"Nope; she's out like old Lottie's eye," Stella said. "Still sound asleep when I left the house."

Duella lifted an inquisitive brow and consulted her watch. "Still sleeping at this hour? Is she ill?"

"Negative. She didn't say anything about not feeling good. She was in bed before nine o'clock last night."

"Oh, goodness me." The Denson twins swapped indulgent glances. "Well, I suppose some of us need more rest than others."

"I guess," Stella said. "Writers are strange ducks, and they keep weird hours and strange working habits. I gave Maude three letters to proofread over a week ago, and she hasn't got them read yet. Guess it's that creative thing in them."

The morning flew by. Guild workers put the finishing touches on church Christmas decorations while they caught up on the latest news. Around noon, Hilda Throckmorton dropped into a metal chair and heaved a huge sigh of approval. "Well, ladies, we have outdone ourselves. This year's Christmas Eve Communion service is going to be prodigiously lovely."

Stella leaned closer to Duella's ear. "Can't she just say that the service is going to be 'nice' again this year?"

Duella patted her hand. "Now, now. Where's your Christian spirit? You know Hilda leans toward drama."

Stella supposed, but it got on her nerves. Still, since her expiration date was long overdue she didn't want to have to account for any misdoings other than what she'd already racked up. Starting right now, she was going to tolerate Hilda, wasn't going to find fault with a single thing she did.

The women began cleanup. They carried the cache of wreaths and cranberry-and-popcorn garlands upstairs to the sanctuary. Sunday evening there would be a hanging of the greens, always a congregational holiday favorite.

When Stella shuffled back through the kitchen she noticed a group of women clustered around Hilda, who was still sitting in the same chair. If Stella hadn't just made the decision to tolerate the woman, she would be wondering why Throckmorton was still sitting on her behind when everybody else was lugging the heavy decorations up and down the stairs. But fortunately she'd made the decision to find no further fault with Hilda.

If it killed her. "Oh, Stella?" Mildred called. "Can you help?"

Stella shifted footpaths and approached the cluster of women. "What's wrong?"

"Oh, dear," Midge fussed. "Someone dropped superglue on the chair and poor Hilda sat in it."

Stella gaped, poker-faced, at the woman sitting perfectly still in the metal folding chair.

Genevieve Harris crossed her arms. "She's stuck. She can't get up without tearing her dress, and it's brand-new."

"I paid seventy-five dollars for this dress," Hilda complained. "The mayor would *kill* me if I cut it up."

Don't laugh, Stella told herself. *Don't laugh. Hilda can now do no wrong.*

"How sad." Stella peered over Throckmorton's shoulder, laughing on the inside. "Have you tried hot water and soap?"

Midge wrung her hands with exasperation. "We've tried everything! She can't get up. What should we do, Stella? You know all the tricks."

Well, yes, she did, but if she laughed she'd be dead meat. But the picture of Hilda Throckmorton trying to squirm out of her dress while glued to a metal folding chair was priceless. "I guess Hilda will have to take off her dress."

"Remove my dress?" Hilda paled. "Yikes. Think of something else."

"Can't," Stella said, though she probably could if she thought long enough. But she wasn't saying anything *bad* about Hilda; she was helping.

"It's just us women," someone reminded. "It's the only way, Hilda, without ruining your lovely new garment."

"Well—if I must." Hilda bent forward and helpful hands began to unsnap and unzip the heavily flowered chintz. Stella's eyes caught sight of Hilda's purse sitting next to the chair. A banded lump of white envelopes stuck out of the lining.

Chain letters?

Her bottom lip firmed. So. Hilda Thockmorton was the copycat bandit. She might have known that Hilda would push her way into the action. But how had she known that Stella had sent the first letter? Had she seen her mailing the letters that day in Ash Flat? That would be purely too coincidental. Maybe she didn't know; she'd gotten the first letter and decided to cash in on the action—

Stella, an inner voice reminded her, *you don't know what those bundled letters contain. You are jumping to conclusions about Hilda, and you vowed to be a changed soul.*

Well, yes, Lord, but bundled letters? What else could they be?

Hargus. Hargus needed to question Hilda. He certainly needed something to his credit, and if Stella questioned Hilda about the letters she'd only get irate.

"Excuse me for a moment, ladies." Stella turned and casually shuffled back to the kitchen, then broke into a trot. Jerking up the phone receiver, she dialed Hargus. Concealing the mouthpiece with cupped hands, she told him to get over to church. Pronto. She had the griff—that's con artist in detective lingo— marked.

Within five minutes, Hargus sauntered into the community hall, trailed by Fred Harridan, retired Burlington Northern man and Morning Shade's ace reporter. By now the women had Hilda swathed in a communion cloth and heading up the stairway.

Hargus threw up a pudgy hand. "Halt!"

The women stopped, hands going to hearts. Hilda gathered the communion cloth more snugly around herself. "Hargus, what do you want? We're busy here."

Hitching up his Dockers, Hargus swaggered toward the matronly woman. "Let's see your purse, Hilda."

The matriarch's face reddened. "My purse? What business is my purse to you, Hargus Conley?"

"Law business." His jaw firmed.

Fred jumped out and took a couple of pictures with his Minolta Dimage S404 digital. Stella wondered if Hilda would sue if the pictures showed the hint of lavender slip that was hanging beneath the communion cloth.

Hilda threw a protective hand over her eyes. "Get that camera out of my face!"

Stella pointed to Hilda's purse, which was now in Mildred's possession, and Hargus took the silent clue. "Mildred, is that Hilda's purse?"

Mildred pivoted from Hilda to Hargus to Stella and back to Hilda.

"You'll need a search warrant to go through my purse!" Hilda crossed her arms. Stella was glad that Pansy was under the weather today and wasn't here to witness this. Throckmorton looked for all the world like one of those Bradley tanks draped in lavender, looking for combat.

"I can get a warrant," Hargus countered, "but I'd rather do this real peaceful-like, Hilda."

They engaged in a cold stare-off. You could hear a pin drop in the fellowship hall; women stood by with bated breath.

"Oh, for heaven's sake!" Hilda relented. "Mildred, give Hargus my purse. I don't have anything to hide." Her rosy cheeks bloomed bright scarlet.

Mildred relinquished the evidence and after a thorough search—even opening one of the festive Christmas greetings—Hargus threw a sour look in Stella's direction and handed the bag back to Hilda. "You swear every one of those is a Christmas card?"

"You can open *yours* if you want." Hilda glowered, arms crossed. "I can assure you you'll not get it otherwise."

Hargus hitched his pants and broke into a friendly grin. "Thank you, ladies. That'll be all. Have a good afternoon."

He turned and walked off with Fred Harrigan trailing him.

* * *

Later, Stella trudged home. Mildred had offered to walk with her, but she'd told her she'd just as soon wallow in her own pity.

When had she lost her worth? The day she turned seventy? No, it was even before that. The day she got her AARP card. Wow—that was thirty-seven years ago. Just turned fifty. Couldn't the age ghouls wait until fifty-five to plague a body? There was not a single purpose for God to leave Stella Diamond here on earth; she was nothing but an irritation and in everybody's way. She'd have bet her social security check those banded letters in Hilda's purse were chain letters, but no, they were innocent Christmas cards. She should have considered that since Christmas was three weeks off. She was losing her edge, her detective moxie.

The copycat bandit made her mad; his letters were sounding more like blackmail than ingenuous fun. Twenty-five dollars. Folks would fall for the ruse, thinking like she once thought; it was all in fun and nothing to get upset about. What's twenty-five dollars?

A fortune to those on a fixed income and who were easily duped. If she did nothing else for her town than solve the copycat mystery, she could die in peace.

God, another week has gone by, and You've still not seen fit to take me, so now I'm asking for a little more time. I know—I'm usually asking the opposite, but this case calls for special compensation. The folks of Morning Shade need me; Hargus can't solve his way out of a brown paper sack, but my mind's still clear, and You'd save me some serious face— since I started the whole fiasco with my letter—if You'd be so kind as to let me crack this case before You bring me home. Seeing as how I've lasted this long, don't seem much to be asking if You'd hold off a bit longer. Even yogurt is still good past its expiration date.

The Lord had no comment—not that she could tell—but Stella was used to waiting. Eighty-seven years of experience wasn't anything to be sneezed at. But she briefly felt a sense of purpose, so maybe He'd said okay.

CHAPTER 21

When I opened the door Saturday morning to find Mildred
Fasco I thought, *'Well, here's another hour shot.* Glancing at the
hall clock, I realized something big must have happened to
bring Mildred out this early. She usually didn't get out and
about until later. I was still dressed in my housecoat and
slippers. "Mildred—come in—it's cold out there."

"*Farmer's Almanac* predicts a hard winter." Mildred
stepped into the foyer, wiping her boots on the small straw
mat that I kept in front of the door for just such nasty
mornings.

"Coffee?"

"Of course—you have any of that froufrou stuff to go in
it?"

"French vanilla creamer?" I laughed. I'd gotten almost
every one of my friends hooked on the flavor, even the ones who
normally took their brew black. "I do, if the bridge club hasn't
used it all." I'd pulled a sneaky one last week: I'd bought
containers of French vanilla and Kahlua cream and hidden them
in the vegetable crisper. I know, I'm selfish, but I like my
creamer, and it's irritating to have my mouth all set for a cup of
coffee heavily laced with the flavored sweetener and find
nothing but a trickle in an empty carton. "Sit down," I invited.

"I'll make a fresh pot of coffee."

"Can't stay long," Mildred promised. "But I thought you'd want to know right away. Abel Brookes has the mumps."

"Mumps!" I came close to dumping the whole can of grounds into the filter basket. "Are they certain?"

Mildred nodded. "Elly called the doctor after church Sunday evening. Sherman thought mumps were probable, but they had to wait a few days to be certain." Mildred shook her head. "Think of all the little kiddies Abel exposed Wednesday evening."

"Kiddies, my foot; I'm thinking of me and Cee. We haven't had the mumps."

"Oh, dear—aren't mumps extremely hard on adults?"

I'd heard they were, and all I needed was to come down with the disease two and a half weeks before Christmas, and Jack Hamel's book due February 1.

"Mumps? Who has the mumps?" Stella shuffled into the kitchen, coming in on the tail end of the conversation.

I greeted her absently. "Morning, Stella."

My mother-in-law shambled to the cabinet and took out a coffee cup. "You're up and around early, Mildred."

"I wanted to get an early start on my day." She fished in her purse and drew out a thick packet of envelopes. " *I* have a bunch of letters I need to mail."

Stella's eyes zeroed in on the letters. "Christmas cards?"

"Just letter letters." Mildred smiled. "You know, newsy little bits to friends and neighbors." She quickly stuffed the packet back into her purse." By now I had set steaming mugs of coffee in front of the two women and put the French vanilla creamer on the table.

Stella took one sip of her coffee then pushed her cup aside. "Thought I'd get started on our Christmas goodies this morning."

My stomach did a porpoise flip-flop. Having Stella in the kitchen was the equivalent of having a bull in the china closet. Years ago my mother-in-law had been an excellent cook, even dabbled a bit in French cuisine for a while, but years of inactivity had dulled her culinary talent. Now she burned meat, scorched potatoes, made pies that tasted like flavored paste. And that was the fruit pies—the creams pies were even worse. I felt sorry for her frustration; I knew I couldn't make a decent chicken casserole myself of late, but at this point I'd just as soon skip the candy-making tradition—which none of us needed— and enjoy a clean kitchen, not to mention having to juggle all that Tupperware containing sticky, fat-and-calorie-laden peanut brittle and Chinese noodle candy littering my countertops until someone finally gave in and threw it away in mid-January.

Sitting down at the table, I gently tried to dampen the idea. "You think we need all that stuff? Seems like I throw away half of what I make each year, and ingredients are so expensive."

For what I spent on sugar, peanuts, Karo syrup, eggs, and chocolate, I could buy a ten-pound box of Godiva and eat myself into a chocolate coma.

"HEY, STUPID!"

Mildred whirled to peer wide-eyed into the living room. I reached for the creamer, reminding her about the Diamonds' latest acquisitions: abandoned parrots.

"My," she said. "Do they always talk like that?"

"Not always." I poured a generous amount of French vanilla in my coffee, stirred it, and then licked the spoon. "Sometimes they say worse. Whoever owned them before must have been ex-navy, because those birds' language can curl your hair if they want."

"YOUR HAIR LOOKS LIKE YOU THREW IT UP AND JUMPED UNDER IT!" *Squawk.*

Mildred's fingers nervously worked to fluff her bangs.

"Quiet down in there." I yelled. "We have company."

"QUIET DOWN IN THERE!" *Squawk.*

"Sorry," I told Mildred. "As soon we get a free moment, we're taking the birds to the Ash Flat animal shelter." I sighed, taking a sip of coffee. "But who knows when that might be?" I'd long ago given up predicting anything relating to the future.

Mildred and I chatted over the clatter of banging pans. Apparently Stella was intent on candy making, so I just let her have at it. It was too early in the day to argue, and I had to write at least a chapter today. Jack promised to read the book's first draft the week after Christmas, so I would have time to revise and polish before I sent the manuscript off to the publisher. At this rate, the book was going to be finished before the first half of the advance reached me—not unusual in the writing world, but difficult on financial planning.

Mildred and I turned to more seasonal topics. We each polished off two cups of coffee and part of a Sara Lee cinnamon coffee cake I'd taken out of the freezer and warmed in the microwave. I'd pretty well blocked out Stella's cooking frenzy; I knew full well I'd be tracking flour onto the living-room carpet. And what was she doing with flour? I thought she was making candy.

I turned to recheck the ingredients while Mildred was telling me about her granddaughter, Becky, and how the girl was a good child but seemed to be going down the wrong path. Mildred wasn't happy about her daughter's remarriage; felt the family situation would only get worse. My eyes fixed on the littered countertop. Broken eggshells, spilled cocoa, Karo syrup running down the sides of the bottle. Stella was situated at the stove, stirring something in a bubbling caldron. The stench was awful.

"What are you making, Stella?"

"CALL THE FIRE DEPARTMENT, IDIOT!" *Squawk.* "IT'S A FOUR-ALARMER!"

"Hush!" I yelled at the birds and winced when I saw Mildred's facial expression. This morning the house sounded like Ringling Brothers tryouts.

"HUSH!" *Squawk.*

Stella turned from the steaming pot, frowning. "Did I put sugar or flour in this pan?" She scavenged through the open canisters on the countertop. "Plenty of sugar here—lots of flour too." Stepping back to the stove, she stared into the pot.

"STINK! MAN THE ROWBOATS, MATEY!" *Squawk.* "MAN OVERBOARD!"

By this time the noise level in the Diamond kitchen had gone off the decibel meter. Frenchie and Claire charged through the door, tails wagging. Stella nearly tripped over the poodles as she carried the pot of hot... something to the sink.

Mildred quickly drained the last of her coffee and set the cup back on the table. Getting to her feet, she smiled. "I have to be running along. I'll never get my errands done."

Stella walked over and openly stared into her purse.

Mildred frowned. "Something wrong, Stella?"

Stella glanced up. "You say those are letters? Care if I take a look?"

"Why ... no." Mildred picked up the bundle and freely handed it to her. "They're just letters."

"Yes," Stella said musingly, "I see." She held an envelope up to the window, turning it first one way then another, clearly trying to read the contents.

Mildred watched, jaw agape.

"Stella," I reminded, wondering what in the world she thought she was doing. Her moods were getting even more strange. "Give Mildred her letters."

"Okay." Stella handed the pack of envelopes back. "Sorry... there's a spot of chocolate on the ... flap."

Stuffing the envelopes back in her purse, Mildred tossed me a concerned look. "I'll talk to you later, Maude. Thanks for the coffee."

I smiled. "Stop by anytime."

I cringed as I heard sugar grains crunching beneath Mildred's stockinged feet; I could only imagine what she was thinking.

When I heard the front door close, I turned to Stella, frowning. "What was that all about?"

"What was what all about?"

"Your looking at Mildred's letters. How rude."

"What's rude about looking at an envelope?" Stella shuffled

back to the sink and dumped the pot's contents down the disposal. *"What* are you cooking? Old shoes?"

"No. It's a new fudge recipe, but I did something wrong."

"It smells like you're boiling road tar."

Somehow we'd gotten off the subject of Mildred's letters, and I didn't have time to pursue the subject. It was close to nine, and I hadn't turned the computer on yet.

"You are going to clean up the kitchen," I reminded her. I rinsed the cups and stuck them into the dishwasher.

"I always do, don't I?"

I left the kitchen on that note, refusing to answer on the grounds anything and everything that I said would be held against me. But for the life of me, I couldn't understand Stella's sudden obsession with people's mail. And I still hadn't gotten around to telling her that I had sent the stupid five dollars so she could stop feeling so guilty. I made a mental note to talk to her over dinner tonight.

"YO! UGLY!" *Squawk.*

Rolling my eyes, I planted my feet squarely on the carpeted stair, determined to avoid an insult fest with a macaw.

Mumps, I thought, my mind going back to the purpose of Mildred's early morning visit. *That's just what I needed.*

On top of that? I got another chain letter. Do these people think I'm made of money?

CHAPTER 22

Captain woke me early Sunday morning, and I managed to get downstairs before Stella for a change. I decided to fix an extra nice breakfast, maybe blueberry muffins, CeeCee's favorite, and my special breakfast casserole.

Last night I'd told Stella I'd answered one of the chain letters: I was Sparrow. I expected a relieved "Me too!" Then she would confess that she'd sent money, and we'd both have a good laugh, and Stella's mood would improve. Instead, I'd gotten barely a glance from my mother-in-law and a curt "That was really stupid, Maude" before she asked for the mashed potatoes.

News that I'd succumbed to the scam didn't faze her; so what was bothering her?

Today I would casually break the news of a second job. I'd have to be careful how I did it, though, because Cee was feeling wiped out from her recent bout with strep, and Stella was still in a blue funk.

I knew they would both assume it was because of them that I had to find extra work to see us through the holidays. That was partly the reason, but not the only one.

I needed to get out of this house. I brought in the morning paper so Stella wouldn't have to go out. The sidewalk was slick, and I didn't want to take a chance on her falling and breaking a hip. I placed the newspaper on the kitchen table and mixed a batch of blueberry muffins. The poodles needed to go out, but they were soon back scratching on the door, shivering and yipping their discontent. I couldn't blame them. This was not a good morning for performing one's necessities outside. Thank goodness for indoor plumbing.

This had been a terrible winter so far—bad weather, bad financial problems. I stood at the kitchen sink, letting my thoughts drift. I knew, as a Christian, I wasn't supposed to worry, and I did trust God to take care of us, but it seemed like I just couldn't decide what to do. I understood that the message of Christmas had nothing to do with money or even paying bills, as worrisome as they might be. And I was trying hard to hold on to the meaning of peace and goodwill the angels brought at Bethlehem, but my Christmas spirit had packed up and gone south.

I heard Stella coming downstairs and went out to tell her I'd brought the paper in. She sat down at the kitchen table and turned to the obituary page. I could hear water running so Cee was probably in the shower. Church didn't start until ten so we had plenty of time for a family morning.

"Says here William Fletcher died," Stella murmured. "Funeral's tomorrow.

"Bad weather for a funeral. Did you know William?"

"No. Seems like I don't know many people anymore. I've outlived most everybody. One of these days my name's going to be in this newspaper, but I'm not going to be around to read it."

"If that happens you'll be in a better place." I took the egg casserole from the oven and placed it on a hot mat before pouring glasses of Cran-Grape juice.

"No reason for you to sound so perky about it." Stella looked up at me and grinned. "In a way I'm looking forward to going, but then again, I'm not in a hurry to get on the bus."

"Is anyone? We know heaven's a wonderful place, but it's

hard to leave the familiar for the unknown."

"Leslie Worthington. I knew him. Used to be sweet on him when we were in school. Land sakes. How many years ago would that be?"

"Beats me. I didn't know you back then." I'll bet she was a pistol when she was younger. She was something else now. Not many women her age were as active as Stella when she put her mind to it.

CeeCee entered the kitchen and bent to pet Frenchie and Claire. The birds squawked a greeting, and Captain wound himself around her ankles. She pulled out a chair and sat down. "Mmm. Look at that breakfast. Are we celebrating something?"

"Maybe. I seem to have a lot of time on my hands, and I've been thinking of doing something about it. The other day I talked—"

Stella cut into my prepared speech. "Anna Wilson died. Probably ate herself to death. Loved fried chicken and okra. That woman had an appetite like a hog."

"How old was she, Grandma?"

"Ninety-nine."

I winked at Cee. *Yep, ate herself to death and took ninety-nine years to do it. Amazing.* I began again. "As I was saying, I've been thinking of finding a part-time job—just a few hours' work a week. I have lots of free time on my hands, and here at Christmas the shops are busy so they need extra help."

"Even the Citgo is crowded," Stella said. "Have to get there early to get a table, and then we just have to take what's available instead of getting our usual space. People don't have a lick of sense when it comes to holidays."

"You're right about that," CeeCee chimed in. "You wouldn't believe how our workload has increased with the Christmas season. It's a wonder postal employees aren't regular Scrooges by the time it's over. But Mom—don't even think about working. You have enough to do here with your writing and running the household. If you want to get out a little, take a basket-weaving class."

"Forget going to work, Maude," Stella agreed. "I'll give you all of my social security check, and I'll take basket weaving with you. Or maybe we could do pottery; I like pottery. We could make one of those big ashtrays to set on the coffee table."

"But we don't smoke."

Stella gave me a look as if she were communicating with a dense child, "You don't have to smoke to own a pottery ashtray."

I sighed. Okay, we didn't seem to be on the same wavelength here. Maybe I should drop the subject and take a job on the sly. Luella had been hesitant when I approached the subject of part-time work. Mentioned something about business being so down ... and I'd hated to pursue the subject, but The Antiques Shop appealed to my taste. It wouldn't seem like work, and I'd be among the priceless treasures of days gone by.

If I did convince them to hire me, I'd have to come up with some way to explain my absences four nights a week. I didn't hold with lying, but maybe a little white fib wouldn't hurt. I could claim I was working at the library those nights. Neither CeeCee nor Stella went near The Antiques Shop. Cee didn't like old things, and Stella contended that she'd lived with junk all of her life. I could make my absences sound like something to do with my writing. Research. That's it. I'd be doing research. Both Stella and Cee were quiet for a change, so I seized the moment.

"Maybe you're right. Come to think of it, I need to do quite a bit of research for my next writing project, and I'm thinking of taking advantage of the local library. I can write during the day and go to the library a few nights a week. What do you think?"

Claire chose that moment to swipe a bite from Captain's food dish. The cat snarled and swatted the poodle across the nose. Claire yelped and ran to Cee for comfort. The green macaw squawked a warning, and the red one shrilled, "MAN THE FORT, MATE; TROUBLE AT HIGH NOON!" Frenchie got so excited he did his business on the floor.

CeeCee had to raise her voice over the hubbub. "Sounds like a great idea, Mom. It would certainly be quieter than trying to work in this madhouse."

Stella accepted the lie without turning a hair. "I'll baby-sit CeeCee's animals while you're gone, except I promised to help at the church for a couple of hours a week, and I have bridge twice a week, Farkle on Tuesday and Friday nights. Other than that, I'll be available."

I didn't point out that eliminated her help for four nights, exactly the same amount of time I'd be gone. At least her heart was in the right place.

"I'll be here the hours you can't be, Grandma," Cee volunteered. "Mom puts up with this zoo all day long. If she wants to get away in the evenings, we need to help her out."

I felt guilty about deceiving them, but at least they weren't upset. And they would be if they thought I had to get a job because they were causing extra expense. I decided to use my first paycheck to buy them each a really nice gift for Christmas.

Cee helped herself to the breakfast casserole and buttered a muffin. "I delivered another batch of chain letters yesterday, but of course you know that. I noticed you both got one."

"Any new leads on who's sending them?" I asked.

"Not as far as I know. Hargus is acting superior and hinting he has a suspect, but I'd be surprised if he has. Anyway, no one's been collared. That Hargus," Stella exclaimed. "Thinks he's so smart. Won't tell me anything. I could help him if he'd just let me."

"I don't want you getting involved with this chain-letter caper," I reminded Stella. "Are you aware that if you're found guilty of sending one of those letters it's a felony, and if the government can prove you sent the letter, I understand you can be imprisoned up to five years and fined up to $250,000—*per letter.* Now that's something to think about." Actually, I'd thought of little else since I'd used Google.com to research the subject. And to think I actually answered one of those letters! "Let Hargus take care of it.

Finding the perpetrator is his job."

Stella bristled. "I guess you think I'm too old to be solving mysteries."

Since that was exactly what I did think, I decided to work around that comment. No use in upsetting her any more than was necessary. "I just don't want you to get in trouble. Whoever is writing these letters won't want to get caught. It could be threatening."

Stella's lip curled in an exact imitation of her favorite TV cop. "I can cover my own back."

"Mom's right, Grandma," CeeCee said. "You don't know what you're up against. There could be some bad trouble before it's over. It's really sad because most people don't realize chain letters are serious business."

Stella's jaw jutted out at that stubborn angle I recognized so well. The more we talked, the more determined she would be to find the culprit. Best change the subject. "Is Gary Hendricks still on your case?" I asked Cee.

"Is he ever." Cee poured her second cup of coffee and reached for another muffin. "You'll never guess what he did yesterday."

I wasn't going to waste my time guessing at something like that.

"He rigged his mailbox with some kind of noisemaker. When I opened the box, it squealed like a pig. I was so startled I dropped his mail in a snowbank and had to get out of the truck to find it. I could see him standing in the window laughing. I tell you, there's something the matter with that man."

"I think he's a case of terminal dimwit." I took the last muffin.

"I like the words *arrested* and *Gary Hendricks* used together. Maybe he'll go too far one of these days, and Hargus can throw him in jail."

I stared at her. "Cee, you don't think ... those chain letters."

"Do I think he sent them? Well, he's the kind that would do anything for a joke—and I mean *anything*. So if he thought of it, he'd do it. But he's smart enough to know it's illegal, so probably not."

We finished breakfast, and CeeCee and Stella helped clean up the kitchen before we all left for our rooms to get dressed for church. So much for telling CeeCee and Stella about my plans— but I guess it's all worked out for the best. I'd get a job for two or three weeks, pretend that I was going to the library, and before I knew it the holidays would be a memory.

The thought made me a little giddy.

CHAPTER 23

Sunday afternoon flew by. I made a big pot of vegetable soup and baked a chocolate cake with fudge icing. Tonight was Stella's bridge group and she'd want to get away early. I supposed I'd have to take her and pick her up when it was over, but she enjoyed the game so much I would hate to disappoint her by refusing to go out in bad weather. Although truth be known, I'd much rather stay home. That was going to be a problem with working nights. I liked being home.

I'd think the homebody Maude came with age, but Stella was older than me and she was a regular gadabout. Made me tired sometimes to see her prancing down the street to the Citgo, outdistancing women half her age.

The phone rang and Stella picked it up. I heard her coming to the kitchen and stopped what I was doing to see what she had on her mind.

She looked upset. "Simon has a cold. Can you imagine? Here it is bridge night and he gets sick. If that isn't just like a man."

"I don't suppose he got sick on purpose."

"Of course he didn't. What did you mean by that?"

Oops. I had forgotten you didn't criticize Stella's friends. Loyalty was a big thing with her. "Nothing, but you sounded like you thought it was his fault he was sick."

"Did I say that?"

"No, I guess you didn't. So is bridge off for tonight?"

"Yes. No sense exposing everybody else to a cold. We're all standing on a banana peel as it is." She lifted the lid on the soup pot and sniffed. "Smells good. Did you remember to add garlic? Garlic's good for you."

"Garlic, basil, and thyme. Seasoned the way you like it."

"You're a good cook, Maude. I believe I could have a piece of that cake before supper if you don't mind my cutting it."

"I don't mind, Stella. Help yourself."

CeeCee came in from taking a walk. Peeling out of her coat, she dropped in the nearest kitchen chair. "Boy, it's really slick out there. You going to bridge tonight, Grandma?"

"No." Stella cut a large square of cake and slid it onto a saucer. "Simon's sick."

"Probably a good thing. You don't need to be out in this weather." Cee paused. "That cake looks good."

"Go ahead, have a piece," Stella urged. "Then I won't be the only one ruining my supper."

"Plus the soup has another hour to cook," I added, still uncomfortable with eating cake before the regular meal.

CeeCee poured a glass of milk and sat back down at the table. "Let's decorate the tree tonight. Everyone else in the neighborhood has their decorations up."

"Sounds like fun," I agreed. "I think we put the decorations in the upstairs hall closet, didn't we?"

"I'll check," Cee offered. "As soon as I finish my cake."

I remembered how she always loved decorating the Christmas tree. We'd had live trees back then, but I had switched to an artificial one once Cee grew up.

Suddenly I missed Herb. Missed him so badly my chest hurt. He'd always made Christmas special, with the right presents for everyone. This year I'd be doing good to afford a fruitcake, but I refused to let my problems intrude tonight. "Lucky I baked Christmas cookies today. We'll have some while we trim the tree."

"And mulled cider?" Stella asked. "I always fixed cider when we decorated at home."

"Herb always asked for it too. I bought cider yesterday, and I think we have the mulling spices. We have to have cider—it's a tradition."

After we finished eating and cleaned the kitchen, I helped CeeCee set up the tree and bring down the boxes of ornaments. Stella watched as we strung the lights first, checking for faulty bulbs as we went. We used tiny clear twinkle lights; they reminded me of stars dangling from the branches.

CeeCee turned on the radio, and the familiar strains of "Joy to the World" filled the room. Captain stalked in from the kitchen, tail twitching as he stared at the lighted tree. The poodles crept in to see what was going on.

Stella held up a silver bell. "Remember this?"

"Of course. You gave that to us on our twenty-fifth wedding anniversary. It's been on our tree every year since then."

"And look at this." Cee held up a ceramic clown, the bright paint inexpertly applied. "How old was I when I made this?"

"Second grade," I replied. "I think the date is written on the bottom." She'd been so proud the day she brought it home from school and placed it on the tree. I hung a small crystal snowflake next to a miniature sled, both gifts from Jean, my agent. I needed to call her tomorrow and wish her a Merry Christmas. Every time I'd called her lately, I'd been upset because of the advance. She was caught in the middle between me and the publishers, and I needed to remember that.

Stella held up a cross-stitched ornament. "Who made this?"

"Pansy. See, here are her initials." I pointed them out on the back of the handcrafted ornament.

"Oh, yes. I remember she made those one year." Stella fastened it to the tree. "I've got one too. I put it away for safekeeping and haven't seen it since."

I opened a small box and took out a four-inch beaded snow-flake, the iridescent droplet glittering in the artificial tree light. My own artwork.

I had taken one of those craft classes once. When I first started my little snowflake, I intended to make enough to decorate an entire tree. Halfway through, I decided I would only make enough to decorate the top branches. By the time I had finished the first one, I knew this was the *only* beaded snowflake I would ever make in this lifetime. I would leave it to Cee in my will, with the stipulation that she display it framed under glass like a treasured antique.

I never took another craft class, either. You either have it or you don't. I don't.

I hung the snowflake close to the top of the tree, next to a light so it would show up to the best advantage.

CeeCee brought mugs of mulled cider to drink as we decorated the tree. Stella had brought her own Christmas ornaments from home, and now she set electric candles in the windows. We all went outside to get the full effect, standing in ankle-deep snow looking at the glowing lights. Reminded me of Clark Griswold waiting for his Christmas lights to come on.

But it reminded me of something more meaningful too. There was nothing like looking at a newly trimmed tree, singing Christmas carols, and breathing in the scent of mulled cider in the air, and unconditional love enveloping the room to set a person's priorities straight. I had so very much to be thankful for: the readers who wrote and shared their lives with me. The fans who plunked down hard-earned money to buy my newest book. God is so very good, and it's moments like this that make me weepy.

"They're beautiful, Grandma."

Stella sighed. "I always had candles in my window. It wouldn't be Christmas without candles."

"And we have to watch *A Christmas Story,*" CeeCee said.

"The movie about the Red Ryder BB gun?"

"That's the one, Grandma. It's a hoot."

"'Better not get a BB gun, sonny. You'll shoot your eye out,'" Stella mimicked, and I thought, *Who says death has to hurt so badly?* We'd all lived to see another Christmas, even though part of us—the part closest to our hearts—was missing.

Back inside, CeeCee wound garlands of artificial holly and pine through the stair banister and brought out a porcelain nativity scene Jake had bought her the first year they were married.

I gazed around the living room, thinking how lovely it looked and how it represented three families. Now, through circumstances we couldn't control, we were struggling to unite into one family unit, and in spite of all the odds, we were making a go of it. *Praise You, Father. Because of You all things are possible.*

Stella sat down at the old upright piano and started playing. "O Little Town of Bethlehem" filled the room, and CeeCee sang along.

I went to the kitchen to get the plate of cookies to eat with our cider. The table was empty. I switched on the light to find Claire with cookie crumbs caught in the hair around her mouth. She scuttled under the table, and I couldn't believe my eyes. There in the middle of my clean floor Frenchie, Captain, and the two macaws were peacefully eating cookies in perfect harmony.

The green bird cocked his head at me. "TURN OUT THE LIGHTS, TOOTS."

I shook my head. Evidently the Christmas spirit extended to animals. I only hoped it lasted. Whoever would have thought I'd ever see Captain sitting beside a red macaw eating a snicker-doodle. Well, I'll be—we had our own version of the wolf lying down with the lamb, except the Diamond household had to be different. We had a cat and a bird. Same concept though.

The red macaw nipped a crumb out from under Captain's nose and lived to tell about it. Would wonders never cease?

I filled a fresh plate with cookies and carried it back to the living room.

We sat talking quietly, watching the lights twinkle on and off. CeeCee's nativity held the place of honor on the mahogany library table, which had belonged to my grandmother. Stella's candles glowed brightly in the windows. Outside sleet hissed softly against the windowpane. Inside the spirit of Christmas reigned.

"Who let the birds out of the cage?" I asked.

Cee set her cup down on the coffee table. "The red one has been trying to open the door. I guess he learned how. Were they out?"

"Out and on the floor with the poodles and the cat, and they were all eating cookies together in perfect harmony."

"Well, that probably won't last. I'd better check on them before Captain gets ideas."

I leaned my head back against my chair, thinking of Christmases past. I'd never had to worry about shopping or paying bills then. This year was different. I didn't want to charge anything, but I couldn't wait until the last minute to buy gifts for CeeCee and Stella either. The weather hadn't helped any. So far it hadn't allowed much more than driving to church, the medical clinic, and the store. Maybe it would be better tomorrow, but the way it was sleeting, I doubted it.

CeeCee let the poodles out for a few minutes. Captain jumped up on my lap. His rumbling purr sounded like distant thunder. The lights on the tree winked at us. The angel Herb had bought on our first Christmas smiled from the treetop. And for a moment—one sweet moment—I thought I saw my husband's face. He smiled. And I knew that everything would be all right. What a gift. What a perfect example of God's love—for me.

Stella stood up and stretched. "This has been a good night. I'm sorry Simon's sick, but I'm kind of glad we didn't have bridge."

"Me too." I dumped Captain onto the floor and stood up. "Bedtime."

Stella and I climbed the stairs, leaving Cee to turn out the lights after she checked on the animals. Her clear soprano followed us up the stairwell, and I couldn't help it. I felt fresh tears running down my cheeks.

"'Silent night, holy night...'"

*   *   *

By the next day the weather had gone from bad to awful. Traffic was almost at a standstill. Cee drove her mail route, and I worried and prayed until she got home safely.

Stella spent the day in the recliner with the television for company, and I actually worked. Confinement can be good. Jack's notes were easier to read now.

I called Jean and wished her Merry Christmas with no strings attached. I guess she was so used to consoling me she immediately launched into her spiel. "I'm moving heaven and earth, but it's the holiday season and things at the publisher are moving very slowly."

Yes, I knew it was the holiday season and I was broke. I felt my pride crack a little further, but I knew Jean couldn't walk on water. "Well, stay in touch."

"Will do—and don't worry, Maude. I have a feeling this is going to be your year."

Right.

I fixed grilled-cheese sandwiches and canned tomato soup for lunch. A pot of chili simmered on the stove for supper. CeeCee would be hungry when she came home, and I wanted something hot to help ward off the winter cold.

"Chili blows me up like I've ingested helium," Stella complained.

"Cee likes it. I'll fix you something else."

"Oh, I guess I can eat it this once. Just be forewarned."

I let it pass, having noticed she could eat anything she wanted to eat but could come up with a dozen reasons for not eating something she didn't like.

"Did you throw away that last chain letter?" she asked.

"I sure did. Unopened. I hope you did the same."

"I kept mine. Might be useful for evidence."

"Evidence of what?" I asked suspiciously. "I thought you had decided not to get involved in this mystery."

"No, *you* decided I shouldn't get involved. I didn't promise anything."

I stared at her, perturbed, but knowing she was right. Thinking back, I remembered she hadn't promised. I definitely was not happy. Why would she be so stubborn when I was just trying to help?

"Stella, I'm not trying to tell you what to do ... "

"Yes you are, and it's all right. I know you mean well, but if I'm not old enough to make up my own mind about what I want to do, I never will be. That's the worst part of getting old; someone is always making decisions for you. You'd think my brain had short-circuited."

"I know that's not true."

"I know it's not true either, but that's what *you* think."

She slipped the poodles the crusts from her sandwich while I sat thinking about what she had just said. "I just don't want to see you in jail."

She grinned. "You're a good daughter-in-law, Maude. I'll try not to make you bake files in cakes."

"I suppose I'll have to be satisfied with that." Actually, I was proud of her. I didn't know many women in their eighties who were that feisty and so determined to control their own lives. "All right, Stella, I'll mind my own business, but if you need help, you tell me."

"You got a deal."

She went back to her recliner, and I retired to my office, where after a couple of games of solitaire I stared out the window at the trees bent low with their icy burden. If we didn't get some relief from this continuous spell of bad weather, those tree limbs would snap. Hit one power line and half the town would be without electricity. Then I couldn't work. I grinned. But it would help with the electric bill.

What am I going to do, God? I'm not trying to make a big commercialized splash over Christmas. I just want to buy something nice for Cee and Stella and pay my bills. Is that too much to ask for?

This was the season to celebrate the birth of Christ, and all I could think of was money. Didn't say much for me, did it?

I heard the front door open and glanced at the clock. Must be CeeCee. Home today a little earlier than usual. She didn't come to my office as she normally did, sitting down to talk before going up to change. She'd developed a habit of dropping in to tell me about her day, and I looked forward to the time we spent just talking. I heard her climb the stairs, not even stopping to pet the dogs.

I followed up to her room. "Hi, honey. Are you all right?"

Her face looked flushed. *"I* don't feel well. My neck is stiff, and I think I'm running a fever again."

Stella had come upstairs after us. "It's this weather. She's been out in it every day."

"And just getting over strep throat," I clucked. "Probably taken a setback."

Stella went to get the aspirin and I filled a hot-water bottle. "You stay in bed. I'll bring your supper on a tray. It's just chili and crackers tonight."

CeeCee made a wry face. "I don't want anything. I'm going to take a nap and maybe eat later."

Stella and I went back downstairs. "If she isn't better in the morning, I'll take her to the medical clinic."

"Either way, she'd better not go to work until she's over this," Stella said. "Are we having anything for supper besides chili?"

"There's ice cream if you want it. Why?"

"Just wanted to know if we were having anything that takes a lot of chewing. I've lost my teeth again."

*　　*　　*

By daybreak, CeeCee was worse. The glands in her neck were swollen and sore. I called Iva and told her to get a substitute to handle Cee's route. It was *sizzling* outside—sleet mixed with drizzle—and I hated driving in it, but Cee needed help. I called the doctor, bundled her up so she'd stay warm, and drove her to the medical clinic.

Stella stayed home with the animals.

The waiting room was full, and we had to sit for what seemed like forever before Cee was ushered in to see the doctor. I passed the time reading magazines six months out-of-date. Finally Cee appeared, looking visibly upset.

"What's wrong?"

"I've got the mumps." She glanced around the waiting room, and then burst into tears. "I feel so foolish! Mumps, at my age. What else can happen to me!"

"Mumps!" Abel Brookes. Abel had given Cee the mumps.

She laughed bitterly. "Grandma insisted that I feel Abel Brookes's forehead. There's no telling how many people he's infected with his germs." She broke into fresh tears, reaching out blindly for a tissue. I pressed one in her hands, keeping my distance. I swallowed, both hands going to my glands. So far they felt normal, but would my luck hold?

We drove home in traumatized silence. I had to concentrate on the icy streets, and judging from the black look on CeeCee's face she was plotting ways to get even with the preacher's kid.

CHAPTER 24

"**F**arkle!"

Pansy, Frances, and Simon threw back their heads Tuesday night and laughed uproariously when Stella failed to score a combination.

"Rats." She handed the dice to Iva Hinkle, who'd joined tonight's game. "Your turn, Iva."

Iva scooped up six dice, rolled them dramatically around in her hands, then flung them on the table. "Nine!"

Stella clapped and then studiously marked a nine on the score sheet.

"Good you could join us tonight, Iva." Simon smiled. "How's your mother?"

"Well these days, Simon, thank you. A friend came over to watch television with her this evening so I get a special night out." She threw the dice again. "Ten!"

It was getting close to nine, and the players were on their last game. Stella stifled a yawn. These late hours were killing her.

"Hargus was in the post office today." Iva addressed her remarks to Pansy.

"He was? Mailing Christmas cards, I suppose."

"No, I don't think they were cards—at least they weren't

shaped like cards. He mailed a big batch—fifty or so."

Stella's ears perked up. They wouldn't be Christmas cards. Hargus didn't have fifty friends. "You sure they weren't cards, Iva?"

"Almost sure, but I could be wrong. Cards come in odd shapes these days."

Leaning closer, Stella moved the dice out of her way. "Could you make out any addresses? Were the cards addressed to Morning Shade folks or folks across country?"

"Why ... I wouldn't swear to anything. I just sold him fifty stamps—and he certainly didn't appear to be doing anything illegal. Once he'd stamped all the envelopes he stepped right up to the box and dropped all fifty letters into the receptacle." Iva suddenly caught her breath, and she met Stella's prolonged gaze. "Why? Are you suggesting that Hargus might be responsible for sending those chain let—"

"My boy!" Coffee cups sloshed when Pansy shot to her feet, firing Stella a scathing look. "Why, how *dare* you suggest such a vile thing? My Hargie wouldn't do one thing against the law. You know how dedicated he is to serving Joe Public! Besides, I've gotten at least *three* of those letters myself. He wouldn't try to fleece his own mother."

Stella hung her head. "Well, I didn't say Hargus—"

"You implied it." Lifting her nose, Pansy promptly abandoned the game. For a moment the occupants at the table sat in stunned silence. Finally Stella ventured, "Anyone know whose turn it is?"

Clearing his throat, Simon said. "I believe it was Pansy's."

"Oh." Stella looked at Frances. "Your turn."

Hargus sent out fifty letters, huh? Stella thought. *Why, that fool. No wonder he had a "red-hot" lead.* Hargus Conley was the copycat bandit or her name wasn't... Boy, her memory wasn't what it used to be.

CHAPTER 25

Early Wednesday morning Stella crawled from a warm bed and wedged her feet into her slippers. The bedside clock read 5:15 A.M. Guilt could play terrible tricks on a body. It can make you lose sleep, be as jumpy as a pea on a drum, and downright ruin your day. Guilt could also make you do things you'd otherwise never consider.

This morning Stella didn't make much effort to walk quietly. Maude would be up in a couple of hours, and CeeCee was so sick with the mumps she wouldn't be stirring for hours. Flipping on the kitchen light, she bent and pulled the heavy black skillet from the cabinet and slammed it on the metal gas burner.

Cast iron made a terrible racket this time of morning.

Reaching in her pocket, she took out her glasses and put them on before she took one of Maude's cookbooks off the shelf. After a moment's perusal, she grunted, took a dozen eggs, butter, cheese, and sausage from the refrigerator and assembled the breakfast items on the counter.

She'd hardly slept a wink last night thinking about what she was going to do. Hargus *could* be the copycat bandit, but she had other leads. Over and over her mind had rehashed the list of chain-letter suspects. Kept her awake most of the night. And she was here to tell anyone—and it was a pitiful few in a town the size of

Morning Shade—but somebody was sending those letters and she seriously doubted it was Pansy's boy—though she wouldn't rule him out yet. She'd already discounted Minerva, Mildred, and Maury Peacock. Hargus was iffy.

Unwrapping the sausage, she dumped the roll into the skillet. When cold meat hits a hot skillet it pops. Frenchie jumped like he'd been shot with a cannon.

Dawn broke through a heavy layer of clouds, shining through the window over the sink. Suddenly Stella stopped what she was doing and put her hands on her hips, forgetting about the egg-dripping whisk in her hand. It was one of those V8 moments! *Why* hadn't she once thought of Lorene Meadows, affectionately known to all at the retirement center as Peaches? The ninety-two-year-old retired postal worker hadn't worked for thirty years, but if there was anyone who'd know the skinny on chain letters it'd be Peaches. And she'd know the profit too.

Stella rapidly broke up the sizzling meat with a fork, her mind shifting into overdrive. Smoke rolled from the skillet, and she knew she'd hit upon a solid lead. This casserole would serve good purpose, by doggy. She'd just take it over to the retirement center and ply Lorene with a little resourceful sausage and eggs.

A high squeal suddenly keened through the kitchen.

Fiddle. The smoke alarm. Stupid, new, fandangle inventions! She tried to fan smoke away with the hem of her housecoat. Then she gave up and took the broom out of the pantry, dragged a kitchen chair to the wall and climbed atop, trying to bat the wailing siren into silence. Meat popped in the skillet, spewing grease onto the stove and linoleum. The alarm made enough noise to wake the dead!

Suddenly the kitchen door burst open. Stella grabbed for support, clinging white-knuckled to the chair.

Maude and CeeCee stood in the doorway. Maude's bed head was a fright. She ought to warn a body before she burst through a doorway looking like that, and poor CeeCee looked like a petrified chipmunk.

"Where's the fire?" Maude shouted.

Stella straightened, her eyes skimming the room. "Fire! What fire? Get me off this chair!"

CeeCee reached out and Stella latched onto her hand. Climbing down, she pitched the broom aside and fell into step with the exited household.

"Animals!" CeeCee shouted. "Someone get the dogs—I'll get Captain—"

"I'll get the birds!" Maude yelled. In a split second the animals were rounded up, and all three women simultaneously tried to push through the open back door. Legs and arms tangled.

"Oh, for heaven's sake!" Maude finally pushed Stella clear, then CeeCee. She fell in behind. The women cleared the back porch, dogs barking, parrots squawking, Captain clawing to break CeeCee's hold.

Lights popped on at Victor Johnson's house. Then in Maury Peacock's bathroom.

Huddled against a biting wind, Stella wrapped her housecoat tighter. Daylight lit the frantic scene. The women stared at the house.

"I don't see flames," Maude said between chattering teeth. "I'll run to the Johnsons' and have him call the fire department. There might be time to save the house!"

Maude bolted toward the drive, clearing the hedge between the two houses in one long sprint.

"Oh my," CeeCee moaned. "What *else* can possibly go wrong? I've got to go in there! Mom's computer—her backup disks with Jack's book—"

Stella restrained her granddaughter. "You can't go in there! Let Herbert Owsley take care of that!"

"But the house could be gone by the time *he* gets here!"

Stella restrained CeeCee, staring at the house, which still showed no evidence of flames. Nothing leaping from the roof, no smoke pouring from shattered glass. "Wonder where it started? I've been worried about that old wiring. Always told Herb that this house wiring was a disgrace and needed to be fixed." Stella sniffed the air. "Don't smell smoke."

CeeCee sniffed the air. "I smell frying sausage."

"Oh no! That's my sausage," Stella said. "I'm making a breakfast casserole."

CeeCee slowly turned to look at her. "At *this* hour?"

"Yeah. I couldn't sleep so I was frying the sausage to make a casserole—only I decided to take it to Lorene at the residential center instead—when that stupid smoke alarm went off."

"The smoke alarm?"

"Yeah—that squealing thing. Wake the dead. Anyway, I got the broom out of the pantry and was standing on the chair trying to get the alarm off when the fire broke out."

"The fire in the kitchen?" CeeCee prodded.

Stella shook her head. "There wasn't *a fire* in the kitchen. I thought somebody said the fire was upstairs."

"Upstairs—I never heard anyone say the fire was upstairs. The alarm woke me from a sound sleep; I threw on a robe, knocked on your and Mom's doors—" She stopped. "You were frying sausage and set the alarm off?"

Stella thought about that for a moment. This could be trouble. "Well, I was frying sausage and, yes, the alarm went off—" She broke into a lame grin. "Good news, honey! There's no fire."

A siren wail filled the early dawn. Front doors opened, sleepy-looking residents peered out into the street.

Maude sprinted back across the lawn, clearing the hedge again, her features flushed from the excursion. "Fire truck's on its way," she panted.

"Never mind, Mom." CeeCee turned on her heel and stomped off toward the back porch.

"Cee! Don't go in there," Maude yelled. "The whole thing could come falling in on your head."

"It's all right, Mother. There's no fire," CeeCee called over her shoulder. "Grandma was frying *sausage* and set off the smoke alarm."

Maude's jaw dropped. "At *this* hour?"

Stella gaped back at her. "I was making a breakfast casserole— smoke alarm went off—"

"Oh, Stella!" Spinning on her heel, Maude marched back into the house. "I'm up this early because you're cooking sausage at this ungodly hour ...?"

She whirled, and Stella had never seen Maude so perturbed— downright ugly acting.

Maude yelled, *"Next time* you want to cook at the crack of dawn, tell somebody!"

* * *

The fire truck pulled away from the curb. Stella waved goodbye to Herbert Owsley. At least *he'd* appreciated the dish of sausage and eggs she'd insisted that he take back home with him. That's the thing about eighty-five-year-old men; they appreciated a home-cooked meal.

A little after eight, Stella put on her coat and boots and carried the insulated covered dish out the front door. Nobody around here was in a mood for something special—that was for certain. She cast a dirty look up the porch stairs. She'd thought about asking Maude to drive her to the residential care center— all the excitement had taken the wind out of her sails—but Maude wasn't in the best of moods this morning. She'd been downright surly over her glass of orange juice, and Stella wasn't allowed to talk about the "fire."

"Just in the way," she told herself as she made the three-block walk to Shady Acres. Not one brave soul sat on the wide veranda this morning. Early risers would be inside beside the fireplace, having their first cup of coffee.

Stella sailed through the front door, sending friendly greetings to the two night nurses. The women were changing shifts, studying charts, writing.

"Morning, Kay. Versaille."

The younger woman glanced up. "Morning, Stella. You're up and about early today."

"Brought Peaches a breakfast casserole." Weren't any use to let a perfectly good casserole—or lead—go to waste.

"Well, Lorene will enjoy that." Versaille stepped over to lift the lid on the steaming casserole and sniff. She closed her eyes. "Mmmm. Sausage."

Stella nodded. "And cheese, onions, and a touch of cinnamon."

Versaille's face clouded. "Cinnamon?"

Stella bent forward and winked. "Secret ingredient."

The woman nodded with a half smile. "You and Peaches have a nice visit."

"There's plenty here if you'd like a dish." Stella grinned.

"I just sent some to the firehouse with Herbert Owsley." Weren't any use to go into that, either.

Versaille reached for her coat hanging on a hall peg. "Can't. I have to go home, feed my husband and four kids, pack five lunches, get the husband off to work, the kiddies out the front door and on the school bus; then I'm going to bed." Versaille was still rattling on when Stella turned down the east corridor, carrying the breakfast casserole to Peaches' room.

A spry-looking woman dressed in a blue cotton robe and white pearls opened the door, peering out at her early morning visitor.

"Peaches! Hi." Stella extended the casserole. "Look what I brought you."

The elderly woman peered at the covered dish, and then lifted her eyes, a smile breaking across her heavily rouged cheeks. "Madeline? You come to see your old mother?"

"No, Peaches. I'm not your daughter—I'm Stella Diamond. Remember?" Peaches had dementia. Some days were good; others were a little foggy. Stella decided she'd hit on one of the foggy days.

Peaches cocked her head slyly. "Madeline?"

"No. Stella." Stella entered the apartment and set the dish on the small eating table. Rooms at Shady Acres were small: kitchen, living room, one bedroom. Photographs of Peaches' smiling family stared back from every nook and cranny. Stella went back and closed the door, then led Peaches to the table.

The woman kept smiling, saying, "Madeline? I didn't know you were coming. You should have called." She fussed with her thinning snow-white bob.

Stella made a pot of coffee from the two-cup Mr. Coffee sitting on the kitchen counter, then dished out casserole, made toast, and tied a bib around Peaches' neck. All the while, Peaches chattered like a magpie.

"Madeline, *how* is your sister? I haven't seen her for the longest time."

Stella buttered toast. "Peaches, you used to work at the post office, didn't you?"

Peaches nodded, suddenly clear. "Fifty-three years."

Good, Stella thought. The fog was lifting.

"Enjoyed your job, huh?"

She nodded. "I loved my job—miss it sorely." She expelled a deep breath. "Getting old is no fun."

"Tell me." Stella poured coffee and then took the chair opposite Peaches. "Do the words *Pigeon* or *Blackbird* ring a bell with you?"

She nodded. "They're birds."

"No—other than birds. Chain letters, maybe?"

The old woman looked up and grinned. "People aren't supposed to send them."

Stella nodded; she was on to something. Peaches might have occasional memory lapses, but Stella bet that Peaches could recall days gone by with a little help, and she'd bet she could still write as clearly as the next person. And what older person couldn't use a little extra cookie-jar money?

"Then you know that sending chain letters is certainly frowned on by the post office?"

Taking a bite of casserole, Peaches chewed thoughtfully. "Why, yes—I suppose I do know that."

"That's good." Stella took a sip of coffee; detective work could wear a body thin. "Have you sent any chain letters recently, Peaches?"

Peaches looked up from her plate. "What a thing to say, Madeline! Accuse your own mother of bank robbery? Why, what's gotten into you?"

Stella went blank. Bank robbery? Who'd said anything about bank robbery?

"No, Peaches." Stella bent closer and patted a blue-veined hand. "I didn't say bank robbery. I asked if you'd happened— oh, say on a whim—to mail out chain letters? Perfectly understandable if you did—no harm's done—just wanted to warn you that you shouldn't be doing that. Twenty-five dollars is a lot to ask, and if the government catches you—"

"You need money?"

"No—I don't need money."

Peaches got up and shuffled to her black purse, fishing around in one of several pockets. She took out three pennies and a nickel. "Here, go buy something pretty."

"No." Stella put the coins back in the purse and zipped the pocket. "I don't need money, Peaches."

Peaches shook her head, confused. Then she turned whiny. "I could never please you, Madeline. Why can't you be more like your sister Belle?" Peaches shuffled back across the room and sat down on the sofa. She sat for a moment, petulance forming on her face.

Deciding that she'd hit a dead end, Stella cleared the table and washed the two plates, two cups, and silverware and set them in the drainer.

She wiped her hands on the dish towel and draped it around the refrigerator handle to dry. "I've got to be going, Peaches. I'll put the rest of the casserole in the refrigerator and you can eat it later."

"Madeline."

Stella turned. "Yes?"

"Go to your room."

Stella gaped at her.

"*I mean* it." Peaches' jaw firmed. She dramatically flung her right arm, pointing to the bedroom. "Go to your room or I'll take a flyswatter after you!"

"Lorene—"

"Now!" Peaches sprang off the sofa—amazing for a woman of her years—and snatched up the swatter hooked to the refrigerator with an angel magnet. Shaking the rubber swatter in Stella's face, she repeated. "Go to your room, Madeline, until you can learn respect for your elders!"

When Stella hesitantly turned to obey, she suffered the smart smack of the swatter across her backside. She jumped. "Hey!"

"Don't you sass me, young woman!" She swatted Stella.

Stella marched into the bedroom and slammed the door. When the door shut, she heard Peaches yell, "Just for that, missy, you're staying in there for another hour!"

Dropping to the side of the mattress, Stella sat there. This was the *last* time she'd bake Peaches anything!

CHAPTER 26

Saturday CeeCee was in misery. "Just stay in bed," I advised. Sleet pelted the front window and I thought, *Well, no wonder she isn't improving.* Kids these days think they're invincible. Why, the way she was in and out of bed would make anyone sick and mumps at her age was serious.

Climbing the stairs, Cee called over her shoulder. "Don't fix me any lunch, Mom. I just want to sleep."

Sighing, I went into my office and thought about my original plan. I probably could be working at The Antiques Shop by now. Luella and Duella, though eccentric at times, were thought to have enough money to burn a wet mule. Even if business was off, they could afford to pay someone for a paltry twenty hours a week.

Their father, Albert Denson, had been president of Guaranty Trust—a wealthy man in his own right. The Antiques Shop was simply a vessel through which Duella could indulge her passion of years gone by.

Around noon I opened a can of chicken noodle soup and dumped it into a pan. While I waited for the soup to heat, I laid two Bayer aspirins on a tray and filled a hot-water bottle. Someone had given me a pillow like thing for Christmas that when microwaved on high for two minutes retained its heat. I'd tried the gift once but gone immediately back to my hot-water bottle. Some things in life could not be improved upon. And Cee might appreciate it.

"I'm sorry to be so much trouble, Mom," Cee murmured when I entered her darkened room a few minutes later. It was all I could do to keep from hugging her. I knew she felt like a burden, but what was a mother for if not to comfort her child? She peered up at me, sheet pulled close to her nose, gazing back as if I could do something more than chicken soup and aspirin.

"Want some potato chips?" I asked. I set the tray on the side of the bed before tucking the blanket around her feet more securely. The inane offer sounded silly even to me, but at this point I just wanted to make my daughter feel better. When Cee hurts I hurt; I suppose mothers all over the world know the feeling.

"I don't think so." CeeCee closed her eyes, swallowing against the pain.

"I brought some nice hot soup. Don't you feel like eating a bite?"

She shook her head. "Maybe later."

"I'll leave the tray—you might feel better shortly."

I left her in bed, doubled over on her side, trying to get warm under the sheet, two heavy blankets, and the spread. I asked myself what kind of mother would allow her ailing daughter to get out of bed to attend church services when she'd been so sick the week before. Then expose her to mumps. I should have insisted that Cee remain in bed that Wednesday for at least another day. Bad weather and Cee's weakened immune system invited a setback, and sure enough, sickness had sailed right in.

Sighing, I went to the kitchen and called Duella. Why, I don't know. I suppose just to see if I could have gotten a job if I'd wanted one. I couldn't leave my daughter now; money or no money, life would go on.

But Lord/I could sure use a Christmas miracle. Seems like everything is piling up on me. I remembered the song we had sung last Sunday morning: "Count Your Blessings." I always enjoyed singing that song, even though in my daily life I sometimes felt like the problems far outweighed the blessings. But even when I was bent beneath the load, I knew better. God had blessed me in so many ways. I thought of people who were homeless, people who had greater problems than I had ever had and knew for sure I was loved and *blessed*. .. but I was still hoping for that miracle.

After my conversation with Duella, I looked toward the sky and said, "Well, that was a dead end." Good thing I wasn't counting on the Denson sisters to pull me through. Supposedly they were broke too.

Oh, well, I'd do the best I could and keep on trusting in the Lord.

By Monday, sleet and rain had brought traffic to a halt. I stood at the kitchen window drinking a cup of coffee, watching it slizzle, trying to fight off a good case of the blues.

Stella wandered into the kitchen, her features pinched. I wondered if she was coming down with something. "CeeCee any better today?" My mother-in-law shuffled to the cabinet for a coffee cup, her slippers wisping against the cold linoleum.

"She was running a temp when I checked her around five this morning."

Around nine I returned to Cee's bedroom and discovered that her temperature now hovered dangerously close to a hundred and two degrees. Shaking my head, I covered my daughter and advised that she go back to sleep.

"You'll have to call Iva," Cee murmured. "I don't think I'll be back to work ever. I'm dying, Mom.''

"You're going to get through this, sweetie. Do you want another Popsicle?" The cold treat was the only thing she'd tolerated in the past twenty-four hours.

By midmorning, CeeCee's temperature rose to one hundred and two and a half. Stella and I bathed her flushed body and gave her three Bayer every four hours, but by late afternoon I panicked and called Dr. Winters.

Angels are among us, and Sherman Winters is mine without question. The good doctor could not walk on water, but he could walk on ice, carrying his small leather medical bag from the medical clinic to our house because the streets were by now impassible. When I let him into our foyer and saw a thick layer of ice coating his burnished gold lashes, I wanted to cry. And I knew then—knew without a doubt—why I live in this little podunk town where people gossip and delve into each other's lives. I live in Morning Shade because there is no other town on earth where a man like Sherman Winters would walk three miles in sleet and ice to help his fellowman.

"I can never repay you for this," I managed, suddenly overcome by emotion.

Grinning, Sherm slipped out of his topcoat and I hung it on the hall peg. "Oh, you will when you get my bill."

I knew that even that statement was misleading. Sherm treated half the town without compensation, said he was a doctor and when folks were sick they needed help.

Stella and I waited outside Cee's bedroom, holding hands and praying while the doctor examined Cee. He was with my daughter for a worrisome long time. When he finally turned toward the doorway, I braced myself. Were mumps ever fatal? I'm afraid I knew the answer.

Giving me a warm smile, Sherm said quietly. "She's a sick woman, Maude, but she'll be fine. Plenty of bed rest—and Popsicles. Mumps will have to run its course."

I caught my breath, faint with relief. "Any particular kind of Popsicle?" There were numerous flavors; I had banana on hand because I happened to like banana myself, but maybe another flavor would be better."

"Banana," Sherm answered.

"Pardon?"

"Banana Popsicles."

"Oh—they're the best?"

"No but they're my personal favorite."

"Oh." I grinned, getting it.

The doctor's face sobered. "Have both of you ladies had the mumps?"

"I've had them," Stella said.

"I haven't."

Sherm shook his head. "Not much we can do now, Maude. You'll have to pray that you've developed a natural immunity to the disease." He gave me an encouraging smile. "Keep CeeCee quiet, plenty of liquids, and watch her temperature. I'll stop by again in the morning."

I walked downstairs with the sixtyish, silver-haired doctor and helped him back into his wool overcoat. "I'm so sorry to disturb you on such a nasty day."

He chuckled. "Wish all my patients were as thoughtful as you." He patted my shoulder, his clear blue eyes brimming with compassion. "Are you taking care of yourself, Maude? You've had a lot on your plate lately."

Tears sprang to my eyes, and I quickly swiped them away with the back of my hand. Someone says something nice to me and I break into tears; I don't understand my moods.

"Thanks. I'm making it." Not profound but truthful, and I knew Sherm understood.

"Well, a fine woman like you should do more than just make it." His gaze held mine, and I knew he was no stranger to loneliness or to times of utter, incapacitating despair. His wife had died two years earlier of a sudden massive heart attack. A vital fifty-eight-year-old woman, the epitome of good health, gone in a matter of moments.

What was the old adage? Eat dessert first.

Sherm understood *lonely*.

When I closed the door, I leaned back against the solid wood and struggled to regain my composure. For the first time since Herb's death I let myself feel—truly feel, void of medication to keep the hurt at bay. The prescription pills lay in my bedside table untouched lately. For months after Herb's death I'd lived on a medicinal crutch, but one day—and even I don't know the day—I'd gradually forgotten to take the pills.

I both resented and welcomed the return to normalcy. Now I had just one more thing to deal with: my own vulnerability.

I was changing bed linens later, thinking about June Cleaver. When Cee was little she liked to watch reruns of *Leave It to Beaver*, a late-fifties sitcom I had watched when I was a child. June Cleaver. Dressed in pearls, hose and heels, vacuuming, fixing dinner, smiling—always smiling—when the "Beav" or Wally did something naughty. There was never any screaming. Husband Ward Cleaver never yelled—only calm, collected meetings of the minds and crisis solved.

I yanked a pillowcase loose from my pillow, laughing as I pictured June with a houseful of poodles, a cat, and two macaws. I bet her pearls would be sagging by day's end.

The phone rang. I waded through soiled linen and fell across the mattress to retrieve the receiver. When I heard my agent's voice, I breathed a sigh of relief. Mentally crossing my fingers, I prayed that her call was meant to assure me "the check was in the mail."

"Your editor called this morning, and Hugh Norton—"

"Vice president of Bethlehem House," I acknowledged— aka the man who signed the checks.

"Yes, Hugh's traveling this week, but he'll be back in the office the first part of next week. Your contract is on the top of the pile."

Top of the pile. The thought didn't comfort me. If Hugh stumped his toe getting off the plane and couldn't work for another week, that meant the check wouldn't be here until spring. I sighed.

"I know," Jean consoled. "Authors tell me they'd love to set up the house employees on the same payment schedule—come to work every day but never have a clue when you get paid. But actually, Maude, the contract isn't the primary purpose of my call."

"Oh?" I rolled to my back and stared at the ceiling. A leak. An ugly brown stain seeped through the textured drywall. Great. More unexpected expense.

"I had a call from a Birkhead editor this morning."

Birkhead. A large publishing house based in New York. The majority of Birkhead books were marketed in the secular market: Barnes & Noble, Waldenbooks, Borders, Wal-Mart. An impressive house, with an even more impressive marketing department.

"And ... ?" I said, certain Jean wouldn't be relaying this sort. of news unless the call had something to do with me.

"And they have put out some interesting feelers concerning M. K. Diamond mysteries."

"Really?" I sat up now, my interest caught. The secular ABA market was huge compared to the Christian CBA market. Not only could the ABA get more books to the public, but because they printed both mass paperbacks and trade size, an author had a better chance to get titles into a major chain. The Christian market printed few mass paperbacks; Christian bookstores focused on the larger trade-size novels or hardbacks. Store shelf space would not accommodate mass paperbacks.

"Maude, I don't want to confuse you or to plant unrest, but as your representative it is my duty to help you evaluate your career and where it's going."

I held my breath, afraid to ask. "Is Birkhead interested in acquiring my work?"

"The call was simply a feeler at this stage. As you know, publishers try not to encroach on other publishers. But Birkhead seemed interested in knowing whether you were satisfied with your present marketing, and if you felt your career is growing. In other words, do you still have complete trust that your books are being marketed with full-house support."

"You know I have mixed feelings about both subjects."

"I know. That's why I felt we should talk."

The subject wasn't a new one; Jean and I had discussed my feelings many times over the years. My present house was tops; I knew writers who would pay in order to publish with Bethlehem Publishers. Regarding author relations there wasn't a better house. They treated me like a princess in most matters. Invited me to attend the yearly CBA conference, paid my expenses, never failed to express in words Maude Diamond's house value. What more could an author ask?

Little, I kept telling myself, yet each time I watched my publisher bring in new authors and do more for them than it seemed they were doing for me, something inside me died. Usually creativity suffered the worst. *Petty,* I told myself. *You have it good so why make a big deal over the fact that after five years with this publisher your print runs have barely increased, and the publisher continues to market your titles as part of a line instead of as stand-alone books?* Occasionally I have stepped out and written a single-title book, which should in all fairness be marketed with the same house enthusiasm as the "fresh, new young voice" or authors with equal sales.

But no one has ever confused marketing and fairness.

Did I want to allow Birkhead to court me? This morning, lying on my bare mattress pad, wondering if I should call the electric company and arrange to pay the bill in two payments this month, I wondered . .. yet I knew the grass was never truly greener on the other side.

Jean's voice jolted me back to the present. "Are you still there?"

"I'm here. Just thinking."

"I know it's hard to sort through the good and bad. We talked and agreed before; you have it good where you are, Maude. But I know you would like to see your books more aggressively marketed."

"Honestly, I don't know what to tell you, Jean."

"Why don't you give the idea some thought? You don't have to decide anything immediately, and you have several outstanding contracts with Bethlehem to complete anyway. This summer perhaps you can meet with Birkhead representatives—if you are still having reservations about your present situation—and hear what they have to offer."

The thought was dangerously tempting to this battle-scarred soldier of the writing world. My armor was tarnished.   .

"I believe what you're saying is this: Your sales should make you a valued author to your house, and accordingly, you want your books marketed to reflect that value."

"That's what I'm trying to say, Jean, and doing a poor job of expressing myself. I am not ungrateful; I know how fortunate I am to be able to publish—so many don't have the privilege, but to be my best, I need to know that I'm appreciated and valued, as much as any employee is valued by big business."

If I dared to make the leap, change publishers, do I expect revisions to disappear, checks and contracts to arrive in an orderly fashion, or to stumble over massive displays of M. K. Diamond titles in every bookstore? No. Writing and publishing go hand and hand, and author and editor strive to produce the best product available. I understood this. And I understood that writers often write for various houses, but I liked the feeling of family—of belonging to one house. But I also understood and struggled with this emotional roller coaster every day of my life, this nagging resentment that my financial woes wouldn't be so acute if my books had more exposure.

"Okay, I'll think about it."

"I know you worry about the lists, Maude, but I'll tell you again, your books *cannot* reach those lists unless they are positioned to get there. You understand that."

"Of course I understand that. I know a book doesn't 'just make it.' But that's my dilemma: my publisher refuses to position my books."

"Then perhaps you should think seriously about what Birkhead has to offer."

CHAPTER 27

That evening the whole world looked like it was made of crystal. Beautiful but deadly. The television news anchor told of automobile accidents. The streets and sidewalks were glazed over. You could hear the crack of breaking tree limbs and a crashing noise followed by the tinkling of shattered ice, like breaking glass. It would take weeks to clean up the mess if the ice ever melted.

Stella hadn't been able to make her daily Citgo run and you could tell it. She was as cross as a one-eyed bear.

I was beside myself worrying about Cee's extra medical bill on top of everything else. Of course I couldn't say anything because it would hurt Cee's feelings and set Stella to fretting about being a nuisance. I felt like barricading myself in my bedroom and refusing to come out until spring, but that wouldn't work because the entire household—including the dogs, the birds, and the cat—would join me.

I sighed, remembering how quiet my home used to be, and then I remembered it also used to be lonely. Well, I wasn't lonely now, but a few moments alone would be nice.

Stella appeared in the doorway. "We have any Ritz crackers?"

"*I* don't think so. Why do you want them?"

"I just saw a neat snack on the cooking channel. You use Ritz crackers with peanut-butter filling, like a sandwich, and dip them in chocolate. Thought I'd make a batch."

And make a mess in my kitchen. I'd already cleaned the birdcage, the litter box, and a puddle left by the poodle. I didn't need more work. Seemed like everything and everyone in this house was proficient at making messes they never bothered to clean up.

"Sorry, no Ritz crackers, and the roads are too slick to go to the store. How about some microwave popcorn?"

"Popcorn gets in my teeth."

That didn't make sense. Her teeth were the kind you took out and washed. You didn't get stuff in them. Under them, maybe. Since Stella wasn't wearing her teeth, I had a feeling she's misplaced them again.

She pushed her lips in and out, looking deep in thought. "You know, I've been thinking about that chain-letter writer. For a while I suspected Maury Peacock."

"That nice man? How could you?"

"Well, I had to suspect someone. And I figured he couldn't be as crazy as he acts, but then I decided he really was. I mean, you couldn't fake some of the stuff he pulls. Pansy called and said he went to the Cart Mart looking for a chain saw. They had a time convincing him he was in a grocery store. Although you'd think he could tell that by looking around him."

"Why on earth did he want a chain saw?"

"Who knows? Scary, isn't it, thinking of Maury turned loose with a chain saw? He probably has limbs down in his yard. Everyone else does."

She was right about that. Thankfully we didn't have many big trees, but the large oak out back had lost several branches. Enough to make a mess we'd have trouble cleaning up. Maybe I could hire someone to cut them and haul them away—but that took money and I'd given up my dream of working in The Antiques Shop. Christmas was only ten days away.

Stella was still yakking about Maury. "*I* worked on that lead for a couple of days, but it fizzled out. That medication makes Maury so goofy he can barely remember his name, let alone write and mail two hundred without getting caught."

"How do you know how many letters were mailed out?"

She blushed. "I…don't know the exact amount, of course. I'm only guessing."

I stared at her, all my suspicions aroused. Would Stella…? *Surely not.* She knew how badly I needed money, but would she go so far as to write those letters? She didn't look away, but she didn't say anything either. My mind was whirling. If she had written the letters, would she be trying to help Hargus find the criminal? Was guilt the reason behind her strange moods?

"Stella, look at me. Did you write that last letter I received in the mail? Are you Blackbird?"

Perhaps it was my imagination, but I fancied she looked relieved. She answered quickly enough. " I am not Blackbird, and I did not write that letter. I can't believe you would suspect me."

Well I couldn't believe it myself. "I'm sorry. It was just a thought and not a very good one, apparently. That's the trouble with something like this; it makes you suspect everyone."

The doorbell rang, cutting short our conversation. I went to answer, wondering who would be out in this weather. Maury Peacock waited on the doorstep, holding a five-gallon can of gasoline. I stared at him, wondering what on earth he was doing out on a day like this, toting a can of gas.

"Evening, Miz Diamond. Heard CeeCee's sick."

"Yes she is, Maury. Has the mumps." If I'd told him once I'd told him fifteen times that Cee had the mumps. I opened the door wider. "Come on in."

I hoped he'd leave the can outside, but no such luck. He carried it in with him, stinking up the living room. Stella hovered in the doorway of the kitchen, eyes slitted and wearing the same expression Captain got sometimes when he was thinking of doing something he shouldn't. Usually involving one of the poodles or the macaws.

Maury held out the can. "Brought Stella a present. Overheard her talking at the Citgo, and she said she hadn't had any gas the last few days."

I glared at Stella, trying to head off any of her remarks, and for once it worked.

"Well, thank you, Maury. I can always use gas."

Poor man.

Maury smiled politely, and I thanked him for the gift and carried it to the garage. When I got back into the house he had settled down in my favorite rocker, gently swaying to and fro. I sat on the love seat across from him, while he rocked contentedly, staring into space as if he had forgotten we were there.

"How much longer do you have to take this medicine, Maury?" I asked.

He smiled hazily at me. "I don't know for sure, but I'm really going to miss it when I have to quit. Makes me feel so good."

"Makes you act downright weird," Stella said. "You sure you're still supposed to be taking both those pills together?"

"Oh, I'm sure, right enough," Maury said. "Go back to see Doc Winters next week. Guess he'll tell me what's what then."

"It's been a long time since you've known what's what," Stella said, and I shot her a look. She wasn't helping the situation.

"How long has CeeCee been sick?" Maury asked.

"Well, like I told you—*fifteen times*—she's had the mumps almost a week, but she had a bad round with the strep throat preceding that so she's been feeling rather run-down."

"I was almost run down yesterday," Maury said. "Crossed the street in front of Hargus's office, and here comes this car barreling out of nowhere. Like to got me. You should have heard the way that driver talked. I'll bet you he never learned those words at his mother's knee."

"You look both ways before crossing that street?" Stella demanded. "You're supposed to, you know."

Maury smiled. "I looked. Didn't see a thing. Like a rocket out of hades. Real strange."

"It's a wonder you've made it all these years," Stella muttered.

Maury got to his feet. "Well, I got to go. Just wanted to check on CeeCee, and bring Stella some gas."

I stood on the doorstep watching as he went slipping and sliding across the yard to his own front door. He had no business out on ice at his age, but it wouldn't do any good to remind him. I'd be glad when he went back to see Sherm. Surely he was well enough to give up his medicine by now.

When I shut the door and went back to the living room, Stella was waiting. "You know last Sunday night when we had refreshments after church?"

"Yes?" I wondered what she was getting at.

"I happened to be passing the third-grade children's Sunday school classroom, and there was Maury, big as life. Guess what he was doing?"

"I haven't a clue."

"He was pinning Easter cards on the bulletin board. Now what do you think of that?"

I considered. "Well, he was either rather early or awfully late with celebrating the holiday."

Stella snorted. "You know what, Maude? You're as weird as Maury."

"I resent that."

She grinned. "Wonder where he got Easter cards this time of the year. They don't go on sale until sometime in February."

"Poor Maury. I wonder if it's safe for him to live alone."

Stella sobered. "I've thought of that. No telling what he cooks for himself. Guess it will be good all around when he goes off that medicine."

CHAPTER 28

Stella climbed the stairs to her room feeling like she'd had a narrow escape. She hadn't lied to Maude; in fact, she had told nothing but the actual truth. She hadn't written the most recent letter. She wrote the first one, and Maude didn't get one of those. She had been trying to get money to give Maude, not get money out of Maude.

She took the letters out of the box where she kept them, every one she had received. Hadn't thrown away a one of them. Not like Maude. She'd just tossed them out like so much junk, but Stella read them over one by one. She'd only asked for five dollars. The new letter writer had started out asking for ten, and then soon upped the amount to fifteen, then twenty-five. Greedy. That's what he was. If you were going to do something wrong, you ought to at least think up your own crime, not latch on to someone else's scheme. Common sense would tell you there wasn't enough money in Morning Shade to support two chain-letter bandits.

Stella took a sort of perverse pleasure in thinking that for a short time in her life she had been a criminal. Sort of added a touch of spice to an otherwise blameless life. How many good churchgoing women her age could say that? Of course, she wouldn't want Hilda to know about her double life. She'd be jealous and want to get one of her own.

Maude, now, she would say what she thought, then let it go. Maude never kicked people when they were down. But if Hilda even suspected you had done something out of line, she would kick you until you went down and then really let you have it. Figuratively speaking, of course. Sometimes she had trouble believing Hilda Throckmorton was a Christian—but then there might be times when Hilda was thinking the same thing about her.

Probably a good thing God did the judging instead of leaving it up to her and Throckmorton. She stashed the letters away and went downstairs to turn on the television. It was about time for the gardening show. She didn't garden anymore, but she liked to watch the show even if it didn't have much in common with reality. Those gardens on TV had no weeds, no bugs, and no problem, just beautiful flowers and wonderful produce.

A fairy tale all the way around.

CHAPTER 29

I was happy CeeCee had improved enough to come down for supper the following night. She had languished in her room until I wondered if she planned to hibernate there. I suppose she missed her babies and Captain, and they must have missed her, if their greeting was any indication. The poodles jumped up, putting their paws in her lap so she could pet them. Captain walked around with his back arched, tail erect, purring. He never acted that glad to see me. Even the birds were happy to see her.

She sat at the kitchen table and ate the chicken and noodles I had fixed especially for her, figuring they would be easy to eat, and banana pudding for dessert. It was good to see her eating again. I'd been worried, although I'd been careful not to let her see how I felt.

Stella spooned up the last of her chicken broth. "I believe I'll have a second helping of noodles. You ought to fix them more often, Maude. I can eat them without my teeth."

CeeCee looked up, her interest caught. "Have you lost your teeth again, Grandma?"

"Seems like it," Stella admitted. "I can't remember where I left them last. They're not on the coffee table, anyway. I looked."

I passed her the bowl of chicken and noodles. "Why don't you keep them in your mouth?"

"Because they hurt. Don't fit like they used to."

Well, that shut me up. Why hadn't I thought of that? She probably needed new teeth. And I didn't suppose Medicare would pay for that. Nor her supplemental coverage either, if I remembered right. So it would be up to me. I sighed. Something else to think about, but Stella couldn't be expected to wear ill-fitting teeth. Nor to live on a diet of chicken and noodles, although they were good, even if I did say so. I helped myself to a second plateful while Cee ate her pudding, avoiding the vanilla wafers.

Being without money was the pits. There was so much I could do if I had the financial stability. I could help Cee for starters.

After supper we moved to the living room, and CeeCee stretched out on the sofa. I brought her a pillow for her head, and Stella even asked what she'd like to watch on TV. At our house Stella was in charge of the remote. I don't remember anyone putting her in charge, but like Captain, she probably figured possession was nine-tenths of the law. She used it ruthlessly too. Just get interested in the late show and you're zapped to a documentary on the life of a rare plant of which there is only one on this entire planet and it's located in the parking lot at the local Wal-Mart.

The lights on the Christmas tree winked on and off, and the blaze in the fireplace warmed me to the bone. I stretched in contentment. There's no place like home on a winter night.

CeeCee half dozed. Frenchie and Claire lay beside the sofa while Captain perched on the back of the couch. My daughter still looked like a woodchuck, but I could see improvement. I kicked off my shoes and leaned back in my chair, preparing to take a nap myself.

The doorbell rang, startling me awake. I got up to answer, wondering who could be calling at eight-thirty at night. Surely Maury Peacock wasn't bringing more gifts.

CeeCee held up an admonishing hand. "I don't want to see anyone as long as I look like warmed-over death."

I nodded and padded out to where someone was playing a tune on the doorbell. Whoever our caller was, he or she apparently was in a hurry to get inside. I opened the door to find Gary Hendricks holding a huge vase filled with about a bushel full of yellow roses.

He flashed a toothy grin. "Hello, Mrs. Diamond. CeeCee in?"

"No ... yes ... I mean... " Cee would have a fit if I let him inside. I moved to step in front of him, but he barged past me, using the vase of roses as a battering ram. I staggered out of the way as he surged toward the living room. Feeling someone had better be there to referee, I trotted after him.

Cee's eyes were wide as saucers, which Gary apparently took to be delight at seeing him. "What are you doing here?" she demanded.

He looked afronted. "I was worried about you. Why didn't you tell me you were sick?"

"I didn't see any reason to tell everyone in town. How did you find out?"

He placed the vase of roses on the coffee table, shoved her feet off the sofa, and sat down beside her. She looked ready to explode. I gave her the "mother's look," the same one I used to flash when she was younger and refused to share the cake at her birthday party. She caught it too, because she swallowed and closed her mouth. I figured I'd bought a little time. Very little.

"Hilda Throckmorton told me. She knew I'd want to know." ·

"Why would she assume that?" You'd think even Gary Hendricks would feel the ice in Cee's voice. Enough to fill every freezer in Morning Shade. But evidently Gary was impervious to anything as subtle as atmosphere.

Stella caught it, though. She surveyed Gary through narrowed eyes. "You ever had the mumps?"

He looked startled. "Why no. I don't believe I have."

"Nothing you'd enjoy at your age." She clicked the remote, assigning the west coast news anchor to the recycling bin in exchange for a few minutes with a foreign correspondent. Watching the news with Stella was an endurance test. You could start off in

California and without any warning suddenly find yourself in New Zealand.

Gary blinked. "CeeCee's no longer contagious. As lovely as she looks, I'd say she's about over them."

CeeCee reached out and took a feeble swat at him.

"Think again," Stella grumbled. "Maude tried to tell you she was too sick to see anyone. You wouldn't listen."

Gary smirked. "As if I'd let anything stand between me and my Christian duty."

I decided I'd better take part in this conversation before Cee did him bodily harm. "Would you like a cup of coffee, Gary?"

"That would be nice, Mrs. Diamond, if I can have it right here sitting beside CeeCee." He reached over and took her hand. Before I went to the kitchen I glared at her to keep her from slapping him. "Did you notice what I brought you?"

Cee peered at the bouquet. "Yellow roses. How nice. Are you sure they're roses, or is it possible you have another little trick up your sleeve?"

"I wanted to get candy. You know what they say, sweets for the sweet, but I wasn't sure you could eat candy, so I bought all the yellow roses Flora had in her shop."

Cee's head jerked up. "Did you tell her who they were for?"

"I certainly did. Nothing's too good for my postwoman."

Cee's eyes flamed, and I had a feeling he was going to learn just how high this girl could fly. I handed him the coffee, shaking my head at Cee at the same time. She clamped her lips shut, and I figured I'd hear about it after he left. *If* he ever left. As far as I could see he had settled in for the night.

Stella had dozed off and was softly snoring. The clock hands crept round toward eleven, and still he sat, hovering over Cee, driving her to distraction. I tried to help, but most of the time he ignored what I had to say. By now she had her arms crossed over her chest, hands hidden so he couldn't get hold of them.

He didn't seem to be aware of her inattention. "I'll be glad when you get back to work. I miss seeing you every day."

"I don't miss your squealing mailboxes and caramel onions."

He laughed, slapping his knee. "Nothing like a little fun to keep a relationship fresh."

"There *is* no relationship, and if there were one, it isn't going anywhere."

Gary laughed as if she had just told the funniest joke of the year. "That's why we get along so well. We both have a funny bone."

"I am not laughing."

I set my popcorn bowl aside, deciding enough was enough. "CeeCee isn't very strong yet, Gary. She needs her rest. It was nice of you to drop by, but I know you don't want to overly tire her."

He started to protest and then backtracked. "No. I suppose not. The evening's young yet, but I'll be running along."

If he thought eleven o'clock was early then he didn't know the Diamond household.

He patted Cee's arm affectionately. "You take care of yourself. I want you to get well enough to come back to church. It isn't the same without you."

Cee pressed her lips in a tight line. He got to his feet, bending over her with puckered lips. She jerked her head to one side and he kissed air. When he started to have another try, she extended her right hand for a friendly shake. He grinned, gripping her hand tightly. A buzzing like a dozen rattlesnakes filled the air. Cee yelped. Gary laughed hysterically, showing me the hand buzzer he had just used to jolt her.

I took his arm and turned him toward the door, afraid if he stayed, I might be in jail by morning. How dare he play his pranks on my daughter when he knew she was sick! I opened the front door and pushed him through.

"Later, Mrs. Diamond."

My tone did not sound cordial. "It would be best if you wait until she is feeling better, Gary. I don't believe she's up to having much company yet."

"You see that she enjoys those roses," he said.

I vowed to empty that vase rose by rose to see what trick he had put in there. The man could not be trusted.

I shut the door behind him and locked it before hurrying back to the living room, where Cee was expressing herself fluently. "That thing even rattled my teeth! Never let that man in this house again!"

" I didn't exactly *let* him in this time. He pushed past me like I was part of the woodwork."

"I can't believe the way he acts. He's crazy."

"He is a little offbeat," I agreed.

Stella opened her eyes. "Loser Boy gone?"

"Finally," I said, gathering up coffee cups. "He definitely overstayed his welcome."

She stretched, yawned. "Nice roses, though."

CeeCee bristled. "I don't want his roses. I want him to leave me alone!"

"Yes, dear." Surely there was one redeeming factor about the man, but I couldn't find it.

Stella switched off the television. "Then tell him to leave you alone."

"*I have.* He won't listen."

Stella nodded. "Some men are like that. You don't want to take him on because it's easier than arguing with him."

For a moment Cee was speechless with rage, and I grabbed the opportunity. "Bedtime everyone! I'll take care of the animals. You two go on upstairs, and I'll lock up."

I turned the poodles out for their evening business, covered the birdcage, and shut Captain in my office. He seemed resigned to his exile, used to the routine by now. The poodles scratched at the door, wanting in. As soon as I opened the door they scampered into their bed, their eyes big under their fuzzy little topknots.

I shut the door to the kitchen and turned out the light after making sure both doors were locked. It had been quite a night. I hadn't really paid much attention to CeeCee's earlier complaints about Gary Hendricks, other than I knew he was a worrisome rascal, but after tonight, I realized my daughter's comments were justified. The man was a nut bar. After unplugging the tree lights and banking the fire, I climbed the stairs to my room.

Probably just nutty enough to send chain letters.

CHAPTER 30

Stella nodded off with one ear half-cocked to Hilda Throckmorton giving overblown instructions on the proper way to arrange a refreshment table. Tonight was the final rehearsal for the church Christmas program.

What Stella had seen of the practice had been good. The kids had messed up, of course. They always did at rehearsal. But she'd never seen them mess up a program, and she'd seen a lot of programs in this church, going all the way back to when Herb finally got old enough to be a shepherd. La, he'd been proud. And CeeCee had been Mary one year. You'd have thought she'd won an Oscar. Come to think of it, maybe being chosen to portray the mother of Jesus was a higher honor than any man-made award.

"Now place the sugar cookies here, the chocolate chips over there, and the brownie squares next to the punch—oh, within two or three inches should do nicely." Hilda's voice echoed through the room like Foghorn Leghorn's.

Stella decided she'd had enough. At her age she should be able to do what she chose, and she didn't choose to be ordered around. So she got up and left.

Shuffling past the youth classroom, she saw Abel Brookes and Becky hovering over a sheet of paper. Abel had a pen in his hand, writing, and Becky seemed to be providing the words.

"No, don't write that," she said. "She'll never believe anything that silly."

"We have to make it sound scary," Abel said. "You want her to answer, don't you?"

Stella stepped back behind the door, where she could peer through the crack. What were those kids doing? Writing a letter? Chain letters?

But why write them at church? The answer almost took her breath. Of course, this was the master copy. They divided up the actual writing. That way they'd only have to write half as many. It wouldn't take them as long as it had taken her. Smart kids.

What was she thinking? Here were two innocent children embarking on a life of crime—well, maybe *innocent* didn't apply to Becky and Abel; no flies on those two. Someone had to stop them. They probably didn't know chain letters were illegal. She glanced around for help, but Hilda had the women lined up to serve. It wouldn't be long until the cast would be ready to come down from the dressing room and then it would be too late— those kids would be headed for juvenile court.

"I can't wait until the money comes in." Becky giggled. "How much do you think we'll get?"

"A bunch. This was a great idea, if we can just pull it off."

"We'll pull it off," Becky assured him. "What could go wrong?"

Land sakes, kids were gutsy these days. Stella's gaze searched the room where the women were, trying to catch someone's eye. She succeeded only too well. Mildred realized something was wrong and hurried over.

"What's wrong, Stella? Don't you feel well?"

She didn't want *Mildred.* Why did she have to be the one to tell her good friend that her little scamp of a granddaughter was headed for a jail cell? It wasn't fair. She moved back so Mildred could see through the crack in the door.

Becky's voice came through loud and clear. You'd think the

girl would have enough sense to lower her tone. "Will you get it in the mail tomorrow?"

Mildred shot Stella a questioning look.

Stella mouthed, "Chain letters."

Mildred went through that door like an Arkansas tornado. "What do you think you're up to now, young lady!"

Becky squealed, and Stella, with great presence of mind, shut the door behind her so no one in the fellowship hall would hear the commotion. But their loud voices drifted under the door so Stella could still hear them.

"Grandma! You scared me!"

"I'll scare you for sure if you don't tell me what you're doing, young lady!"

Stella cackled, picturing Becky looking to Abel for help. He would turn red as fire, shuffle his scuffed tennies.

"We were writing a letter. That's all."

"A *letter?*" Mildred's voice raised two octaves. "And *who* would you be writing a letter to?"

"J-just writing," Able stammered.

"I'll take that letter." Stella imagined Mildred holding out her hands. "And don't give me any sass."

Becky would reluctantly hand it over. Mildred would scan the written words. "You were sending this to your mother?"

Becky would nod—Stella's imagination suddenly braked to a halt. *Her mother!* Becky was writing to her mother?

Mildred's tone dropped to one of gentle admonishment. "And what did you hope to gain by it?"

"It was my idea," Abel defended. "Becky didn't have anything to do with it."

Stella had to give it to the kid; that was brave of him, considering that Becky had been hanging over his shoulder telling him what to write. Becky probably lifted her chin.

"No, it isn't all Abel's fault. I helped."

Silence, then Mildred's voice. "You were planning to tell your mother you had been kidnapped and to send a ransom."

Both must've nodded.

"Five hundred dollars is very little for your precious life, Rebecca." Stella pictured Mildred tucking the letter in her jacket pocket. "Now, you listen to me. This is called extortion. It's against the law. You might have thought it was a harmless prank, but it could have landed you in a lot of trouble."

Becky would have paled by now. "Sorry, Grandma. I didn't mean to do anything wrong. It's just that I'm so mad at Mom for getting married again. I felt like I had to do something."

Mildred's expression would have softened. "I know it's been hard for you, Becky, but you're handling it the wrong way. Someday you'll be grown, and maybe you won't make any better decisions than your mother has made. Don't you think you need to cut her some slack?"

Becky would agree, shamefaced. "I didn't intend to get Abel in trouble. You won't tell on him, will you?"

Of course Mildred would shake her head negatively. "I won't tell, and Stella won't either. I'll speak to her. But I don't ever want to hear of you doing anything like this again. Now, go get in line before the cookies are all gone."

"Sorry, Grandma."

"Sorry, Mrs. Fasco."

"Oh, and Becky?" Mildred's voice again.

"Yes, Grandma?"

"You're worth ten thousand times five hundred dollars. You do know that, don't you?"

"Sometimes—not always. Mom's not very good with words lately."

"Who said anything about Mom?" Mildred's voice dropped tenderly. "In God's eyes your life is priceless. Remember that, honey."

Abel and Becky shot out of the room and past Stella. Stella looked at Mildred. "I'm sorry. I heard *letter* and *money* and jumped to a conclusion I shouldn't have jumped to."

"I'm glad you did. I shudder to think what would have happened if they had actually sent that letter." Mildred sighed. "I'd better get back to the serving table before Hilda comes looking for me. I don't want her to get wind of this."

No, that wouldn't be good. Stella stood in the empty classroom, thinking. She could mark Becky and Abel off her suspect list. Seemed that no sooner did she put someone on the list than she was forced to remove them. If this kept up, she'd soon eliminate everyone in Morning Shade—except the letter writer, and then she'd have the culprit.

To borrow from Sherlock Holmes, "Elementary, my dear Watson."

CHAPTER 31

The macaws wandered around the kitchen on tiny-clawed feet, getting in my way. I'd stumbled over the green one twice and he squawked, nailing my bare toe. Needless to say we had words. One of these days I was going to trip and break something, and I'd be in a fine mess.

I switched off the stove burner and poured steaming vegetable beef soup into a bowl. Sticking a single poinsettia bloom into a bud vase, I set the vase on the tray. Cee was steadily improving, the swelling nearly invisible to the naked eye. I'd feared that being roused from a deep sleep for the predawn trek because of the fire alarm would cause further harm but she had weathered it with no ill effect. Her eyes still looked like two burnt holes in a blanket, but Sherman—

Odd, how I'd suddenly dropped the professional *Doctor* and had began calling Sherm by his given name.

Sherm. I tasted the name on my tongue, uneasy at first with the informality. For some reason I felt disloyal to Herb, but that was insane. *Sherman Winters—Dr. Sherman Winters.* Now was that hard, or utterly too personal for a woman to say? I have friends who remarried practically as quickly as they'd lowered their spouse's casket into the ground—and more than a few had regretted the impulsive leap. Would I be handling Herb's death differently if CeeCee and Stella hadn't kept my mind off his death and focused on daily struggles? I couldn't say. Loneliness was a hungry predator, and sometimes the mind would resort to the unthinkable when the pain hurt too much.

I picked up the tray and carried it to the front room. CeeCee was on the couch watching Dr. Phil. I wondered if she really benefited from the daily consulting session with the good doctor, but I had to say he was a pretty cute Texan. My daughter glanced up when I set the tray on the coffee table.

"Thanks, Mom."

"Sorry lunch is so late today, but I was on a roll and I hated to stop until I finished the chapter."

"It's okay. I'm really not hungry."

I eyed the open bag of salt-and-vinegar chips discreetly stuffed behind the pillow and knew why.

"Grandma gone?"

"She's not back from the Citgo yet."

"Did you ever find out where she disappeared to the other day?"

"She said she'd spent the day at Shady Acres with Lorene."

"Oh. I bet she enjoyed that."

"She was pretty tight-lipped about the visit."

In fact I hadn't been able to pry anything about the visit out of her. At first I thought she was pouting, embarrassed about the fire-alarm incident, so I hadn't worried overly much about her absence. I'd taken a fruitcake out of the oven and set it on the counter to cool, then gone upstairs to see if she was all right, only to find she was gone. Rarely had Stella left the house at eight and not returned until almost dark. I'd even had Hargus out looking for her, but he couldn't find her anywhere. When she did come home, she slammed the front door and hiked straight up to her room without saying anything to anyone. I was relieved to see her, but I'd been worried sick, and by the time she'd slammed in the door I was ready to call the State Patrol.

She could have had enough consideration to call and let me know where she was, but other than a foul mood, Stella seemed no worse for wear, and since I didn't think it was my place to ground an eighty-seven-year-old or take away driving privileges—which she so rarely exercised these days—I swallowed my impatience and informed her that in the future I would appreciate a phone call if she was going to be gone all day. That's when she told me she had spent the day with Peaches, though lo and behold, I couldn't imagine what those two women found to talk about the entire day—especially since Lorene's dementia was getting worse all the time.

When a commercial came on, CeeCee slowly swung her legs off the sofa and sat up. She stared at me—one of those blank, I-still-feel-like-dying looks. The pillow had flattened the back of her hair. She reached for the spoon and halfheartedly took a spoonful of soup. "I've been meaning to ask, Mom. You haven't gone to the library like you'd planned. I'm okay, honest. You don't have to be here twenty-four-seven."

"I know I don't, but the weather's so bad I can't make myself get out."

I knew the flimsy excuse was just that, but without revealing the web of my intricately-laid-out-but-never-materialized, part-time-job plan, the white fib was the best I could do. Which reminded me: I needed to call Duella and wish her and Luella a Merry Christmas. Who knows; maybe I could get her to change her mind and give me a few hours in January. I could still use the extra money, and honestly if. I didn't get out of this dog-yapping, bird-screeching, cat-licking zoo, I was going to blow my cork. Excusing myself, I left CeeCee and Dr. Phil alone (plus a few million other watchers) and disappeared into the kitchen to make my call.

Duella's chirpy voice answered on the second ring.

"Duella? Maude."

"Oh, so nice to hear from you, Maude. How is CeeCee today?"

"Improving, thanks. I wanted to wish you and Luella Merry

Christmas."

"Well, how nice! And the same to you and yours, Maude."

We chatted for a few minutes, and then I threw in the suggestion about part-time work in January. "Life should be more sane then," I promised her. "I'd be glad to help with inventory or whatever." I knew she'd said that she was broke last time we talked, but she couldn't be serious. *Tight* I believe was the appropriate adjective.

Still, I couldn't miss the almost imperceptible sigh on the other end of the line. "Oh, that would be so nice—but I believe that Luella and I can handle the workload. But thanks so much for offering, Maude."

Well, I wasn't *offering*—money would exchange hands.

Duella sighed more audibly. "It isn't as if the store is being overrun with shoppers. Holiday business is so off this year."

I *tsked*, aware that bad weather was affecting every business owner's holiday cash flow this winter. The most voiced complaint I heard was that no one could get into the Christmas spirit, or if they did, they couldn't get to the stores to shop.

"I'll work the whole month of January if you should change your mind and need me," I offered again.

"Well, we'll see. Luella and I need to pinch pennies ..,"

The confession brought a smile to my lips. The colorful spinsters often expected hard times and always prepared for the worst. Herb used to tell me it was because their generation lived through the Great Depression.

Funny. I thought that was what I was living through

I hung up and had no more than turned around before the phone shrilled. Shooting the cordless a hateful look, I snatched it up and pushed the talk button.

Jean was on the other end.

"Hi, Jean." I always had to be careful about the greeting. I talk fast so *hi, Jean* comes out *hygiene* if I'm not careful.

"Maude—Happy Holidays!"

Yeah, yeah, rah, rah. "The holidays will be a lot brighter if you're calling to tell me the contract's signed and the check's in the mail," I predicted brightly.

"Well... nearly."

My heart hit the floor. Another delay! "What's wrong now?"

"Oh, Hugh Norton contracted the flu on his recent business trip. He's flat on his back in bed—but he's on antibiotics and hopes to be back in the office early next week."

"And if the flu hangs on?" Which, with my luck, it probably would.

"Well. . . then he'll be back in the office no later than the first of the year. You know how holidays play havoc with house schedules."

Oh, I knew; I had firsthand knowledge, unfortunately.

"Maude ... can I help financially—"

I stopped her right there. "Thank you, Jean. But I'm fine."

That's the kind of agent I had; I knew she was about to offer a check to see me through the immediate crisis, and I refused to start that. I would survive this holiday; God would provide. He always did, no matter how weak my faith—and it was getting dangerously low right now. With that unnerving thought I closed my eyes and reminded Him I was teetering awfully close to the edge, so if He could spare me a minute, I'd sure appreciate His attention to my fiscal crisis.

Jean and I said our good-byes and mentioned how much we appreciated one another, wished each other a final Merry Christmas, and hung up.

I headed for my office and heard one of the macaws shout, "HEY, EGGHEAD!"

Yep. That's me, a real bonafide egghead. I should have given up the uncertainty of writing and gotten a real job fifteen years ago. Entering my workspace, I wondered what the going rate was for abusive-speaking macaws. Enough to buy Stella and Cee a Christmas present? I grinned.

CHAPTER 32

Mom! CeeCee shifted on the small sofa, trying to get comfortable. The house was as empty as a tomb. Grandma was off somewhere, and Mom was either out or deep into writing. Her eyes switched to the birdcage and bumped into a pair of black orbs.

"WHAT'S UP, SWEETIE?"

"Nothing, Green Bird. Pure-dee ole nothing."

She shifted, trying to find a scrap of comfort. The tight ache in her jaw was relentless; she couldn't alleviate it with hot packs, cold packs—anything. Mumps. At her age. If there was ever a year that she wouldn't want to live over, this would be the one. Jake's death, the move from California back to Arkansas, living with Mom and Grandma. The throb in her jaw intensified.

Did anyone ever really experience true love? In California, almost all of her and Jake's friends had divorced—or never married in the first place. Maybe it was her small-town upbringing, but living together outside of marriage never seemed right to her. Certainly it wasn't God's plan.

Only sometimes she thought she'd have been a lot smarter living with Jake instead of marrying him. He'd wanted the 'no promises' arrangement, argued that they needed to know each other better before they "took the plunge." That's how Jake looked at marriage:

free-falling from a cliff without a parachute. CeeCee, on the other hand, thought marriage was sacred, serious. Forever.

Shifting, she sat up and irritably tried to untangle her feet from the heavy afghan. "Mom!" Dropping back to the pillow, she sighed.

"BAD DAY, MORON?" *Squawk.*

She'd had worse. The day the team doctor called to tell her that Jake had collapsed during a workout at the gym. The harried drive to the hospital only to discover that the blood clot had claimed her young husband's life instantly. The day she had to sell her beautiful home, the furs, the jewelry Jake had given her. The Mercedes.

The day she'd bitten into that caramel onion—

Her thoughts halted. What made her think of Gary Hendricks, the loser? Probably because his practical jokes had worn as thin as his insane pursuit. She was not ready for a relationship. It was too soon. And though Stella said God made a mate for everyone who was intended to have one, CeeCee had had her mate, and she didn't care for another one, thank you.

Her postal coworker Ty Hardin surfaced to her mind. Sweet, unassuming Ty. Now there was a man worth his salt. His wife, Marlene, had died early in their marriage, and he still grieved for her. He wouldn't so much as look at another woman—not in a male-female way. CeeCee didn't think grief should last forever, but the romantic side of her thrilled at the idea of a man loving one woman so much, so deeply that she couldn't be replaced. Not ever.

She swiped at a hot tear suddenly rolling down her cheek. "Change the subject, CeeCee. You're getting maudlin."

The phone shrilled, startling her. She snatched up the cordless and pressed the button. "Hello."

"CeeCee, CeeCee, my little sweet pea, pea. Flower of my heart."

She closed her eyes, wanting to barf. *Gary Hendricks.* "Hello, Gary."

"Still can't talk because those ole mump-ti-dee mumps got you down?"

"Right." She rolled her eyes.

Squawk. "MORON ALERT! BEEP, BEEP, BEEP."

CeeCee slapped her hand over the receiver. *"Hush!"*

"SHUT UP."

"Quiet!" she told the bird.

"SHUT UP."

"How about Gary Wary dropping by with a milk shake, huh? A strawberry one—thick and creamy?"

"No, thanks. I not very hungry lately."

"Oh."

She pictured the way his bottom lip drooped at rejection.

"Well, how about ole Gary stopping by with an armload of books? Romance, mystery, maybe a few inspirational titles on how to cope with mumps at thirty-one!" He hee-hawed.

Like there was such a title.

"No, thanks."

CeeCee didn't want to hurt his feelings, but how was she going to make him understand they had no future? It was much too soon for her to think about dating. Her marriage might have been imperfect, but she had loved Jake. And secondly, she and Gary had nothing in common. She was sure that somewhere out there in this big, wide world Gary had a mate: at the zoo.

Forgive me, Lord.

Somewhere out there was a mate for Gary, and he needed to look for her and leave CeeCee alone. "Gary?"

"Yeah, Toots?"

"I..." How did you dismiss a suitor kindly? "I've ... decided—after a good deal of thought—to ... to ... observe a period of mourning."

Silence. Then, "Did you say you'd decided to observe a period of mourning?"

"Yes."

"Who are you? Jackie Kennedy or somebody?"

She nodded rapidly. "Yes!" She hadn't thought about the

former first lady until now, but yes, she was declaring a period of mourning for her late husband.

"You're going to wear sackcloth and ashes an entire year?"

"Maybe longer."

The statement was followed by a lengthy period of silence. Guilt flooded CeeCee. Now she wouldn't be able to accept a date for a whole year, but at this point the idea didn't bother her. It was quite possible she might never date again. She'd had her chance at love and failed. But she had walked away from the ashes with the knowledge of why the marriage failed. She had never once consulted God about a mate—a man she intended to spend a lifetime with—her future children's father and role model. She had blithely fallen in love with a football hero who had the morals of an alley cat, and God forgive her, been so caught up in Jake Tamaris's spiritually bankrupt world that she'd fallen prey to the delusion.

"CeeCee. That means you can't date for a year."

The porch light was on but nobody was home.

"Yes, Gary. That's what *mourning* means."

Strained silence came across the line, and she suddenly felt drained. She shouldn't have to deal with these kinds of things, not when her jaws ached and it hurt to talk, let alone think.

"Well...," Gary said as though her statement was starting to penetrate kryptonite. She could hear pages rustling, as though he was rapidly thumbing through a book. "If that's the case, what are you doing one year from tonight? Can we make a movie date? I have my social calendar right here and it looks like—yes, December 19 next year is open. Good news."

Stuffing the end of the pillowcase in her mouth, she screamed. What was it about the word *no* that this man didn't understand? He couldn't be so dense that he failed to recognize there was no attraction here—not from this woman.

The day she had buried Jake she had walked away from the gravesite and promised God that the next time—*the next time*— she would consult Him about a husband. Grandma's favorite saying had come to her mind that warm spring afternoon: All good things come to those that wait upon the Lord. Well, when and if she ever met a man who held her interest, God would be advising her. No more going it alone for CeeCee Tamaris, and certainly not with a man as hungry as Gary Hendricks.

"A year is a long time. We'll see."

Coward, her conscience accused. *Spineless wimp. Do not raise his hopes.* A year—two years, five years—down the line and she would *never* think of this man as anything other than a nuisance.

"Okay." His tone was resigned now. Hurt. "Take care of yourself, CeeCee."

"Thanks, Gary. You too." She paused. "Gary?"

"Yes?"

"Merry Christmas."

"Yeah, same to you, CeeCee."

She should have felt relief when she hung up, but she didn't. She felt awful. Bad, and nothing like the Christian she professed to be. She'd read somewhere that when a person tacks Christ's name beside his, he'd better live by the same rules as the Master. Surely there should have been an easier way to tell Gary that she wasn't interested.

She punched the OFF button and let the phone drop to her chest. *Rude,* CeeCee. Rude and simply unforgivable at this time of the year.

* * *

Stella took a sip of fruit punch and kept her eyes peeled for Clifford Johnson. Strains of "Deck the Halls" filled the Shady Acres recreational center. The retired politician was wearing a foil halo onto which he had tacked a piece of mistletoe, and he was now working his way up and down the tables, making women scream and blush with delight with a holiday kiss.

If he got any closer to Stella she was making a run for the ladies' room.

"This seat taken?" Pansy set a plate of festive goodies on the table and sat down before Stella could issue an invitation. She'd finally gotten over Stella's perceived insult concerning Hargus and chain letters. "I see Clifford's at it again."

Stella humphed. "If he starts this direction I'm outta here."

"Oh?" Pansy fussed with her hair, rearranging a sprayed lock. Tonight Stella's bridge partner was decked out like a Christmas tree: black slacks and a black sweatshirt with a blinking Merry Christmas emblazoned across the front, gaily wrapped Christmas boxes hanging from her earlobes. Stella bet local radar had her on screen the moment she stepped out of her room.

Pansy grinned and then tittered nervously. "Why? Clifford's not so bad—very successful in his day."

Stella eyed her friend and swore that Pansy had set her cap for one of Clifford's disgusting smacks. Happened every year, but this year Stella was outsmarting the senator. She kept her eye on the man, but her mind was elsewhere. All the fun had gone out of the season—not that the season was about fun. It was about the birth of the Savior. Stella shouldn't have to remind herself of the true meaning of Christmas, but still, this probably was her last one and these chain letters had put a kink in her colon. And the real pits? She couldn't even talk to Simon, Pansy, or Frances about her dilemma without implicating herself in the mystery. She straightened her purse handle, rearranging the bag sitting in her lap, ready for quick deployment. Clifford was working his way down the line, getting closer.

Frances threaded her way through the multitude, holding a plate of cookies above her head.

"Yoo-hoo!" Pansy motioned for the retired teacher to join them.

"My—what a party!" Breathless, Frances sat her cookies on the table. Confetti in the shapes of tiny poinsettias and silver and gold Christmas trees were scattered across the white linen.

"Isn't this fun!"

A real blast, Stella thought.

Pansy started in on how she was behind on her shopping; only five days left and she still hadn't finished Hargus's quilt. She had started the quilt shortly after Labor Day, and that's all they'd heard about since—the Ohio Star pattern. How pretty it was. How proud Hargus was going to be of Pansy's masterpiece. Stella figured about the only "masterpiece" Hargus recognized was bottled. Masterpiece barbecue sauce on a plate of ribs.

"OOOP, OOOP, OOOP!"

Whirling, Stella saw a grinning Clifford, mistletoe halo perched above his head, leering over her. She should have known; turn her head three seconds and Clifford would make that silly diving-submarine sound and zero in on his next victim.

"OOOP, OOOP, OOOP!" When Clifford dove for the kiss, Stella calmly turned her head and his mouth encountered a hair ball. The back of Stella's head.

Spitting, Clifford flushed several shades of red. He fumbled in his back pocket for a handkerchief and promptly scrubbed his tongue.

"What 'ave you 'ot on your 'air!"

"WD-40," Stella said. She wasn't the fool he thought her to be.

He shot her a not-so-amused look, and with another *"OOOP, OOOP, OOOP!"* he moved on to the next table.

"You should be ashamed of yourself," Pansy hissed under her breath. "Poor Clifford—he's just being friendly. Where's your holiday spirit?"

"He can be friendly with somebody else." Stella reached for her cup of punch, morose now. The only way to salvage her holiday spirit was to break this copycat chain-letter case.

"She's right, you know." Frances's eyes followed Clifford through the crowd, her cheeks touched with rosy pink. "Clifford shouldn't be kissing the women without the women's permission."

"I'd give him permission," Pansy stated.

"That's why he doesn't ask." Stella set her cup back on the table. She ought to go home; *Law and Order* was coming on and tonight was supposed to be a new episode. If only she had someone like those detectives to help her break this case. *Ooh, baby—that would be nice.*

"Earth to Stella!"

Stella glanced up when Pansy's voice penetrated her musings. "What?"

"I said," Pansy leaned in, "what's wrong with you lately? You haven't been yourself in weeks."

Stella's shoulders briefly lifted. "I don't know. I can't seem to get in the holiday spirit this year."

"Oh." Frances made a moue with heart-shaped lips. "Christmas is always such a lovely season. Aren't you feeling well?"

"It's not that—I feel as good as anyone can feel at eighty-seven."

"Then what is it, dear?" Pansy perked up, all ears now.

"I guess it's Maude having to work so hard to make ends meet." That's the only reason Stella had sent the first chain letter—an honest attempt to help out. "Then CeeCee feeling so bad with the mumps. All those birds and dogs running through the house. Makes a body tired."

"Well, sounds to me like you have a full-blown case of Christmas blues." As if to reinforce Frances's diagnoses, Elvis's "Blue Christmas" blared over the Muzak.

"Oh, honey, I know how you feel. Sometimes I feel that I'm in Hargus's way," Pansy sympathized. "Seems like I'm just underfoot with no purpose."

Stella nodded. "Know what you mean, Pansy. Maude never lets on, but I know she feels I'm a burden."

"Nonsense." Frances leaned over and patted her hand. "Maude adores you, Stella. We all adore you."

"Hilda Throckmorton doesn't adore you," Pansy reminded,

then—attention diverted—she whispered, "Oh, look. Clifford's coming back this way." She fumbled in her purse and took out a small canister. Misting a couple of shots in her mouth, she swallowed and then dropped the breath spray back in her bag.

Stella shook her head. Man crazy. Pansy's face fell like an undercooked soufflé when the elderly politician rushed past their table and made a beeline for Ethel Curry.

"Flitter," Pansy mumbled. "Well, as I was saying, don't feel so bad, Stella, ole girl. Hargus brought my Christmas present by this afternoon."

Frances frowned. "So early?"

"You know Hargie. Every year he can't wait until Christmas Day to give me my present."

Stella recalled the set of socket wrenches he'd given his mother the year before. Complete with a rolling toolbox.

You had to wonder about that boy.

Frances pressed closer, apparently trying to hear over Elvis's wail. "What'd he get you this year? That new J.Lo perfume you've been wanting?"

"No," Pansy mused. "Not the perfume."

"What?" Stella asked. "Another one of those fancy nightgowns you've got a drawer full of?"

"Of course not—I've told him I didn't need another nightgown or robe or slippers."

"Then what?" Stella asked.

"A lube gun."

Stella stared at her. "A lube gun? One of those thingamajiggies that you oil your car chassis with?"

"Yes—oh, that naughty rascal. I don't know what to think about him. He said I'm so hard to buy for—I don't like gowns or robes or slippers—so this year he thought maybe if he bought me a lube gun, and I didn't use it, he could borrow it." Her smile seemed a tad faint. "He's so practical—guess that's my fault. I always said, 'waste not; want not'."

"A lube gun." Stella had heard it all. Still she knew that Hargus loved his mother and respected her—even though his taste was in his mouth. Pansy was needed; Stella wondered what that felt like. It had been a long time since she'd been needed. And now, she couldn't solve a simple mystery involving chain letters.

"OOOP, OOOP, OOOP!"

Startled, Stella whirled and Clifford swooped in for the kill. He planted one noisy, smacking kiss smack-dab in the middle of her forehead. Every eye in the room turned to gawk.

Stella felt her cheeks ignite in a five-alarmer. "Get away," she hissed.

Clifford planted another kiss, then *OOOP, OOOP, OOOPed* off in the opposite direction, taking aim at ninety-nine-year-old Thadian Wilson.

Stella picked up a Santa Claus napkin and scrubbed the evidence off her forehead. Clifford's OOOPing sub echoed in the background.

She hoped that annoying ship sprang a leak with Clifford in it.

"Oh," Pansy swooned, clasping her hands in ecstasy. "You are so lucky, Stella Diamond! Clifford has *never* kissed me."

"Really." Stella scrubbed harder. "Are you bragging or complaining?"

"I believe Clifford has his eye on you, Stella," Frances mused. "You might make a match if you wanted."

Stella glared at her. "Are you out of your mind? At my age?"

Pansy giggled. "You know what they say. For every old pot there's a lid."

"I hardly consider myself an old pot," Stella retorted, feeling this conversation was getting out of hand.

Misery on Clifford and his *OOOP, OOOP, OOOP!* She'd like to whop him over the head with a plate full of Ethel Curry's rock-hard cookies. That would knock the *OOOP, OOOP, OOOP!* out of him. Poor Ethel. That woman never could boil water. Her husband was supposed to have died of a heart attack, but Stella figured acute indigestion had played a big part in his sudden departure.

When Clifford looked her way again, she narrowed her eyes, lips tight. Just let him try! She'd had all the hanky-panky she could take for one night. Evidently he got the message, because he looked startled and zoomed away in another direction.

Pansy sniffed. "Why did you look at poor Clifford like that? You've probably scared him so much he'll not come back our way."

Stella bit into one of Frances's cookies. "Clifford is skating on thin ice. If I hear that *OOOP, OOOP, OOOP!* One more time, I'll pull that man's plug on his Ho! Ho! Ho!"

CHAPTER 33

Christmas Eve morning. Christmas will be low-key in the Diamond household except for the very small gifts I bought at Wal-Mart—good ones, but small. I didn't want it to be this way. I'd had plans to make this year's celebration extra nice.

To think that once my thoughts were consumed with bestseller lists. Funny how your perspective can change. Oh, I'd still love to be on that list, but the idea doesn't consume me—or not as much as it once did.

I stared out the window at the snow-covered landscape, wishing I could change our situation, but there was nothing I could do. I'd given up working at The Antiques Shop. Cee had been too sick for me to leave her. Slow in overcoming the mumps, she'd needed me, and of course I *wanted* to take care of her.

I wandered into the living room to plug in the Christmas lights, feeling I needed something to brighten my day. The bare, empty space beneath the tree reproached me. I was sure Stella and CeeCee had noticed, but they hadn't said a word.

CeeCee was too weak to shop, and Stella always gave us each twenty dollars. It was up to me to provide Christmas this year, and I had failed. I sat down in my favorite chair, staring at the tree lights. *Where did I go wrong, Lord? I have tried so hard this past year to be everything to everybody. I've taken Stella and Cee into my home even when I really didn't want to at first. My writing is getting harder to do, and the money is slow coming in. I can't carry this burden alone any longer. Please help me.*

I could hear Stella stirring around upstairs. She'd be coming down soon. At least the sidewalks were clear and she was getting out to go to the Citgo again. Her disposition had improved tremendously, and she usually came home bursting with news about the regulars and their problems.

I was getting some work done between running up and down stairs to check on Cee. For a blessing Gary Hendricks had stayed away. I don't think CeeCee could have handled many more visits from him, and a few more tricks like that hand buzzer and I would have had a few choice words of my own to say to that young man.

I had gone through the vase of roses he brought her, looking for surprises, and found a plastic frog, one of those motion-sensor contraptions that croak when anyone gets in its range. The sound it made was so realistic that Captain pounced on the frog and had to have it wrestled away from him. He hadn't taken it well. I still had the scratches to show for my part in the battle.

CeeCee wanted to throw the frog in the trash, but Stella claimed it to take to her bridge meeting, where she tricked Frances into getting off her dignity long enough to look for a wayward frog. Frances didn't plan on doing anything after she found it—just point it out for someone else to get rid of. According to Stella it caused quite a commotion. Apparently no one stopped to think how unlikely it would be to find a frog in your living room in the middle of an Arkansas ice storm.

Stella came downstairs wearing her teeth for a change. I found them for her last night, grinning at me from a shelf in the medicine cupboard in the upstairs bathroom. I heaved myself up out of the chair and marched to the kitchen to fix breakfast. If the world were scheduled to come to an end tomorrow morning at 6 a.m. the women in the Diamond household would have to eat breakfast before they could attend the ceremony. We never missed a meal nor did without very many snacks. The amount we spent on salt-and-vinegar potato chips alone would finance a third-world country.

Stella was already at the table thumbing through the paper. "I wondered if you were up yet since I didn't smell breakfast cooking."

"Seems like I'm having trouble getting started this morning." I opened the refrigerator door, wondering what I should fix. About all I could see were bacon and eggs and maybe fresh orange juice. The juice would be something healthy to offset the high-cholesterol breakfast. I had intended to start eating healthier, but like everything else, I hadn't got around to it.

While the bacon sizzled in the pan, I started coffee perking. Maybe I'd feel better after my early morning cup of caffeine. The poodles were prancing in front of the back door, wanting out. Captain marched back and forth in front of his feeding dish, and the macaws were trying to outdo each other by seeing which one could scream the loudest. I gritted my teeth, trying to get myself under control. My nerves were shot from all of the stress I had endured the past month. I needed some relief, and I needed it now.

Stella rattled the pages of the newspaper. "Did you know Tom Morrison?"

"No I didn't," I snapped.

She looked at me appraisingly. "Tell you what, Maude. You need a vacation."

"Yeah. A vacation from life."

"When that advance comes in, why don't you get away for a while? We'll get along just fine without you for a few days."

I blinked back tears. Of course I couldn't afford to take a vacation, but it was sweet of her to think of it. "Oh, Stella, I'll be all right. It's just Christmas coming on top of everything else."

She nodded. "Seems like it's coming at a bad time this year, but you know, Maude, Christmas isn't just packages under the tree."

"I know that." I felt slightly offended that she felt she had to make that point.

"I was thinking about it last night. A lot of people at Shady Acres don't have much family. I'm lucky. I've got you and CeeCee and this nice home where we can live together. I know we'd rather have our husbands with us, but if we have to be alone, then I'm glad I'm alone with you."

I was bawling at this point. "Oh, Stella. We *are* lucky. Thank you for pointing it out to me."

I hadn't wanted her to move in here, and I suppose she had known it, but I couldn't imagine life without her now. She was irritating sometimes, funny at times, and downright enjoyable at times, but she was never boring. I hoped I could be as classy when I reached her age.

I turned the bacon and cracked eggs. Stella went back to her paper. "Adella Thompson. I knew her."

"So did I. What did she die of?"

"Doesn't say. A short illness. Well that's a blessing. I hope when my time comes to go, it will be quick. I don't mind going; I just don't want it to hurt."

I laughed. "I suppose we all feel that way."

CeeCee entered the kitchen. "Well, you sound jolly. What's for breakfast?"

I turned to find her smiling at me. "You actually feel like eating breakfast?"

"I think I'm finally on the mend. How about a scrambled egg?"

"Coming right up. And there's some peach yogurt in the refrigerator. Think you might want that?"

"Sounds good. Grandma, how are things down at the Citgo?"

Stella looked up from the newspaper. "About the same. That girl with the pink hair has dyed it green for the holidays. Wears a pair of those red Christmas ornaments for earrings. Gave me quite a turn first time I saw her, but I'm getting used to it by now. Sort of looking forward to what she does for Valentine's Day."

CeeCee laughed. "She's just expressing herself."

Stella grunted. "I can express myself without looking like I'd dropped in from outer space."

She turned back to the obituary pages. "Clement Douglas. Got run over chasing the fire truck. Must have thought he was a dog."

"Stella!" I stared at her, scandalized.

She grinned. "Just wanted to see if you were paying attention."

We finished breakfast, and I washed the dishes while Cee went upstairs to shower. It was good to see her up and around, although she was still pale, and I'd guess she'd lost close to ten pounds. A rough way to lose it too. Stella was back in her recliner, resting up. Tonight was a big night for the church ladies—the Christinas Eve service, with refreshments later of course. Church people seem to do a lot of eating. Maybe because there are so many other things they can't do, they take advantage of the one indulgence allowed. At any rate, between church breakfasts, luncheons, teas, and plain refreshments, which usually mean cookies and punch, we seem to spend a lot of time in the fellowship hall.

Although Stella had done a great job with the spaghetti dinner, Hilda hadn't asked her to chair tonight's festivities, keeping the reins firmly in her own hands. I always enjoyed the Christmas Eve service, but tonight I dreaded going. I still was having a hard time with that barren space under the tree. I wished I could charge something, but my credit card was gasping already. Practically maxed out.

I set out the ingredients to bake a Lady Baltimore cake, Stella's favorite recipe. If I couldn't provide gifts, I could at least fix their favorite food for Christmas dinner. Turkey, bought at the after-Thanksgiving sale, with stuffing, broccoli casserole . .. what else? Fruit salad, for Cee.

I started feeling better. Cooking does that for me sometimes. Maybe I could use Gary's roses to make a centerpiece. I thought about how little Cee would like that and changed my mind. A bowl of fresh fruit and nuts would be less controversial. And special treats for the dogs and the cat. Sunflower seeds for the birds. When you don't have what you want, make do with what you have.

CHAPTER 34

Stella had to be at the church in the early afternoon to prepare Communion glasses, so Maude drove her there. The streets were nearly clear now, but icy patches still remained. The debris from the storm had mostly been hauled away, but the broken trees were a mute testimony of the deadliness of the ice.

Stella had just as soon stayed at home. She knew what it would be like at the church, everyone rushing around getting in the way, and Hilda cracking her verbal whip and trying to run the show. Where that woman got the idea she could run anything was beyond her. Everything Hilda put her hand on turned into a circus.

Maude parked close to the entrance to the fellowship hall. "I'll see you later. Cee's not planning to come tonight, and I think that's wise. She's still not feeling very well."

"Maybe we could have Gary Hendricks drop by and see her," Stella said.

"Bite your tongue. That's all it would take to give her a relapse."

Stella laughed and got out of the car. "Well, you be sure and come. I'll need a ride home."

"Watch out for slick spots. Maybe I'd better walk you to the door."

"I can take care of myself." Now why did Maude have to sound like her keeper? She got so tired of people thinking she had to be watched over and helped just because she was old. Wait until they got to be her age and see how they liked it.

"No offense meant," Maude said.

"None taken." There had been, but she'd learned to overlook it and go on. You had to overlook a lot of things when you got old.

Maude drove away and Stella went inside. The noise was so loud she felt like clapping her hands over her ears. Women were dashing around with dazed looks on their faces. Pansy and Frances were stirring up cookie dough, wooden spoons clacking against the big Pyrex bowls. Mildred and Harriet were slapping on tablecloths like they were in some sort of race, and right in the middle of all the ruckus stood Hilda, shouting orders like some windup doll stuck in overdrive.

Stella stared transfixed at the church's self-appointed leader of the women. Hilda's ample frame was encased in a suit of fire-engine red; under it was a Christmas green blouse. Around her neck hung a necklace of marble-sized red beads with a gold cross pendant. A gold angel pin decorated her broad bosom, and matching angel earrings adorned her ears. The woman looked like a Christmas decoration herself. Where did she find a getup like that?

While Stella watched, Hilda flapped her hands like a bird in flight. "I mean it. If anyone disrupts this service, they will answer to me. I intend for everything to be as perfect as possible."

Stella removed her coat and went to help with the Communion glasses. Minnie Draper looked up and smiled. "See you finally got here."

"I'm here. Looks like Hilda is running in high gear."

"She's in fine form," Minnie agreed. "Been that way ever since she came. Guess she's trying to impress Pastor Brookes."

"Humph! Who put her in charge anyway? I don't recall that being the law."

"Well, don't rile her any more than she already is. I think

she'll have a breakdown of some sort if anyone crosses her. Her face is almost as red as those beads around her neck."

Stella snorted. "Sort of eclipses everyone else, doesn't she?"

Hilda rushed to oversee the placing of floral arrangements on the table, pushing Mildred Fasco out of the way. From the look on Mildred's face, Stella figured she was having a hard time holding on to her Christmas spirit.

Gary Hendricks, treading where no sane man would dare intrude, stuck his head through the doorway. Stella turned her back to him, hoping he wouldn't notice her. Everyone else was too busy to pay him much attention.

"Hello there, ladies. Need any help? If so, I'm your man."

Hilda whirled on him, lips firmly pressed, eyebrows raised. *"No!"*

Gary blinked, opened and closed his mouth like a beached fish, and vanished without another word.

The Communion glasses were ready, so Stella and Minnie started putting out the nuts and mints. Anna Weatherby had brought a plate of her famous fudge, and Harriet had made those creamy mints for which she was famous. Stella poured nuts into cut-glass dishes, placing them exactly where Hilda indicated.

Several children had come into the hall, most noticeably the preacher's kids. You could count on them being underfoot, Stella thought. Looked like Elly could control them, but for all her quiet ways, or maybe in spite of them, she seemed to be outmatched. They descended on the refreshment table like a crowd of hungry crows.

"Now, boys and girls," Elly chirped, "we don't bother the refreshments. Those are for later. Why don't you go get ready for the service?"

This had about as much success as talking to the wind. Stella leaned over the table, staring at a little girl with dark hair and mischievous eyes. "Touch that and I'll pinch your nose."

The girl looked startled. "No, you won't."

"Sure about that?"

The child nodded, but she backed off. Stella grinned. She still had it. No kid ever got the best of her. Except maybe her own. Herb could talk her into almost anything. She'd sure been crazy about that boy. Still missed him. This was her second Christmas without him and it didn't seem right.

She stiffened. Here came Abel and Becky. Wonder what they were hatching up this time? You could bet they were up to something. They were about as ornery as kids could get, and smart too. They would probably grow up to be outstanding citizens, making their own children toe the line. That sort usually did turn out that way.

They approached the table. "Hello, Mrs. Diamond," Abel said. "How are you tonight?"

"Three steps ahead of you. Don't try any of your tricks with me."

Becky was all wide-eyed innocence. "Us? Why, Mrs. Diamond. How could you?"

"Been writing any letters to your mother lately?" Stella asked. Becky blushed and shook her head.

Stella relented. "Well, I shouldn't have said that. It's none of my business. Why don't the two of you run along?"

"We will." Becky stared at something past Stella's shoulder. "Is that stove working all right?"

Stella turned to look before she realized she'd been had. She whirled just in time to see both Becky and Abel grab a handful of nuts. She snatched a dish towel and took after them. From the looks on their faces they had never been chased by an eighty-seven-year-old woman slapping at them with a dish towel and breathing fire and brimstone.

They ran.

Stella made it to the doorway, where she had to sit down and rest. She was old. Too old to lose her temper like that. But she felt a sneaking glow of pride. Not a bad footrace for a woman her age.

She had almost caught them, too, when Hilda got in the way. She laughed, thinking of the way Becky had bounced off Hilda's backside. Bet Mildred would hear about that.

In fact, Hilda was already sounding off. " *I* declare, Mildred. It looks like you could keep that granddaughter of yours in line. She almost knocked me down."

Mildred put her hands on her hips. "It would take more weight than Becky packs to knock you off your feet."

Hilda swelled up like a weather balloon. "*I* beg your pardon?"

"If you hadn't been in the way you wouldn't have gotten hit." Mildred went back to cutting cake into equal squares, ignoring Hilda.

Stella figured it would be a good time to sit still until everyone got busy again. She needed the rest anyway. It wasn't that she begrudged the kids the nuts, but they shouldn't have tried to fool her like that. She grinned. Did a good job of it too. It would serve them right if Abel grew up to be a preacher and married Becky. What a preacher's wife she would make. She wouldn't let someone like Hilda push her around. If there was any pushing to be done, she'd back Becky against Hilda any day.

CHAPTER 35

I drove to the church wishing I had stayed home. I could have asked Mildred to give Stella a ride. She would have been agreeable, but that would have meant putting Stella and Becky in the same car. I couldn't do that to Mildred.

I stopped at the Citgo and got two cartons of Rocky Road ice cream, my contribution toward tonight's refreshments. I could have baked a cake, but after working on my own Christmas dinner, I was tired of cooking.

The stars gleamed against the black velvet of the sky, and I should have been counting my blessings, but I wasn't. Instead I was going over my complete list of grievances, demanding God pay attention. He didn't seem to be listening.

When I reached the church, the fellowship hall was a madhouse. Women scurrying in all directions, children running and screaming, and smack-dab in the middle of all the ruckus stood Hilda Throckmorton decked out like a Christmas nightmare and sounding like a drill sergeant addressing a bunch of raw rookies.

"Ladies! I say, ladies, let's pull together now. We need to stop this squabbling and get along."

"Birds in their little nests agree," Elly chirped. This got her a disdainful glance from Hilda.

I placed my two semi-melted cartons of ice cream in the freezer portion of the refrigerator and tried to hide behind the other women. The last thing I needed was Hilda Throckmorton yelling at me. The way my nerves felt I might yell back, which wouldn't add much to the peace and harmony of the Christmas service.

On second thought, it might clear the air. There were a few faint rumblings of discord like the low mutter of thunder. It sounded like a storm of rebellion was brewing.

Duella and Luella arrived, late as usual and breathless. Luella's hair was a strange shade of plum with red overtones, which actually went quiet well with her gray suit and lavender blouse. Duella wore black with her usual red hat, this one with a flashy Christmas tree pinned jauntily to the crown.

"Sorry we're late," Duella explained, "but we had a customer and we couldn't leave until he did."

"I hope he bought something."

"Yes, he did. A lovely Rhode Island block secretary in the Chippendale style." Luella sighed. "I would have liked to have kept it myself, but Sister thought we should sell it, and she was right, of course."

Duella shook her head. "We can't keep everything we fall in love with, and the price we got for that secretary will come in handy with the winter bills to pay."

I knew all about winter bills, and it wasn't a subject I wanted to talk about. The noise was getting on my nerves. All my troubles seemed intensified—no job, no family gifts, no peace and quiet. Suddenly I missed my old life with Herb, instead of Stella, snoring in the recliner at night, before CeeCee came bringing her menagerie and Stella hunting for her teeth.

Plenty of time to write, Herb to help with the bills, no stress, no clutter, no problems. So much had happened in the past year and a half, I couldn't absorb it all. I'd been overwhelmed with no time to get back on my feet.

Hilda put Duella and Luella to arranging the silverware.

"Remember now, I want this to be perfect. If you have any questions, ask first before you do anything."

"As if there was anything complicated in putting out silverware and napkins," Stella muttered.

I jumped. I hadn't realized Stella had come to stand beside me. "Has she been like this all afternoon?"

"Pretty much. About driven everyone batty. Only good thing is she's kept Gary Hendricks out of here so he can't pester me about CeeCee."

"Did he ask if she's coming tonight?"

Stella shook her head. "He probably would have if he'd gotten the chance, but he couldn't get past Hilda. Sort of reminded me of Frenchie and Captain."

I laughed outright. "Stella, you're a stinker."

Hilda bore down on us. "Ah, there you are. I want the two of you to mix the punch. You'll find all the ingredients over there."

She walked away and Stella muttered, "Aye, aye, Madame Important Woman in Charge. We'll make the punch."

I was ticked too. Who did Hilda Throckmorton think she was, snapping out orders like this? Defying her would only cause a fuss though, so I meekly followed Stella to the punch bowl. "Where's the recipe?"

Stella made a face. "Oh my, I forgot to bring it. We'll have to make it from memory."

Which would have been all right, except my memory and Stella's don't always run on the same wavelength. We ran into trouble the first jump out of the chute. I poured in orange juice, and she dumped in enough sugar to rot the teeth of every church member at Living Truth.

"Stella! That's too much sugar."

She stuck out her lower lip. "I like it sweet."

"We're supposed to be making punch, not syrup."

I added pineapple juice and she poured in cranberry juice.

"Not so much, Stella. Leave room for the Sprite."

She slapped the bottle of juice down so hard it spurted out the top. "I've been making this recipe for more years than you've been alive. Don't tell me how to make punch."

I jerked off my apron. "If that's the way you feel, I'll let you run the whole shebang."

Stella started bawling. "I'm just an old woman in everyone's way. Go ahead; tell me to my face. I'm a burden."

"You're not a burden, for goodness' sake. Don't make a scene."

"Don't be mad at me, Maude. I'll let you make the punch your way, even if it is wrong."

Frances and Pansy came hurrying over to take Stella's part. "You should be ashamed, Maude," Frances said. "You know how easily Stella gets upset."

Hilda pushed herself into the group, wringing her hands. "Can't we all calm down? It's Christmas Eve and I wanted everything to be so nice. Surely you can make punch without having a fight."

If she had stayed out of it, I'd probably have smoothed things over with Stella, but Hilda was the last straw. I threw my apron down on the counter. "I believe that does it. I'm going home."

I stormed out of the fellowship hall, not caring what anyone thought. I'd had enough. This was a sorry Christmas all the way around, and I was tired of fighting it. I reached the foyer and glanced into the auditorium with its stained-glass windows and air of peaceful dignity. We were here to celebrate the birth of God's own Son, the Prince of Peace. What did it matter how we made the punch?

This was a night of celebration, of family gatherings. How could I have been so hateful to Stella? She *was* old, and I had argued with her in front of the entire women's group. Of course she was upset. More than that, I had threatened to go home leaving her at the church alone. She'd have to beg a ride from someone. She would be so humiliated.

Lord, I'm so sorry. I've acted awful just because I don't

have a lot of money. Mary and Joseph didn't have much money either, but they trusted You to provide. I'm sorry I forgot to rely on You. Sorry I've made Christmas so miserable for everyone, and I'm sorry for the way I've treated Stella. I'm going right back down there and ask her forgiveness, just as soon as I ask You to forgive me. You have blessed me so much, and I've been so blind I didn't even notice. Forgive me, Lord. I'll try to do better next time.

I felt a peace in my heart that had been lacking for months. Help had come. Not the financial help I wanted, but the strength and peace that come from trusting God. I went back to the fellowship hall, where preparations were still in full swing. Stella sat at one of the tables looking so lost my heart melted. I had done that to her—my temper, my mouth.

I sat down beside her and took her hand. Her lips quivered, and tears filled her eyes. "Stella, I'm sorry. I wasn't really fighting over the punch. It was just all of the problems I've had to deal with lately."

Her voice trembled. "I'm sorry I'm such a burden. If I could get a part-time job maybe I'd be able to move back to Shady Acres."

"Oh, Stella, you're not a burden. I love having you live with me. I'd miss you if you left. Please don't think this outburst had anything to do with you. It's just that I'm such a failure."

Her eyes opened wide. "A failure? You? What are you talking about? You took me in—and don't try to tell me you wanted to, because you didn't and I know it—and you took CeeCee and those poodles of hers. You cook, clean, and support us somehow. You've taken three women from different generations and made us a family. You're not a failure; you're the most successful woman I know."

I hugged her. "Oh, Stella, can you forgive me?"

"I will if you'll forgive me."

I laughed, feeling relieved. "I'll bet that's the best punch they've ever had."

"Or the strangest."

I sniffed. "Do you smell something burning?"

A haze of blue smoke drifted through the room. "The church is on fire," Hilda boomed. "Everyone out!"

Frances jerked open the oven door. "The cookies are burning."

Suddenly the fire alarm clanged. Stella clapped her hands over her ears.

In what seemed like no time at all, sirens sounded, growing louder. A look of sheer horror crossed Hilda's face. The fellowship door burst open, and three brawny firemen rushed in dragging a large hose.

"Where's the fire?" one shouted.

Stella walked over to stand in front of them practically yelling over the alarm. "There's no fire! We burned the cookies!"

The firemen looked at her, bewildered. "The cookies?" one of them asked.

Frances pointed at the still-smoking lumps of burned dough. "The cookies."

His expression cleared. "Oh, right. The cookies. You don't need us then?"

"Not unless you can turn off that alarm."

"Sure, we'll take care of that." One of them did whatever was necessary, and a blessed silence fell on the gathering. The fireman touched his hat. "Maybe you'd better warn us the next time you bake."

They left and Frances scraped the burned cookies into the wastebasket. "Well, this certainly will be a Christmas Eve service to remember."

I guess I should have known the evening wouldn't be complete without one final climax. There was a low moan, like the wind sighing through the pine trees, a crash as of fallen timber, followed by a stunned silence.

Hilda Throckmorton had fainted.

*   *   *

Later Stella and I drove home in a state of holiday bliss. The Christmas Eve service had been inspiring, and the fellowship later had gone off without a hitch. Hilda, extremely chastened, had been persuaded to sit down in a place of honor with a cup of punch, while Frances and Pansy mixed a fresh batch of cookies and the rest of us pulled it all together. The punch was delicious, although it didn't conform to either my or Stella's recipe. We promised to remember what we put in it so we could make it again.

Stella sighed. "You know, Maude, no matter how big a mess we make of things, God always brings it out all right. He takes good care of us, doesn't He?"

"He does at that." And I was going to try to remember it the next time I got into trouble, although if the episode with the punch was any indication, my memory wasn't all it should be.

When I turned the corner onto our street, I spotted the electric candles glowing in the windows, their shining rays spilling out on new-fallen snow.

Contentment filled me anew. Life wasn't so bad.

I pulled the car into the garage, and Stella got out and proceeded into the house. She was like a kid when it came to parties—anxious for the fun to begin. We'd invited Maury Peacock, Victor Johnson, and the usual people from church. Nearly everyone but Gary, and I felt bad about that. I think the poor man needs attention, but far be it from me to suggest that to Cee.

By nine o'clock my front room was spilling over into the kitchen and hallways. Friends and neighbors mingled amid the sounds of laughter and Christmas carols combined with the smell of freshly brewed coffee and evergreen. I still had to get through the gift exchange later, arid I wasn't particularly looking forward to giving only candles and body lotion, but I knew deep in my heart that neither Cee nor Stella would mind. It was my own pride that stood in the way.

"Oh, dawdle." I stood in front of the refrigerator and lamented my rapidly depleting ice-cube supply. Maury Peacock had just walked into the kitchen to bring an empty plate. "Maury," I called, "could you run over to your house and bring me a couple of trays of ice cubes?"

Maury paused, apparently mulling over the request. Then he slowly shook his head. "I'd love to, Maude, but my doctor says not to run or overexert myself in any way while I'm taking this medicine."

It took a minute for me to realize he'd taken the request literally.

"No … I mean would you *walk*—walk *slowly* over to your house and bring back some ice?"

He nodded solemnly. "Well, I believe I could do that. Just so's I don't run."

Victor Johnson had the green macaw in an uproar. The colorful bird hung upside down in the cage, trading insults with my neighbor. You'd think Victor had more brains than to argue with a bird.

Around 9:45 the doorbell chimed, and I stepped away from the punch bowl to admit the late arrivals. Probably Pastor Brookes and his family, only now able to leave the church. But when I opened the door I found Hargus on my doorstep with a wide-eyed Duella Denson. In handcuffs.

Handcuffs. I suppose if I hadn't been thunderstruck I might have wondered why poor, sweet Duella was wearing iron, but I couldn't do anything but gape.

"Stella here?" Hargus took a hitch in his britches.

"Why … er … Duella?" I found my voice about the same time Duella's tear ducts kicked into overdrive.

Streams of hot water left pinkish ruts through Duella's rouged cheeks. "Maude—Hargus arrested me!"

"Arrested you!" I emphasized the word so loudly because I couldn't believe he'd do such a thing. Half the guests standing in the front room went suddenly as silent as a mole.

"Citizen's arrest—I'm authorized." Hargus nudged The Antiques Shop owner into the living room, and I shut the door.

Already traces of the biting wind had swept through the foyer. Trailing Hargus, who was leading Duella, into my office, I wondered what in the world was going on. And where was Luella? In fact, those were the first words out of my mouth. "Where's Luella?"

"She's home," Duella sniffed. "Hargus arrested me there— I had just put Luella to bed, and then stepped out the front door and walked to the postal box when he drove up, siren wailing."

"For goodness' sake, Hargus." I glared at Pansy's son. "Take those cuffs off Duella this instant."

"No can do, Miz Diamond. Caught her red-handed, ready to mail a batch of chain letters."

Lowering her face in her hands, Duella boo-hooed.

"Chain letters!" Stella burst through the kitchen doorway, her face alight. "Did someone mention chain letters?"

By now every guest had assembled in the front room and doorways, their eyes pinned to the excitement.

"Caught the copycat bandit in the act." A satisfied smirk dominated Hargus's animated features. The word *smug* came to mind.

Stella looked crestfallen when she saw the new arrival. "Duella? Hargus, are you nuts?" She glanced back at the bawling prisoner. "You've been the one writing those letters?"

Dabbing at the corners of her eyes with a hanky, Duella tried to explain. "Yes . . . I'm so ashamed of myself . . . I didn't know . . . I didn't know I could do time! I thought with business so down and money so tight that maybe I could cash in on a little excitement. I didn't think anyone would miss a few dollars . . . and the cash would mean the world to me and Luella. I'm Hummingbird." That said, she promptly burst into fresh tears, and I thought, *Well, land sakes. All that talk about the Denson sisters' being rich as Rockefeller was just that—talk.*

"Wait a minute!" I held up one hand. This didn't make a lick of sense. Duella Denson didn't have a devious bone in her body. Why would she be mailing chain letters in order to acquire money? "Just hold on," I demanded when nobody seemed to hear me.

A deadly silence fell across the group. Carols played in the background. Only Duella's wrenching sobs were heard. I stepped forward and put my arms around the shopkeeper's quaking shoulders and hugged her. She was going to make herself sick. "Hargus, what is the meaning of this?"

Hargus took another hitch in his pants. "Like I sez, Miz Diamond, I caught Duella mailing a stack of chain letters in the postal box near her home." He grinned, his eyes focusing on Stella. "Cracked the copycat case wide-open—sure as shootin'."

I couldn't believe what I was hearing, and I sure couldn't believe that Duella Denson had done anything wrong.

"Did you really mail those letters?" I asked Duella softy.

She pressed the hanky close to her nose. "Most of them. When I got the first letter from Pigeon, the idea seemed like a good one. So I wrote a few and mailed them. Even went to Ash Flat and rented a postal box so I wouldn't reveal my true identity. Pretty clever, you have to admit. A bit of money trickled in—enough to fuel my imagination. *Why,* I thought, *this could really work!* And it didn't seem to be devious or criminal. All those bird names had me so *confused!* Then I got another letter last week, one that I didn't send, but I figured by now there were more than me in on the action. Then I got careless and decided to mail a new batch of letters from here instead of driving to Ash Flat. That's when Hargus drove up and slapped the cuffs on me."

"So you're the culprit." I guess if I lived to be a hundred I could still be surprised. Stupefied, actually. Who'd have ever thought poor, sweet Duella Denson was putting the make on her friends and neighbors? But then wasn't I guilty of the same crime?

"Oh, no." Duella shook her head adamantly. "I didn't mail *all* the letters. There were—are—at least three other birds in on the action—

Pigeon, Sparrow, and Blackbird."

Hargus sobered. "The jig's up, Duella. I caught you red-handed, and chain letters are mail fraud."

Duella appeared faint.

"Now, hold on a minute." Stella broke in, suspicion lining her face. "If Duella didn't send all those letters, who else is involved?"

Hargus snorted. "Miz Denson would say anything to distance herself from the crime—or crimes—she's responsible for. Several counts—at least five previous letters—"

"Wait a second," I interrupted. I felt my cheeks blaze, and the sudden heat had nothing to do with my age. This wasn't exactly how or where I wanted to make my particular confession, but I couldn't let Duella take all the heat.

Thirty sets of eyes switched to me. I could have died. "I did write five letters, and I sent someone five dollars," I confessed. "But what bird are you, Duella?"

Duella adamantly denied the charge. "I never got a dime from you, Maude. Honest."

Clearing my throat, I repeated. "Well—I don't know who sent the first letter, but I answered one to make Stella feel better." I swallowed. "I told you, I'm Sparrow."

Stella blinked. "Make *me* feel better?"

"You," I acknowledged. "I figured from the way you'd been creeping around and acting so guilty you must be Pigeon, and you had sent money on the first letter—so I thought if I sent money and then admitted to you that I sent it, you would feel better about what you'd done."

"Well." Stella dropped her gaze. "Actually, I did send the first letter. I'm Pigeon."

The room's occupants groaned out loud. The confession didn't surprise me.

"I sent the first letter. I thought since Maude was having such a financial squeeze that if I sent the letter, we'd have a little extra cash. Went clear over to Ash Flat, rented a postal box, and used a fake name. I figured I could bring in extra money—a lot, the way I had it calculated." Stella took a deep breath. "But it didn't work out the way I planned. Remind me to give you the ten bucks I got for the effort."

Duella sighed. "Chain letters aren't a sound investment."

"Why, Stella—" Once again my mother-in-law had rendered me speechless.

"Now, you just hold on." Hargus peered over Stella's shoulder at me. "That only accounts for one letter. Duella had to have sent—" he stopped, thought for a minute, appeared to be counting—"oh, skip it."

"No, go on, Hargus. Finish what you were about to say," I demanded, sensing there was more to the ending of this story than met the eye.

"I didn't send all the letters!" Duella exclaimed again.

"Well—" Hargus cleared his throat sheepishly—"since you mentioned it, I guess I have to admit that I sent the last letter. I rented a post office box in Ash Flat, too—and made up a fake name. I'm not stupid. I'm Blackbird."

Well, you could have heard a feather drop in the room. A mosquito tiptoe across the floor. A flock of birds leave the room.

"Now, it's not what you're thinking." Hargus hauled up his pants, sending Pansy an apologetic glance. "I sent a letter, yes, but only to yank Stella's chain and foil the person who was upping the ante. I figured Stella was trying to make a mountain out of a molehill with this chain-letter caper, until I got one myself. And she was never going to quit ragging on me until I pretended to look for this copycat bandit. I sent the letters, hoping she'd get wind of it— and sure as shootin' she did. I planned to return the money if anybody fell for the scam— which they didn't. I was just having a little fun."

"You're not funny," Stella told him. "And you did not solve this case. Remember that."

He glowered at her.

And to think I thought this Christmas would be uneventful.

"Then all this chain-letter business has been, if not innocent, then certainly without criminal intent."

Someone in the room quickly spoke up and reminded me that it didn't make a hill of beans' difference; if you sent a letter asking for money you were perpetuating mail fraud.

Oh my. To quote someone more profound than Maude Diamond, "Oh, what a tangled web we weave, when first we practice to deceive"—or something like that.

Since Cee was out of the room, and Iva Hinkle hadn't come tonight, Stella, Hargus, and Duella agreed that since no *real* harm was done it was best to drop the matter.

We put it to a vote and it carried unanimously.

And we swore everyone else in the room to secrecy, made them promise they'd keep their mouths shut about the unfortunate incident.

The cuffs came off Duella, who promptly accepted a cup of punch and apologies all the way around. I figured everyone was happy, but evidently not.

"Now wait just a minute," Simon said. "You don't mean you're going to drop the whole thing?"

"And why not?" Stella rounded on him. "No one meant to do anything wrong. It was a simple misunderstanding."

"My redecorating homes was a simple misunderstanding." Simon's jaw jutted out in a virtuoso display of temper. "And *I'm* doing twenty hours a week community service. How come you, Stella, Duella, and Hargus can walk away with no repercussions?"

Stella and Hargus went off like Roman candles, but Simon didn't back down. "What's sauce for the goose is sauce for the gander. You're no better than me."

I sighed. Why had I ever thought anything would be simple? Particularly when Stella and Hargus were involved? If Simon hadn't kicked up such a stink reminding everyone that he was doing twenty hours a week community service because he had thoughtfully redecorated a few area homes—with no criminal intent in mind—Stella would have been home free. But if there's one thing folks in Morning Shade are, it's accountable; we take responsibility for our mistakes. With that in mind I called for another vote.

"I know this isn't the 'law,' but I recommend that Hargus, Duella, Stella, and I—for our part in the 'crime'—join Simon each week for the next six months in giving twenty hours to our community for retribution."

"Why," Hargus sputtered, "you can't do that—this matter calls for a judge and jury!"

I gazed around the room at familiar faces and grinned. "Oh, Hargus. In Morning Shade, the folks *are* judge and jury."

Unconventional but true.

Mildred Fasco spoke up. "Maude, Morning Shade doesn't have enough community work to keep four more people busy twenty hours a week."

"Hmm." She had a point.

Someone one else chimed in. "I hear they need volunteers over in Shiloh. Hospital needs volunteers real bad."

"Shiloh?" Well, there's the solution. Shiloh is larger than Morning Shade.

"Shiloh's eighteen miles away," Hargus complained. ·

"Don't make me no mind," Stella said. "I'm not going to be around to serve my sentence."

"Me either," Duella said. "I mean—I'm willing to go to Shiloh twenty hours a week—not what Stella's implying."

I called for another show of hands, and the sentence again passed unanimously. *Great,* I thought. *Me and my big mouth. Now Stella has twenty hours a week of community service in Shiloh Memorial Hospital to stir up new trouble.*

I don't know about anybody else, but personally I think with all the well-intentioned crimes going around, this part of Arkansas was going to be the cleanest place on earth once the convicted got through with their community obligations,.

And I swan if I didn't hear my small inner voice remind me, *But Maude, you* said *you'd like a twenty-hour-a-week part-time job.*

Not keeping Stella out of trouble, Lord. Let's be reasonable.

So ended Morning Shade's newest whodunit: the copycat bandit. And I thought to myself, *What* else *could possibly go wrong in this peaceful little Arkansas town?*

EPILOGUE

It was close to midnight when I closed the front door and turned off the porch light. I was bone tired but relieved to have the mystery solved.

I think Stella was a little disappointed to learn that need had played a larger part in the copycat case than intrigue, but she seemed content to temporarily lay her hat and magnifying glass aside. She and Hargus had reached a rickety truce. Zero for zero on accredited cases. I wondered how long they would stay that way, neck and neck. Eyeball-to-eyeball. If I knew my mother-in-law—and I was afraid I did—she would find a new case ... or make one.

CeeCee ambled into the living room carrying three steaming mugs of hot chocolate. The day had been long and tiring, and I was looking forward to a few moments alone with family.

We sat down—Cee beside me on the sofa, Stella in her recliner. I noticed my mother-in-law's eyes droop with fatigue.

"Want to open gifts?" I yawned.

"Mine first!" Cee was on her feet, off to the bedroom, then back, balancing an armload of brightly decorated Christmas gifts. Oh, to be thirty-one once more.

"My goodness!" I sat up straighter, staring at the various shapes and sizes of boxes. "What is all this?"

"Presents." CeeCee grinned. *"I* went through yours and Grandma's dresser drawers last week and *voila!* Christmas presents!"

Stella and I began to open the boxes she shoved our way, and we all had a good chuckle. Inside were gifts of Christmases past—lingerie, sweaters, funky clothing that we'd tucked away in drawers and forgotten about. But we thought we were walking in tall cotton now.

I held up a garish blouse Cee had given me when she was sixteen. Purplish blue with row upon row of ruffles. "Shall I wear this to meet the queen?"

CeeCee bent double, holding her hands over her mouth with merriment. "That's awful, Mom. What was I thinking?"

"You think *that's* bad ..."

My eyes shifted, and I broke out into hysterics when I saw Stella on her bare feet, toothless, preening like a peacock, modeling the weirdest-looking hat—fuchsia with iridescent green feathers. "Like it?" she deadpanned.

"Atrocious!"

"That's what I thought when you gave it to me the first year you and Herb were married."

My sides actually hurt from laughing. Gifts that once had meant little were now rich with meaning.

I handed out my simple gifts, and lo and behold, Cee and Stella loved them. The way they carried on over those candles and body lotion you'd have thought I'd given them a million dollars.

"Mom, you've made it a truly special Christmas," CeeCee said. She leaned over and gave me a tight hug. "I still miss Daddy so much, but tonight's been easier than I thought it would be." Then reaching into her pocket, she said quietly. "The only thing 1 have for you is my thoughts, Mom. Here—1 wrote this for you."

I opened the handmade card fashioned on white construction

paper. On the front Cee had drawn a childish illustration: a flower, a tree, and a bird in a bright blue sky. But inside the message was anything but childish.

Dear Mom,

I don't remember the day you brought me home from the hospital, but you do. I'll bet you looked at me and couldn't believe the miracle you once carried close to your heart was alive, breathing, and totally dependent upon you. You wanted everything perfect for me. Perfect childhood, perfect marriage, perfect life.

But by now we both have learned that life isn't perfect. What is perfect is your love. It's never failed me. It's seen me through the good and the bad, and the best part, I know it's constant and something I'll always have whatever happens.

Over the years together we learned that your dreams for me weren't always my dreams for myself. But that's okay. We made it through those years, stronger in our love for each other. Mom, I want you to know that being your child is the greatest gift on earth.

Thank you for being my mom. I didn't choose you for my mother, but I would now in an instant.

Merry Christmas. I love you.

CeeCee

Swiping a tear, I thought whoever said that giving had to be expensive hadn't met my family.

*　　*　　*

Later I sat in the darkened living room, shoes cast aside, feet propped on the coffee table, going over the night's stunning events. When that advance check came I had to find a way to slip some cash to Duella without hurting her pride. I couldn't bear the thought of the Denson sisters sitting alone at the back of The Antiques Shop fretting over unpaid bills. The way I figure, we're all in this thing called life. Same boat. We need to all row together. I believe that's what God intended.

Only the tree shed a blinking light. If this was Stella's last Christmas on earth, then it was my most significant. Oh, I missed Herb—saw him every direction that I turned tonight— but I'd made it through the memories. And I'd make it through a couple more months of deadlines, insecurity, angst—well, *writing*. So I guess I'm made of sturdier stock than I suspected.

The knowledge brought warm fuzzies to my heart. My hand rested against Captain's furry coat, rising and falling with the cat's soft purring. Outside, snow drifted softly on my perfect world; the birds slept peacefully in their cage. The dogs were nowhere in sight but I suspected they were curled up on CeeCee's bed, getting hair all over the comforter....

"Hey, Maude?"

I opened my eyes and smiled at Stella. "I thought you were in bed asleep."

"I was—then I woke up and remembered I have something for you." Stella rummaged in her housecoat pocket and took out an envelope. "It came in the mail this morning—been meaning to give it to you all day."

"For me?" I studied the envelope. It was the size of an advance check, with a Bethlehem House return address. But I knew it couldn't be the check. Hugh was still out sick, and mail didn't reach my door overnight.

"Open it," Stella encouraged.

So I tore into the envelope and took out a check. For a moment I simply stared at the piece of paper, so emotionally overcome I couldn't find my voice.

What a mighty God I serve.

I held in my hand a foreign royalties check—on a book that was over five years old and long forgotten. But there it was, a beautiful. $3,728.32 that I never expected—actually never even dreamed about. But God knew.

The enormity of answered prayer swept through me, and I blinked back hot tears. *Here it is, Maude. Remember this moment the next time you're running low on trust.*

A check that would be pocket change to some but was a windfall to me. It served to remind me that my Father kept His promises. In my head I heard the verse *"Be silent, and know that I am God!"*

Sighing, I folded the check and laid it beside me on the sofa, my heart so filled with gratitude that I still couldn't speak.

"Something good?" Stella asked.

"A miracle," I confessed.

Nodding, Stella smiled, glancing toward the lighted Christmas tree. "Well, it's the night of miracles."

"Yes," I murmured. At that moment I vowed I would never again underestimate God's love, and yet at the same time I wondered how long it would take me to break the promise.

Knowing Maude Diamond, probably not long, but I was going to try harder.

That's the least any of us can do. Just try a little harder.

ABOUT THE AUTHOR

Lori Copeland is a popular bestselling contemporary and historical author who writes Christian and clean and wholesome stories. Her books have been nominated for the prestigious Christy Award and received two Romantic Times Lifetime Achievement awards. Copeland's novel Stranded in Paradise is now a Hallmark movie.

She lives with her wonderful husband, Lance, in the Ozarks. She has three grown sons, three daughters- in-law, and many exceptionally bright grandchildren— but then, she freely admits to being partial when it comes to her family. Lori enjoys reading biographies, knitting and participating in morning water-aerobic exercises at the local YMCA, and she is presently trying very hard to learn to play bridge. She loves to travel and is always thrilled to meet her readers.

When asked what one thing Lori would like others to know about her, she readily says, "It's good to know that since I'm far from perfect— I'm forgiven by the grace of God." Christianity to Lori means peace, joy, and the knowledge that she has a Friend, a Savior, who never leaves her side. Through these books, she hopes to share this wondrous assurance with others at this Christmas season.

Lori would like to invite you to "like" her page on Facebook. https://www.facebook.com/Lori-Copeland-49638671412/timeline/

35575368R00152

Made in the USA
San Bernardino, CA
29 June 2016